LOVE
AND
PAKLAVA

ALYSSA JARRETT

Geek Chic Press LLC

Editing by Kristen Tate at the Blue Garret

Cover design by Nick Jarrett

ISBN: 978-1-963875-04-1 (Ebook)

ISBN: 978-1-963875-05-8 (Paperback)

Published by Geek Chic Press LLC

PO Box 1193

Oakland, CA 94604

 Formatted with Vellum

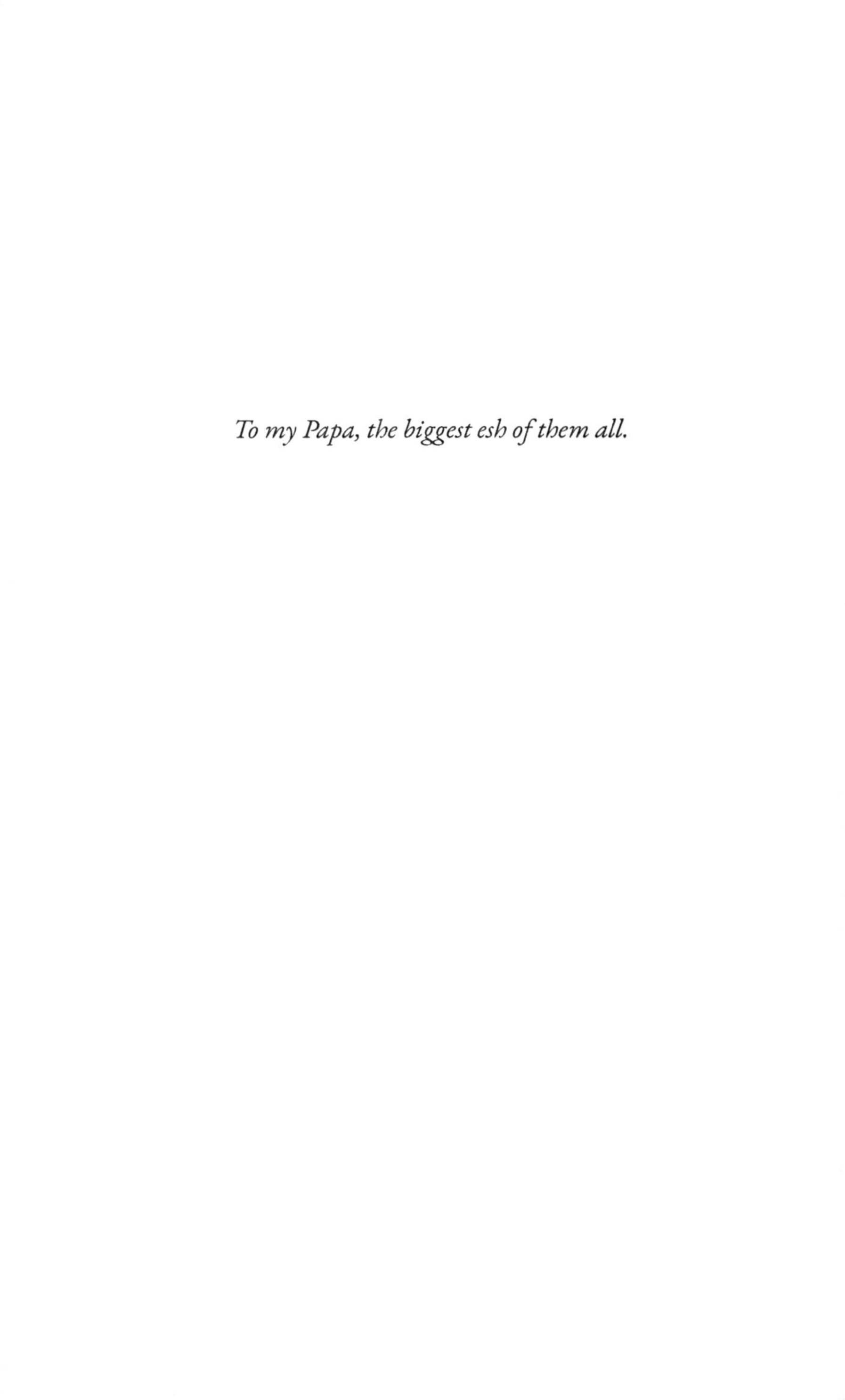

To my Papa, the biggest esh of them all.

content notes

This book includes references to childhood neglect, drug and alcohol abuse, incarceration, death of a parent (historical, off-page), swearing, and explicit sex. Reader discretion is advised.

Love and Paklava is at its heart a romantic comedy that celebrates love, culture, and connection. While its primary focus is bringing joy, I could not authentically write about the Armenian American experience without discussing the Armenian Genocide, a tragic chapter in history that continues to shape Armenian identity and resilience.

If you would like to learn more and support organizations dedicated to Armenian history and humanitarian efforts, I encourage you to explore the following resources:

Armenia Fund (armeniafund.org)
Armenian General Benevolent Union (agbu.org)
Armenian National Institute (armenian-genocide.org)
Armenian Relief Society (ars1910.org)
Children of Armenia Fund (coaf.org)
Fund for Armenian Relief (farusa.org)

chapter
one

I love living in the city. The skyline of glass towers kissing the clouds. Public transportation packed with commuters. Art and culture tucked into every corner. Knowing you could spend your entire life exploring and never run out of things to do, places to see, and people to fuck.

I love cities like I love dicks: the bigger, the better.

As I stomp through San Francisco's Tenderloin neighborhood on this brisk November night, I know for a fact that I love this city more than most people. Pearl-clutching suburbanites and tech bros don't want to stare at poverty because poverty stares back. They grew up with functional families and silver spoons. The first time I saw drug paraphernalia, on the other hand, was in my home, not on the streets.

I make a quick detour to drop off extra dinners at a nearby encampment before picking up the pace on my way to my destination. After my nine-to-five of giving mani-pedis and a myriad of other beauty treatments as a nail tech and aesthetician, I start my second shift playing piano at jazz clubs in SF's grungiest haunts.

Tonight I'm working at Ms. Maven's, a Black-owned

piano lounge and cocktail bar that's been offering soul and spirits for decades.

"What color you got on today, Tori?" asks Jerome, Ms. Maven's longtime bouncer, as I approach the entrance.

I pull my hands out of the pockets of my leather jacket and wiggle them for his benefit. It's not my manicure he's inquiring about. In my line of work, surrounded by acetone and electric files, I have to keep my own nails simple so I can focus on my clients.

Instead, I express my personality with my crown jewels: the full-finger rings I wear like claws. Of all the accessories that clock me as alternative—my black wardrobe, half-shaved head, tattoos, ear gauges, and facial piercings—it's my claws that everybody knows me by.

"My tried-and-true," I tell Jerome, showing off my favorite set: brushed stainless steel inlaid with amethyst studs.

He nods with approval. "I see whatcha doing. Matching that purple hair of yours so Mr. Manhattan won't take his eyes off you."

I peek inside the club, intrigued. "He's back already?"

"Third time this week," Jerome says, shaking his head. "Keeps asking if you're playing. I don't give out nobody's schedule—if they keep coming around and spending good money, they'll figure it out themselves." He follows my gaze. "You gonna put the poor boy out of his misery, or should I?"

I always appreciate when security guards and staff are proactive about protecting performers from unsavory characters. It wouldn't be the first time Jerome has had to kick someone out. But we both know that won't be necessary with Mr. Manhattan.

"A face that pretty looks much better wrapped around my finger, don't you think?" I toss my hair, claws sparkling under the streetlamp, and give him a wink.

Jerome chuckles. "No wonder you're always giving your food away. You're too full from man-eating every night."

"Damn straight," I say over my shoulder as I enter the club. Scanning the small crowd stationed at the bar, I pinpoint our subject sipping the cocktail that gave him his nickname.

"And tonight I'm getting stuffed," I mutter under my breath, locking eyes with my target from across the room.

Everybody looks more attractive under the lounge's low lighting, its reddish hue washing seductively over the black leather seating. As I walk past Mr. Manhattan, swaying my hips just so, I can clock his exact type. This isn't a pathetic loser who escaped his parents' basement. Dressed in too-tight black jeans, a white tee, and a sleeveless hoodie to show off his tattoo sleeves, he's a dirtbag who gets plenty of tail. He likes the chase, and so do I.

I appreciate his sharp angles and dirty stubble as he objectifies me. I don't mind the salacious staring. An object is all he is to me, too. A complete stranger with a hard cock. I don't need to know his name, learn about his job, or meet his friends. The best part about casual sex is keeping it casual. I won't be making room for him in my life, and if I never see him again, who cares?

"I get off at ten o'clock," I tell Mr. Manhattan, running a claw down his forearm as I walk by.

He smirks, licking his lips. "You sure will, baby."

Cha-ching. Dirtbag is in the bag. Now that I've confirmed my late-night plans, I can concentrate on the performance I'm actually paid to do.

I exchange brief pleasantries with tonight's band before settling in at the piano for a quick soundcheck. With my beauty business taking up the vast majority of my time, I don't have grand ambitions of hitting the road and touring for months on end. I'm well-connected in San Francisco's jazz scene, so my network is large enough to keep me busy. I'm a gig worker through and through, and between rotating around various clubs and filling in where needed, my calendar is fully booked.

Not to sound like a grating girlboss or startup guru, but I enjoy the hustle. Nobody like me who was born and raised in New York City and lifted themselves from the lower rungs of society has ever taken it easy. If anything, San Francisco can feel sleepy to a native New Yorker, so maxing out my schedule is my way of moving at my naturally rapid pace.

The seats start filling up with old hepcats and couples celebrating date night off the beaten path. Not a tourist in sight, just how I like it.

With my hookup locked down, I'm feeling good—until half past eight, when the emcee introduces the band. The saxophone player gets a raucous cheer from a group of friends and family seated at the tables in the front row, and my heart twinges with a pang of sadness. Only a few people in the audience clap politely when my name is called, forcing me to plaster on a smile and fight back my disappointment that the people I care about most aren't here.

I remove my claws, revealing the STAY SHARP tattoo inked across my knuckles. It's for the best that I keep busy. My closest friends certainly do. Casey, Som, Glen, and I used to be tied at the hip as part of supermodel Alex Waterston-Gardner's entourage, but over the years the group has expanded to include boyfriends and new friends. It's not the close-knit family it used to be, and I've been feeling more and more like the odd one out. Especially when everybody else is partnered in one way or another, and I'm the only one without a seat in this game of musical chairs.

In the past, it wouldn't be out of the ordinary for my friends—aka the glam fam—to be in the audience whooping it up after every one of my solos. Now, when we're not on the job, I'm usually flying solo.

As my fingers dance across the piano keys, I try to remind myself that the lone wolf life isn't new to me. I raised myself out of the rubble of a broken home, paid my own way through beauty school, and built my career, brick by brick, serving the most famous social media celebrity in the world. I earned my claws, and I'm not afraid to use them. Preferably scratching up a dirtbag's back in a public restroom.

Thankfully, tonight's set is pretty standard, so I don't have to give it my full attention. Even if I flub a note or two, jazz musicians are known for improvising.

Instead, I spend each song eye-fucking Mr. Manhattan at the bar. My playing gets more passionate with every scene I imagine: shoving him into the nearest stall, getting pounded until I see stars, digging my rings into his shoulders so hard they draw blood.

I can't be bummed about my friends being missing in action if I'm too preoccupied with getting some action.

That's not quite true. The glam fam isn't missing—our mutual friend and marketing extraordinaire Tania Beecher is in town, and they're making her beautiful for her big day.

Well, not *the* big day, but the first of many as she speeds toward the altar. Soon the glam fam will be done planning Tania's outfits for her engagement photoshoot in Yosemite, and tomorrow we'll make the long drive to the national park and scope out the perfect locations.

The trumpeter blasts his horn in my direction, the universal sign for a fellow musician to wake the fuck up. I give him a brusque nod, hearing him loud and clear.

Get your head in the game, Tori, and focus. You're still an important part of the friend group. You chose to do Tania's nails and brows the day before so you could squeeze in this gig. There's no reason to blow this out of proportion.

Now, blowing a dirtbag until he turns into a puddle at your feet? That's a better use of your time.

We finish playing our last song, and I'm not sure who stands up faster—me or the audience giving their ovation. On Thursdays, the club closes at ten-thirty instead of midnight, which only gives me a half hour to get paid and get laid.

As I wait with the band for the club owner to dole out our cash, I catch Mr. Manhattan's eye and motion toward the restroom. "Meet me in five," I mouth, holding up my hand for emphasis.

He saunters off with the smugness of someone who's used to having sex on tap, and I don't blame him. Most people would get offended by being perceived as 'easy,' but when time is of the essence, the last thing I need to be is hard to get.

But as soon as I shove the bills into my pockets, my plan gets shot to hell when Tania bursts into the club.

"Tori!" she gasps, out of breath. If it weren't for her casual attire of a peacoat over jeans and riding boots, you'd think she sprinted off a movie set. Her full face of makeup is immaculate, and her curly brown hair has been blown out with gorgeous shine, a gray streak twinkling like tinsel. "We've got an emergency."

My brain short-circuits, confused how anything bad could happen to Tania when she's looking that good. She grabs my arm, and I let her lead me toward the exit. It's not until I step into the nondescript black van idling at the curb—one of many that Alex's team uses to evade the paparazzi—that I realize this might be the first time Mr. Manhattan's been stood up in a bathroom stall.

In an instant, I've gone from getting fucked to being fucked.

"Is everyone alright?" I ask, scanning the van. Hairdresser Glen Cooper is in the driver seat, per usual. Chauffeuring us ladies around is his act of chivalry as the only man in the glam fam. Stylist Casey Holbright is riding shotgun, shopping bags stacked high on her lap because they clearly ran out of space in the rest of the vehicle. Lastly, makeup artist Som Srisati is seated in the very back with Alex Waterston-Gardner, aka Princess Alex. Everybody's safe, but Tania's still upset. So what's the emergency?

"We're fine, physically at least," Tania reassures me. She pats the seat next to her in the middle row, before plastering on her best damsel-in-distress expression. "Victoria Townsend. Tori. My lash lord and skincare savior. We're facing a catering crisis, and you're our only hope."

I blink, unconvinced. "A catering crisis? This late at night?"

She nods grimly. "I just called my parents to remind them that they're scheduled to book the caterer in Fresno tomorrow, but it turns out my brother talked them into an impromptu trip to New England to see the seasons or whatever." She rolls her eyes. "As if the ancient redwoods in our own majestic state weren't enough. But the point is—it took weeks to secure this appointment, and I can't risk missing it."

Despite the luxury concealer covering her dark circles, I can tell Tania's exhausted. As the owner of a successful marketing agency, now based in the California foothills, she's usually the consummate planner, but it's been a monumental feat to pull off this Valentine's Day wedding in record time. Even though they were technically engaged in April, Nolan's line of work put wedding planning on pause until the fall, giving us only three months to make it all happen.

I can't blame Tania for the accelerated schedule, not when she's marrying a man who risks his life on a daily basis. And no, Nolan Wells isn't a firefighter protecting Yosemite's forests or a park ranger battling blizzards and bears. We never thought a tightly wound, former Silicon Valley executive would fall for the world's greatest rock climber, but somehow they're a perfect match—even if Nolan would much rather be scrambling up cliffs than posing on them in formalwear.

"Okay, but what do you want me to do about it?" My words come out a bit harsher than I intended. To be fair, though, a good railing is the best attitude adjustment, and that opportunity's been taken away from me. "We're supposed to drive to Yosemite tomorrow to scout photoshoot locations. All of us." I gesture to the rest of the glam fam in the van. "Fresno's in the opposite direction."

I feel ridiculous pointing out the obvious, especially since Tania was born and raised in Fresno and doesn't need a refresher on the geography of the Central Valley. But I've played enough video games as a kid to know when I'm being treated like a non-player character on a side quest while the real heroes get to battle the final boss.

Tania hesitates to reply. "Why can't you just reschedule it?" I suggest. "It's not like—" Before I can finish my thought, I clamp my mouth shut to avoid offending her. Because what I'm really thinking is, it's not like Fresno is a culinary mecca, at least not like San Francisco, where I live, or New York City, where I'm from.

But Tania's too perceptive to miss what's between the lines. "I get it, Tori. Not all of us can be best friends with celebrities who have Thomas Keller on speed dial." She cranes her neck toward the statuesque blonde who's typically the center of attention. "No offense, Alex."

Alex perks up from her phone, probably posting for her 500 million social media followers. If it wasn't for her, I wouldn't have such an amazing job in the first place. "Oh, none taken! And I'd pull some strings if I could, but TK's booked solid for the next two years."

Tania squeezes my hand, sorry written across her face. "If I could come up with another solution that wouldn't derail my entire wedding planning timeline, I would. But Dikran's Deli is the best Armenian restaurant in my hometown, and as someone with Armenian roots, the place holds a lot of sentimental value to me. This is Dikran's busiest time of year, and they're super old school. No email, no e-signs, nothing. If I don't book this contract tomorrow, there's no guarantee I'll be able to reschedule. Then I've got no caterer, and I'm back at square one."

My lips retreat into a fine line. I'm not heartless—I know how important Tania's wedding is to her and how tormented she feels about this mishap. She's so Type-A that it must be killing her that her family dropped the ball. It's not like she can reschedule her engagement shoot photographer in the literal eleventh hour either. She's caught between a rock and a hard place to book.

The sympathy on the faces of my friends doesn't make up for the fact that I'm the most expendable person here. Casey's coordinating Tania and Nolan's attire, and best believe she has several outfit changes up her sleeve. Som and Glen may be my roommates, but they're such a tight twosome on their own—both personally and professionally. Nobody ever gets just their hair or face done, so wherever one of them goes, the other follows. And even if Alex didn't require security detail wherever she goes, her posing skills are unmatched.

Tania gives my hand another squeeze, sensing my feeling of alienation. "I'm not asking you to take on this mission because you're unimportant, Tori. I'm asking you because you're outrageously important, and I know you'd never let your friends down."

She's right. I'm ol' reliable, loyal to a fault. My mom's been dead for nearly a decade, and my dad's been dead to me for much longer than that. I have no siblings or extended relatives in my life, so it's not like I'm close to anyone else. My friends are all I have left, and it would take way more than a wedding-related road trip to make me desert them in a time of need.

I sigh. "So where is this deli?"

~

EMAIL FROM TANIA BEECHER to Tori Townsend on Thursday, November 10, at 11:32 p.m.

TO: Tori Townsend
FROM: Tania Beecher
SUBJECT: Catering notes for Dikran's Deli

OMG THANK YOU, thank you, thank you, Tori, for taking care of this catering order. You are a lifesaver, and I owe you big. I know it's super late, but I'm sending you these notes from my dedicated wedding email address to keep everything organized. Everything you need to know should be included, but let me know if you have any questions!

1. **Get there first thing in the morning.** I don't remember their exact hours, and they don't have a website or social media (like wtf), but it's always a madhouse every time I visit. Make sure you beat the breakfast rush, or you'll be waiting forever.
2. **Tell them to increase the guest count to 200.** I originally quoted fifty guests—just our closest loved ones—until Nolan offhandedly invited all his free solo climbing buddies. For someone in such a solitary sport, he has an obscene number of friends.
3. **Remind them the menu needs to be vegan-friendly.** I have no idea how this will be possible given how much butter is in pilaf, but I trust them to work their magic for Nolan and his fellow plant-based brethren. Especially when their

Armenian cucumber salad is the best on the planet. I had an ex who hated cucumber, and I should have ended it on the spot.

4. **Ask them for the Armenian friends and family discount.** I mean, we're not actually related, but our community is so small, we might as well be.

5. **Make sure to work with Vahe.** The owner Queenie calls the shots, but she's not always available. I get bad vibes from one of her granddaughters, but there are two of them and I don't remember which is which. Her grandson Vahe is the one who's most involved in the business. Plus, he's a total sweetheart. You'll love him. I have a good feeling 😊

chapter
two

The drive to Fresno the next morning is uneventful—why wouldn't it be when I arrive before the sun rises?—but I can't shake the darkness of my thoughts. No matter what genre of music I played on the way here—calming instrumental jazz, upbeat power pop, vindictive black metal—nothing manages to cheer me up. Not when I keep ruminating about how everyone else is on their way to a winter wonderland, and I'm sent on a mission to tie up a loose errand all by myself.

I should have thrown a hissy fit, refused to be treated like a lowly servant, and stayed in San Francisco. That would show them.

But what if it didn't? If I were to make this all about me instead of supporting Tania during one of the most stressful periods of her life, I'd be breaking the only bonds of friendship I have left. Despite my moodiness, if there's one thing I can't allow myself to be, it's a disappointment. I may not have a smile on my face, but I'm going to do what's been asked of me, even if that means being banished to the armpit of California.

Okay, that's not fair, I know. As I park along the curb of Dikran's Deli, I'm trying not to judge a book by its particularly weathered cover. This downtown isn't the kind of quaint neighborhood you'd visit for its Sunday farmer's market. It's gray, gray, gray—from the clouds of smog overhead to the dilapidated factories as far as the eye can see. It's such an unexpected setting for a business relying on foot traffic that at first, I'm certain I have the wrong address.

But when I step out of my car, it's not the red-and-white-striped awning or giant sign that reads BAKERY that gives it away. It's the thick scent enveloping the air, and there's nothing armpit-like about it. It's earthy and yeasty, and my stomach growls at the prospect of fresh-baked bread in the morning. Perhaps I'll be able to turn this day around, after all.

I stomp my black combat boots to the entrance, but they're a tad lighter than I expect. Am I excited? God forbid I have a pep in my step. Gross.

But no sooner do I pull on the deli's door than I realize the danger of getting your hopes up.

Fuck. It's closed.

But the intoxicating smells and the fact that the lights are clearly on tell me someone's there. I peer through the window, my warm breath fogging up the glass, until I see a large man appear behind the counter.

"Hey!" I shout, jostling the locked handle. "You mind?"

The man looks up, bewildered. He hesitates for a split second, but I must not be that unsavory of a character, because he walks around the counter and unlocks the door instead of screaming at me to get lost.

He opens the door no more than an inch. "Sorry, we don't open until eight. Can you come back at that time?"

I check my smartwatch. This is what I get for thinking ahead. I wanted to avoid the hellish Bay Area commute, but I beat my map app's best estimate and now I'm two hours early. What the hell am I going to do for that long in this industrial wasteland?

"Can you come back to the beginning of that sentence and try again? Because that's not going to work for me."

We scan one another from head to toe, sizing each other up. I'm wearing the same steel and amethyst steampunk-inspired claw rings from last night, which I tap impatiently on the glass door. If I don't get what I want, I'm not above sinking these sharp talons into anyone who stands in my way.

But this guy's not budging. He doesn't seem bothered that I look like I keep boa constrictors and alligators as pets. And why would he? He's so massive he fills out the entire door-frame. If I had to guess, I'd say he's at least six-foot-five, with the same domineering physique as my favorite bouncers.

Just because he could punt me back to my car without breaking a sweat, that doesn't mean he doesn't have a weak-ness. I detect it as I'm appreciating his lush, dark waves and trim beard: the sympathy in those deep brown eyes.

"Please. I live in San Francisco, and I came all this way because my friend is getting married. Her family had an appointment to discuss catering, but calendars got crossed, and they can't make it. So it's just me."

If my hard-ass, ball-buster self can't convince him to let me in, I can play the damsel in distress. Come on, Baker Bro, let's end this charade like you don't care about a desperate plea for help.

He loosens his vice grip on the handle and pulls the door back. "Come in. I've got a bunch to get done before we open, but take a seat and I'll see what I can do."

I'm feeling victorious after my doe-eyed performance, but I thank him profusely lest he get a whiff of entitlement off me. I enter the shop before he can change his mind and take in my surroundings.

I've never been inside an Armenian deli before, but it's not unlike the ones I would frequent when I lived in Queens. Small tables along the perimeter, and a huge refrigerator on the right. Through the fridge's glass doors I spot countless wrapped packages and aluminum trays. A sign taped to the door lists prices of foods that are familiar yet foreign at the same time. Some sound like dishes I recognize—paklava instead of baklava, tolma instead of dolma—but there are plenty more I've never heard before.

While I'm trying to decipher what a msalosh might be, the man pours a mug of coffee from a pot on the counter. "Cream or sugar?"

I turn away from the fridge and take in the gesture. Well, look at that. If he's instinctively hospitable to strangers barging into his business, Baker Bro must be a well-adjusted son who was raised right by a father who gave way more of a shit about him than mine did about me.

"Neither, thanks," I say, trying to keep the twinge of jealousy out of my voice. It's not his fault if his family was functional. "As you could probably tell," I continue, motioning to my monochromatic dark outfit, "I prefer my coffee as black as the soul I don't believe I have. People who dilute theirs with a bunch of crap should stick to chocolate milk—"

Which is exactly what his mug looks like it's filled with. He's unwrapped more Sweet-N-Low and cream packets than most restaurants offer to customers.

Before I can take my foot out of my mouth and apologize, he laughs. "It's okay. You're right—I would stick to chocolate milk if it was caffeinated. Luckily, my masculinity isn't defined by how sweet I make my beverages."

He takes a big swig, looking at me over the top of his mug. Is that an actual twinkle in his eye? My cheeks grow hot, and I will the blush that must be rising to stay beneath my pale complexion.

He's not the kind of guy I usually go for. Sure, he's got the body of a linebacker, and the chiseled jawline and sloped nose that make a man look distinguished, but there's not a rough edge on him. No tattoos or piercings that I can see, and he's wearing a long-sleeved flannel and an apron like he's never taken drugs at a music festival or fucked a stranger in a jazz club bathroom. You know, the first two random examples I could think of, unrelated to my own life.

"So . . . are you gonna stand there without telling me your name?"

I pick up my mug and blow on the top, always prepared to get burned by men I've just met. "Tori. Technically, it's Victoria, but nobody calls me that without getting stabbed in the eye." I wave my hand with a flourish, so he can get a good look at my claws, but they don't faze him.

"That's too bad. Vahe and Victoria has a nice ring to it."

He laughs jovially as my eyebrows hit the ceiling—so this is the grandson Tania was talking about.

"I thought you said you had a bunch of stuff to do." I flick my head toward the back of the deli, away from me. But then my stomach growls, as if protesting my dismissal of the one person in this joint who can prevent us from succumbing to starvation.

Vahe chuckles. "Including feeding you breakfast. You're lucky you were sent on a mission to find a caterer instead of a mechanic, because it's nothing but auto shops around here. If it weren't for me, you'd be wandering around, chomping on loose lug nuts."

I gulp down my coffee, baffled by this man and his bizarre sense of humor. He dons a pair of oven mitts and disappears to the back kitchen before returning with a metal baking sheet, topped with fresh pastries. They're all different shapes, from braided ropes to pretzels and spirals, and the fresh scent wafting from them makes my mouth water.

He smiles at the look on my face. "Yeah, I tend to have that effect on people—lighting up a room and all that jazz."

I try to frown, put off by Vahe's unwavering cheeriness,

but it's unconvincing. The way my heart is pounding and my eyes are laser-focused on the spread before us are proof that I couldn't be more excited to dive in. "What are these little pillows of paradise?"

Vahe refills my mug. "Choreg. They're like Armenian biscuits. A bit plain on their own, but my grandfather always ate them with his morning coffee, so I grew to love them."

I grab one shaped in a spiral. "How much?"

Vahe scoffs. "I would never treat a new customer like a business transaction. I'm not going to forget you committed such a grave offense, but I'll forgive you if you help yourself."

I thank him, shaking off a pang of guilt. I walked in here fully intending to complete such a transaction and leave as quickly as humanly possible. Before my stomach can twist itself into knots over my blatant self-centeredness, I alleviate the hunger with a bite of the choreg. At the first taste, I'm so overcome with pleasure that I wouldn't be surprised if the moisture in my mouth drifted further south.

"Oh god, I needed this," I spurt between big bites. The choreg is so warm and buttery, denser than a croissant and softer than any bagel. I'm taken aback by how ravenous I am, and before I know it, I've inhaled half a dozen. It kills me to wash the remnants down with the rest of my coffee, but I drain my mug and sigh. "That has to be one of the best things I've ever eaten."

Vahe looks away as I'm licking crumbs off my lips and clears his throat. "I'm, um, glad you enjoyed them. I'd hate for you to walk away unsatisfied."

It may be the hot, heavenly bread I gorged on, but I'm flushed. With overt innuendos like those, there's obviously a sexual undercurrent that's making us both uncomfortable. But I'm on a time crunch and itching to rejoin the glam fam. If I wrap things up soon, I can meet everybody in Yosemite and still participate in the photo shoot scouting. Plus, it's not like I'm going to hook up with a baker in Fresno, no matter how delicious his pastries are. Time to shut down any chance at intimacy and return to the transactional.

I slap down my credit card on the counter. "Seriously, Vahe, they were too amazing not to pay you for your services. Now all that's left is to nail down this catering order, and I'll be on my merry way."

Vahe mutters under his breath. "Find it hard to believe you've ever been merry in your whole life."

"Excuse me?" The deli isn't officially open yet, but I'm still a customer. A paying customer if he wasn't such a weirdo about hospitality.

"I said you got it, ma'am!" he calls out as he walks to the kitchen. "Just take a seat. I'll take care of your request once I finish the remaining batches for the morning rush."

I know this time he won't be returning with something else scrumptious to clear the air. This must be my punishment for putting my needs above his generosity because I can recognize when I'm being iced out.

∼

VOICEMAIL ANSWERING *message for Dikran's Deli*

HI THERE, you've reached Dikran's Deli, this is the owner Karine Derderian—ha! Can you imagine? I haven't been called by my full name since I swapped dentists in 1972. Anyway, this is Queenie, and don't you forget it.

My grandkids keep telling me the deli needs a website and an email and social media and a page on something called Yelp —and frankly, I'm tired just saying all that. What do I need them for anyway? You can't order tolma over the godforsaken internet. The peppers would get mushy, and all the filling would spill out. Not on my watch!

If you want the best Armenian food in Fresno, and you don't live in Fresno . . . well, that's on you. Get your tookus up and drive over here. It'll be worth the trip, I promise you that.

What was this message supposed to be about? Our hours? We're open when we feel like being open, and we close when we want to close. You'll find out when you get here. Check the sign on the door if it's not obvious.

If we're closed and you need to leave us a message, you can call this number. Which you did because you're leaving a voicemail.

Start yapping when you hear the beep, and we'll get back to you in a timely manner—as long as your definition of timely is anywhere between thirty minutes and five business days.

Okay, that's all you get. You know the drill. [*beep*]

chapter
three

When I was early in my career, working the front desk of a nail salon while putting myself through beauty school, I'd occasionally have to deal with a disgruntled customer. The Karen who'd come barging in, coffee in hand, to demand that we shift around our schedule to accommodate her without an appointment. In those moments, I'd hold back every urge to dump her unicorn-mocha-choco-frappuccino on her head. Instead, I'd flash the fakest smile and tell her, "Why yes, we take walk-ins!"

And then I'd make her wait. No magazines on the table, no TV overhead to distract her from the ticking hands of the clock. By contrast, I had plenty to keep me busy: filing paperwork, decluttering the salon, reorganizing the shelves of nail polishes, and a myriad other to-dos. Not once did these customers from hell ever outlast me. Around the forty-five-minute mark, they'd toss their drinks in the trash, gather up their hideous handbags, and storm off in a huff—not without threatening to leave a one-star review, of course. Call me petty, but when you're working in low-paying jobs where people treat you like you are less than human, you get a thrill exerting your power in even the smallest ways.

My point is, Vahe may think I'm one of these Karens, but I know what game he's playing. And unlike entitled customers expecting a walk-in, Tania had an appointment scheduled. I should have checked what time Dikran's Deli opened—that's on me—but I'm not leaving until I've completed my assigned mission. And if there's anything that could override my impatience, it's spite.

Vahe probably assumes I'm going to sit down like a lump on a log, pouting and playing on my phone. But he doesn't know anything about me other than my preference for black clothes and caffeinated beverages. I may live in San Francisco and be on the payroll of the world's most popular influencer, but I'm not some spoiled coastal elite. I've been in customer service my entire career, working for whip-cracking managers who espoused the same slogan like nails on a chalkboard: *"If you have time to lean, you have time to clean."*

So that's what I'm going to do. While Vahe is preoccupied baking in the back, I'll make myself useful up front. Starting with the obvious, I step around the counter and brew another pot of coffee to replace what we drank, then open cabinets until I spot the cleaning supplies. For the next thirty minutes, I make quick work of all the tasks I used to take on before opening for business: wiping down the tops of fridges, disinfecting surfaces, sweeping the floor, and getting the glass to sparkle.

It's not particularly interesting or exciting work, but when I notice the frames on the wall that need dusting, it's like traveling through time. You can't miss the signage outside declaring that Dikran's Deli has been in business since 1925, but only when you take in these photos does the weight of one hundred years settle on you. It's like the whole family tree is hung on these walls, with faces smiling in black and white or weathered sepia tones. Five generations from what I can tell, from the patriarch Dikran himself celebrating the grand opening to what looks like a recent snapshot of Vahe with his arms wrapped around two women, likely his sisters, who are holding a gaggle of bright-eyed, curly-haired children between them.

"Can we help you?" an angry voice bursts through the front door, and I whip around in surprise. Standing in front of the counter are presumably the very sisters I was studying in the photograph. They're both about the same height and share the same dark brown eyes, but the one leading the way has blown out her natural curls and is wearing a frown as sharp as her cheekbones.

"As you can see, we're not open," she says tersely, "so unless you have a really good reason to be here, we'll assume you're trespassing and call the cops."

My eyes bug out. This is escalating quickly. "Whoa, now hold on a minute—"

"What's going on here?" At the sound of our voices, Vahe's rushed back, concerned. "Mari, I thought you were taking the kids to the Chaffee Zoo today."

Mari, the angry one, gestures to their sweaters, which I'm now realizing are both animal prints—hers in leopard and her sister's in zebra. "That was the plan, until Queenie called in a fuss, saying she broke a nail while cooking for the senior center's Friendsgiving dinner tonight. The woman she normally gets manicures from is out of town, so now it's our problem."

Vahe stares blankly. "That doesn't make any sense."

Mari's annoyance grows exponentially. "You're telling me! It's the one weekend we can take off before the holiday rush so we can spend quality time with our kids, but Queenie's never let the fact that she can no longer drive stop her—not when she has her grandchildren to chauffeur her around. So the husbands are on zoo duty while we try to find a salon that opens earlier than ten a.m."

As someone who's never had a functional family, I know better than to insert myself into someone else's domestic drama—preferring to slip out of the room unnoticed—but there's something about a beauty blunder, especially with someone's high-maintenance grandma, that I can't resist.

"Um, I'm a nail artist." All three heads turn in my direction, as if they've just remembered I'm still here. Like a fucking square, I wave at them. "Well, I'm a licensed aesthetician, so I can do way more than nails, but manicures are kinda my thing."

They notice my claws holding the microfiber duster. I'm so used to wearing them that it's a hassle removing them for simple tasks. If they're confused about why a nail technician would cover her fingers with full-knuckled rings, they don't admit to it.

"I'm sorry, who are you again?" Mari asks in a tone that's not at all sorry, not waiting for me to reply before turning back to Vahe. "You know you need to run it by me before you hire more staff. We've already scheduled the kitchen deep cleaners for next week."

I toss the duster onto the counter nonchalantly, unintimidated by someone throwing their weight around. "Vahe didn't hire me. If anything, he was nice enough to open early for my catering appointment, and I was simply making myself useful while he finished up in the back. I'm Tori Townsend, by the way." I deliberately stick my hand out to the other sister first to show her I don't care one bit who's the so-called boss here.

"Anush," the curly-headed sister says with a smile, shaking my hand. "You'll have to excuse Mari." She leans in conspiratorially. "Nobody's been able to convince her the customer is ever right. That's why she balances the books instead."

Mari grabs the duster to return it to its rightful place in the cleaning supply cabinet. "And you're damn lucky I do. If I weren't accounting for every decimal, our great-grandfather's legacy would be buried along with every kitschy cupcake shop and hipster coffee bar that's folded after the hype runs out. Ironic how every passion project with a mission to revitalize this neighborhood dies before its second tax season. Cool vibes don't pay the bills."

I laugh a little too loud, startling Mari, who certainly wasn't intending to tell a joke. But if there's anything I can get on board with, it's a curmudgeon with a sense of humor that's Sahara-level dry.

Anush points at the metal baking sheet on the counter, bare except for the crumbs I left in my wake after inhaling every piece of choreg. "We all have our specialties. But it looks like you're already acquainted with Vahe's."

"Yes," I admit, "which is saying a lot because I'm notoriously difficult to please. He's, uh, clearly good at what he does." I wave my hand up and down in his Vahe's direction. The gesture was meant to compliment his culinary skills, but it comes off like I'm referring to the muscular body beneath that tight-fitting apron and oven mitts. Not that I noticed.

Vahe must be overheated from the stuffy kitchen, but when he avoids my gaze, his flushed face takes on another meaning. Is he blushing at the compliment?

He coughs, glancing at the clock on the wall behind him. "We're about to open, and I still need to finish up back there. Where's Queenie anyway?"

We swivel our heads as if the matriarch is going to pop out from behind the refrigerator or underneath one of the dining tables, but there's no one in sight. The three siblings groan.

"Is she still in the car?" Mari wonders aloud, striding outside with Anush at her heels. Vahe returns to the kitchen to check if she's entered through the back door, which leaves me on my own with no one covering the cash register. My customer service training tells me not to abandon my post so close to opening hours, in case any hungry customers come in demanding caffeine and breakfast pastries. But what if Queenie's taken a fall or had a stroke? She may be in need of serious medical attention.

I briskly follow Mari and Anush out the door, which slams back with a loud chime. The sisters look up, startled, but their wide eyes already give away that Queenie's nowhere to be found. My head swivels around the front of the deli, scanning whether Queenie's wandering in the street, but I can't see anything other than the dilapidated gray exteriors of the surrounding industrial park.

My childhood was too rough to have any memories of my own grandparents. In fact, given how my deadbeat dad was in and out of jail and my mom spent what few pennies she could scrape together on cheap beer, I can't recall ever meeting them. But I know that the elderly can get disoriented and go missing. It sounds far-fetched that someone with cognitive decline would be cooking for a senior community, but perhaps she's mistaken one of the auto body shops for the bakery. I'd be confused too if I expected to take a whiff of fresh dough and could only smell gasoline instead.

There's no way Vahe is going to prioritize straightening out Tania's wedding catering order if his grandmother is one case of bad luck away from ending up on the six o'clock news. The sooner I can help find her, the faster I can wrap up this errand and get the fuck out of Fresno. If that means I have to knock on every door within a ten-mile radius, then that's what I'll do.

But my mission gets cut short once I round the deli toward my car and a flash of movement catches my eye. On top of a tall ladder is a hunched woman, struggling to lift a large sign with big, bold letters that read 100 YEARS OF TRADITION. "Queenie?"

Even if she didn't perk up at my incredulous voice, I can tell I have the right person the way her permed jet-black hair sits atop her head like a crown. Not to mention, she's wearing a matching black fringed shawl like a royal robe—one which I'm deathly concerned is about to get tangled up in the ladder and cause her to take a Humpty Dumpty tumble, cracking her skull on the sidewalk.

"Who's asking?" Queenie's voice is gravelly, like my mother's after decades of chain smoking. She swivels in my direction but doesn't stop whatever task she's trying to accomplish. "You certainly don't look like the staff at the old folks' home."

I follow her suspicious, kohl-rimmed glance to my clawed fingers, which prompt me to remove the rings and shove them into my pockets. "I'm not. I'm here for a catering appointment, but you've got your family worried sick. You mind handing that to me so we can get you down from there?"

Holding the ladder to keep it steady, I reach up to grab the sign out of her hands, but she jerks back. "I own this building, missy, and I will not be told what to do with it!"

I'm impressed by both her obstinance and grip, but there's no way she's winning this one. I had a belligerent client try to smack me across the face as I was trimming her mangled cuticles, and she almost got kicked out with a broken wrist.

"I get it, you're the boss," I say calmly, pulling the sign back. "So why don't we order that strong and strapping grandson of yours to take this off your hands? Especially since I hear they're in urgent need of a manicure."

Queenie raises her permanently drawn eyebrows. "Strapping, eh? Single too, for what it's worth, but you must already know that about Vahe the way you've butted into my family's business."

Damn, get me ice for that burn. By now, our standoff has turned into a tug-of-war, and I can only hope that my face is hot from us huffing and puffing so Queenie can't tell I'm blushing. And here I thought I was stubborn.

"Give the sign to me, Queenie. You're going to get yourself seriously hurt."

"Get your paws off it, or I will kick you off this ladder!"

"I'd like to see you try!"

We grapple over the sheet of metal like Som and Glen calling dibs on the hottest guy in the club, shouting over each other to give up the fight.

"What the hell is going on here?" Vahe bursts around the back of the deli, panic across his face. I'd be horrified too if one of my customers got into a physical altercation with my grandmother, had I known her. But I can't help but take advantage of Queenie's moment of distraction.

"Ha—got it!" I exclaim, but the victory dies on my tongue when the force of yanking the sign out of her hands topples me off the teetering ladder. In a split second, I release the sign in an attempt to avoid going down like dead weight. It flies from my hand and makes an awful sound as it crashes behind me, but it's too late. My foot's slipped off, and I'm tumbling backward.

In this real-life trolley problem, I don't expect Vahe to save a complete stranger over a dear relative, so I brace myself. If I'm lucky, falling from a ten-foot ladder won't spill my flesh and blood all over the concrete.

And yet it's not the cold, hard ground I make impact with, but rather Vahe's warm, hard chest. With his formidable wingspan and upper-body strength, he manages to prevent both of us from an untimely death by stabilizing the ladder with one hand and catching me with the other.

"Are you alright?" he says as he lowers me to the sidewalk. "What happened?"

Notes of honey and vanilla hit my nostrils as I breathe him in, simultaneously calming me down and shooting a shiver down my spine. Sinking into Vahe is like diving into the most heavenly desserts, and I have to brush him off before I get so caught up that I reach out to take a bite.

"I'm fine," I insist through gritted teeth.

Queenie and I exchange haughty glares. "She started it!" we blurt out at the same time.

Vahe pinches the bridge of his nose. "I don't care. Either way, I believe it." He rubs his forehead. "Queenie, what were you doing up there anyway? We thought we lost you."

The matriarch scoffs. "Your father's been putting off installing that sign for months—by the time he gets around to it, our centennial will be over. Since I already broke a nail, I might as well take care of it while I'm here. Now where is that blasted thing?"

Mari and Anush emerge at the sound of Queenie's complaining, but their relief dissolves as quickly as it appears. At first, I'm offended that they're openly grimacing at me, until I turn around and see where those hundred years of tradition landed.

Right through my car's shattered windshield.

~

A LIST of things Tori Townsend needs to scream about (in no particular order)

1. Movies about BDSM or kink in which the main character is wringing their hands about how "dark" and "fucked up" they are. You can like getting spanked without it being a moral failing. Just enjoy it!
2. Every time I've checked my phone for the time, got distracted while doomscrolling, then immediately forgot the time the second I put my

device down. If I didn't have the attention span of a gnat, I wouldn't get trapped in this hellish cycle.

3. The next man who says "body count" with a straight face is going to be the first on my actual body count when he pushes me into serial killing.

4. Salon clients who abuse the privilege of getting their hair or nails done as an excuse to treat beauticians like shit. I am a licensed professional—not your maid. Show some damn respect.

5. People who play what I like to call the Trauma Olympics. As someone with capital-T trauma, I have had days where I felt worse about missing the bus than getting backhanded by my mom. Life can suck for so many reasons, and I see no point in ranking who has had it worse.

6. That said, whoever perpetuated the notion that anyone over the age of thirty is too old to blame their parents for their lot in life. I don't let my piss-poor upbringing hold me back from making something of myself, but I have carte blanche to bitch about it for as long as I see fit.

chapter
four

Just my fucking luck. I've lived in San Francisco for years and not once have I been a victim of a smash and grab, but within minutes of arriving at a quaint family bakery, my car looks like a casualty in a horror movie. The windshield is cracked into a million spiderwebs, and the sign has lodged into the driver's seat. Had I been sitting there my death would have conjured flashbacks to the logging disaster from *Final Destination 2*.

But I'm not one for silly superstitions. Because if I never left my car and stepped into this deli I wouldn't be facing hundreds of dollars in repairs—all thanks to an elder who's even more ornery than I am. Now I'm convinced she's named Queenie because she's a royal pain in the ass.

I can hear Vahe shooing his sisters and grandma back into the deli, all of them bickering in a bastardized blend of Armenian and English, but their voices are drowned out by my self-righteous indignation, boiling me from the inside out. I shouldn't even be here. I should never have agreed to Tania's ridiculous request to drive hours out of my way and pick up the pieces of her catering plan. Why couldn't she have rescheduled? When my friends tell me to jump, why do I insist on asking how high?

The answer must be about three feet, because that's how far my body jolts forward when a hand grazes my balled fists.

"Whoa there!" Vahe rocks back on his heels to avoid getting hit by my impulsive swing. "I'd let you punch me if it would help anything, but then both me and your car would be damaged."

I don't bother apologizing for nearly clocking him. He's probably written me off as a monster who attacks unsuspecting senior citizens, in front of their century-old businesses, no less. Not that I feel guilty for getting into an altercation with his grandmother when she clearly instigated it—okay, not *that* guilty anyway. There's no reason to say sorry and assume any culpability. I'm better off driving away and pretending none of this ever happened—if my car was in any shape to be on the road, that is. So now I'm stuck in this dreary ghost town, hundreds of miles away from home, risking a bullshit lawsuit from a squabbling family who'd rather see my skull crack open than accept my help.

"You can let it all out, you know."

I jerk my head in Vahe's direction. "What?"

He gestures toward the deli. "I told them to get back inside so you can have some space. Because you're about to blow."

"Oh yeah, I wonder why?" I wave at the post-apocalyptic disaster scene that is my car. "Are you going to tell me to look on the bright side and smile, sweetheart?"

"I wouldn't dare." The corner of his mouth tugs into the tiniest of grins. "I mean, it always works for me, but I can respect when someone's not in the mood for silver linings. So, fuck it. Let it out instead."

"Let what out?" If Vahe was any other stranger, I'd flick broken glass in his eyes and tell him to get lost. But I'm morbidly curious to hear his suggestion.

He places his hands on his hips as if an authority on the subject. "You traveled to a frankly depressing part of town at the buttcrack of dawn, only for your car to get wrecked by some cranky old biddy who couldn't admit fault if her life depended on it."

I chuckle at the thought of having more in common with Queenie than I gave her credit for. Vahe continues, as if I'm not the only one who has things to get off their chest. "I may have only caught the end of that episode, but it wouldn't be the first time Queenie's gotten handsy with customers, whether in a not-so-nice or way-too-nice way."

"Who hasn't, honestly?" I admit, my mood lifting without my consent. I've had the day from hell, and it's not even eight o'clock. I should want to roll around in my rage, like a pig in shit. Why is it so difficult to stay angry around this man?

Vahe approaches me slowly, like a lion tamer trying to subdue his circus act. "So here's how it's going to go, Tori." He checks his watch. "We open in fifteen minutes. My sisters will handle the morning rush and keep Queenie in line until I've had a chance to clean up this glass and drop off your car at the mechanic next door. Even if Willis didn't owe me for making him the hero with fresh nutmeg cake at his kid's bake sale, he'll fix your windshield free of charge after I tell him you got caught in the path of Hurricane Queenie. Her reputation's well . . . documented around here. He's running a one-man show though, so it will take him a while."

I anticipated that my day would be shot, but I'm pleasantly surprised that my wallet's being spared. Since Vahe isn't yelling obscenities and chasing me out of town, it's clear he's taking the blame for my bad luck. And if there's anything I love, it's making a macho tree trunk of a man grovel a little.

"That's a start," I say, raising an eyebrow. "But I've got a lot of pent-up aggression to get out, and who knows how long it will last."

Vahe steps forward, placing his palms on my shoulders. His grasp is assured, and when I don't claw his eyes out, he sighs a slow exhale, knowing his lion isn't going to commit murder.

"That's why I'm recommending a very particular antidote. I'll keep the pastries coming and the coffee pot fresh, for however many hours it takes for your vehicle to look brand new. But first, you must let it all out. There's nobody else around, so bellow into the abyss. Yell until there's no air left in your lungs."

I swivel around, self-consciously. "Are you serious? Why the hell would I do that? That would be unhinged."

Vahe shrugs. "When I first started working in the bakery to make some extra cash in the summers during high school, there used to be an aluminum swinging door that separated the kitchen from the front counter. On its own, there was nothing wrong with it, but after going back and forth between rooms for what felt like a thousand times per shift, it became a nuisance, especially when my hands were full carrying piping-hot trays of food. One day, I got so frustrated, I took my dad's power tools to it, so I'd never have to deal with it again."

I squint, both to process the moral of Vahe's story and to better imagine his hearty biceps in the throes of manual labor. I can't resist wondering what other kind of drilling he'd be good at.

"My point is," he says, registering my confusion, "is that I wanted to do my job unencumbered, and I didn't care one bit what other people thought once the hallway was in full view. Sometimes a door needs to be ripped off its hinges, and anyone who's around to witness it will have to mind their own damn business."

He makes a good point, underlined by a fire flashing in his eyes. If this is how he pushes pastries, then Dikran's Deli must be rolling in both literal and figurative dough, because this man could sell me anything with that unwavering conviction.

I check to make sure a line of hungry customers hasn't formed around the block. But with the rest of his family inside and nobody else loitering nearby, I place my claws back on my itching fingers and seize the opportunity.

With the deepest breath I can pull into my lungs, I do what I haven't indulged in since I was a toddler throwing a tantrum because my mother yet again forgot to remove the crusts from my PB&J.

I scream. Roaring without reservation. Not the high-pitched squeal that splits your ears as you're watching mean girls get their comeuppance in a slasher film, but rather the deep, guttural cry that escapes from your chest after being trapped since the day you were born. It doesn't take long for me to realize this scream is not about my broken windshield. I scream at every patronizing man who told me to be happy on demand, at every Karen who treated me like a servant, at every teacher and boss who declared I had an attitude problem. I scream for my dearest friends who are slipping away from me in real time. I scream for the father who left and the mother who stayed but was never present, not really. I scream as an only child lamenting the siblings her parents couldn't afford to have, as a high school senior applying for beauty school loans because they drank what should have been her college fund. And I scream as a thirty-something outcast who had no idea she was a razor's edge from unleashing a torrent of anguish in front of a golden retriever in human form.

Eventually, my voice gets so hoarse that my yelling devolves into coughing, and I have to hunch with my claws digging into my knees to avoid toppling over. Vahe slaps my back as if expelling the evil from my body. I'm much lighter than I was before—although, that could just be an asthmatic response from being stuck in this smog-hole of a city.

"Did you let it all out?" Vahe calmly rubs up and down my spine, warmth radiating from his palm.

I take a minute to breathe slowly through my nostrils and wipe the tears that have unwittingly escaped my eye ducts. "I . . . needed that. I wasn't expecting catharsis with my coffee, but I feel better. Thanks to you. "

Vahe beams at the first genuine compliment I've given him and not his cooking. In fact, he's so overcome with joy that before I know it, he wraps me up in his arms and gives me a big squeeze. But the hug is over in a second—before my body can decide to tense or go slack—because as soon as my eyes bug out of my head and I gasp, he sets me back down.

"Sorry," he blurts out, snapping his hands back like they're a measuring tape he's retracted. "It won't happen again. Not until hell freezes over, I promise."

"Or earlier." The words fall out of my mouth before I know what I'm saying. Vahe's jaw drops. "Whatever, it's fine. Don't read into it, alright?"

Vahe's crossed arms makes his skepticism obvious, and I don't blame him. I can't even interpret my own mixed signals. In any other circumstance, he would have suffered a finger ring straight to the face. Everything about my hard exterior is like barbed wire around a wild animal exhibit with a massive sign warning Do Not Touch. Nobody manhandles me without getting their eyeballs gouged.

And yet, here I am, not only tolerating Vahe in my personal space but also reassuring him that I may allow it again. Did I scream out my brain without realizing it?

"We're chill," I insist. "Completely back to normal."

He uncrosses his arms with an amused twinkle in his eyes. "That's good to know because I'm not the only one with a to-do list. While I'm dropping off your car and trying to get this opening shift on track, I'll need you to finish what you started."

"Nearly killing your grandma?" I exclaim incredulously.

"You and me both, but no." Vahe motions like he's going to put his arm around my shoulder but recognizes his error midway through, awkwardly pointing to the deli instead. "I'm talking about that favor you sort of, kinda agreed to earlier. Before she pulled a 'This is Sparta' moment and sent you careening toward the pavement."

We're almost at the entrance when I stop short. "Are you serious? I should be filing a restraining order against Queenie, not her fingernails."

Vahe sighs. "I know, which is why I'm not accusing you of elder abuse. If anything, Queenie *is* the elder abuse. But I need you to babysit her so I can do my job and my sisters can enjoy a day at the zoo with their kids. I know you're trapped here against your will, but you'd be doing me a real solid by keeping Queenie from messing with the plumbing or whatever dangerous task she's compelled to complete now that her nails aren't holding her back. A manicure is exactly what we need to get her out of our hair and at her Friendsgiving soiree where she belongs."

He opens the door, and with the dread I'm feeling, its annoyingly upbeat chime should be replaced with a funeral dirge. "Unpaid labor serving the literal pushiest woman I've ever met—how thoughtful! You're not selling this since I don't see what's in it for me. What's stopping me from waiting at the mechanic's and avoiding your family entirely?"

Vahe waves his arm toward the auto shop next door. "Be my guest. I'm sure you'll love hanging out in a freezing icebox without central heating and listening to Willis's conspiracy theories about how aliens put fluoride in the water to control our minds."

I weigh my options. I could abandon ship, but then I traveled to Fresno for nothing. I'll have to explain to Tania that I didn't take care of her catering order because I refused to humor a stubborn senior. Queenie may be a tough cookie, but at least she's not a full-blown nutjob.

Vahe must know as well as I do that we both need something from each other, but he pushes through my hesitation anyway, seizing the opportunity to convince me once and for all. "Your labor will absolutely be paid, by the way—and not just in cold, hard cash. Because you haven't tried my famous paklava yet." He bends to my ear and unleashes an agonizingly slow whisper. "Letting that sweet . . . flaky . . . buttery heaven hit your lips for the very first time is priceless."

There's no way he's not aware of how sexual that offer sounds, and I'm falling for it hook, line, and sinker. If the bribe of delectable baked goods isn't enough to win me over, now images flash in my mind of Vahe feeding me, as sticky, sugary syrup drips down the side of my mouth. I lick my lips in lustful anticipation, simultaneously turned on by his negotiation tactics and turned off by how easily they work on me. I'm a horny sucker who should have relieved my urges before I left the house, and now he's got me right where he wants me.

Wanting *him*.

***Common phrases** in Western Armenian (and when to use them, according to Queenie)*

"Hello"

- Armenian script: բարեւ
- Transliteration: *parev*
- Queenie commentary: A decent way to start a conversation, but unless you're Publishers

Clearing House showing up with a giant check, you'll need to bring more to the table.

"Good morning"

- Armenian script: բարի լույս
- Transliteration: *pari luys*
- Queenie commentary: Awfully assumptive since you don't know the kind of crap I've had to put up with this morning, but as long as you don't annoy me with mindless chitchat, it will be good enough.

"How are you?"

- Armenian script: ինչպես ես
- Transliteration: *inch-bes es*
- Queenie commentary: If you know me, you won't have to ask this question because I'll make it abundantly clear how I'm doing. And if you don't know me, then what's it to you anyway?

"I'm fine."

- Armenian script: լավ եմ
- Transliteration: *lav em*
- Queenie commentary: The deli could be burning down, or I could be actively dying, and I would say this just to get some doofus to stop talking.

"I'm not fine."

- Armenian script: լավ չեմ
- Transliteration: *lav chem*

- Queenie commentary: On the other hand, the second I am inconvenienced, you will hear about it. Loudly.

"Farewell"

- Armenian script: Երթաս բարով
- Transliteration: *yer-tas parov*
- Queenie commentary: A bit formal, if you ask me, but hey—if you're a paying customer, then you can talk as hoity-toity as you like.

chapter
five

They say when it rains, it pours. That was true as I was racking up spaces on the bad luck bingo card: my car getting wrecked, almost face-planting on the pavement, and deciding to run this ridiculous errand in the first place. But it's also true with this morning rush. One minute I'm screaming into oblivion with nobody in sight, and the next customers have parked bumper-to-bumper along the perimeter to get their hands on hot coffee and fresh Armenian bread.

It's a good thing Vahe's too preoccupied with pushing pastries because I need to cool off after the rollercoaster of emotion I've ridden in the short time I've been here. Being hungry and horny is a dangerous combination, and only one craving can be satisfied in public. Which is why the only hole I'm stuffing right now is my mouth.

Whatever hopes Mari and Anush might have had to get back to the zoo with their families are dashed when a queue of people starts crowding the cash register. Now it's all hands on deck. Except for Queenie—or especially for Queenie—depending on how you look at it. While her grandkids are running around taking orders, packing to-go boxes, and restocking the fridge, she's playing politician.

I take another big bite of tahini bread, watching her make the rounds. Every time she stops at a table, they're happy to see her and conversations last way too long to be merely cordial. The clientele is mostly folks around Queenie's age, and it's obvious from the way they're catching up that they're old friends, likely for decades.

I anticipate being perturbed by this chummy environment, but this isn't some sanitized version of small-town America, like Star's Hollow from *Gilmore Girls*. Many customers must work nearby because they've dressed the part: mechanics in grease-stained coveralls and construction workers in well-worn carpenter pants. I catch snippets of a variety of languages—Armenian, of course, but Spanish and Hmong too. As someone who grew up in Queens and has lived in the Bay for over a decade, much of it in San Francisco's diverse Mission District, I find Dikran's Deli comforting. I'm not accustomed to places that are predominantly white, even though I'm white myself, so I tend to avoid them at all costs. The real terror, for me, isn't a working-class neighborhood that's rough around the edges. It's country clubs and HOA meetings and a home-to-American-flag ratio that starts giving off vibes from that Jordan Peele horror flick . . .

". . . get out."

I perk up from my table, which is covered in choreg crumbs, to see Queenie lording over me, hands on her hips, in mid-monologue. "Excuse me?"

She waves her right hand in front of me, and it takes me a beat to realize she's not shooing me away. She's showing me the broken nail on her index finger. "I said my granddaughters and I want to get out of here, so let's take care of business. Or are you not a nail lady?"

I resist rolling my eyes. Just once I'd like to hear a male technician referred to as a nail man. "Licensed aesthetician and nail artist, yes. We didn't have time for formal introductions while grappling on that ladder, but the name's Tori. What can I do for you, Queenie?"

She ignores the reminder of our recent scuffle and slides into the chair across from me, nails fanned out. She's so comfortable assuming the position that I almost forget we're not in a salon.

Queenie huffs. "I was peeling those blasted potatoes for the grapevines and caught my nail before I knew what happened."

Only half of that sentence makes sense. "Grapevines?"

"The Grapevines, the retirement community in Sunnyside, off the 180." Queenie points in a random direction as if I should be familiar with the finer details of Fresno's neighborhoods.

I explain I'm not from here, and without asking me where I live, she's off to the races. "To be honest," she says, "I don't like its new name, because everybody knows it as the Old Armenian Home, but I can see why they changed it. Some people get weird about ethnicity. My family's owned this deli for a century, and we still get folks thinking only Armenians are allowed in." She gestures toward the long line of customers. "You can see the rainbow in here. I don't care if you're white, black, or purple—"

"So what color are we thinking today?" I interrupt, not wanting to spend the morning educating an octogenarian about racial microaggressions. "I can't match the exact red you've got on, but purple is my favorite color." I flash my amethyst finger rings before taking them off one by one and grabbing my travel case out of my bag. Queenie deliberates over the options before selecting the deepest, most regal shade of violet. "Excellent choice. That will be sure to impress everyone at the Grapevines. Friendsgiving dinner, I hear?"

We settle into our respected roles as I clean off the tabletop and pull out the supplies I need. I remove her existing polish, relieved I don't have to soak off any gel, as Queenie dives into the ins-and-outs of tonight's event: the holiday decor and how much each item cost; every course and how tasty she expects it to be based on who's cooking it; and, of course, all the juiciest gossip about the guests.

"A lot of the gals are giving Marge a hard time for playing the field after her husband's passing, but I knew him, and he was a total bore. Most men are, frankly, but good for her for fixing herself a sampler platter while she still can."

She makes me laugh so hard I almost clip one of her nails clean off. Given her off-color comments on color, I was expecting her to be problematic about everything, but I'm pleasantly surprised by her sex positivity. I'm still mentally holding her at a distance, given her questionable beliefs and behavior earlier, but my icy exterior starts to thaw.

"Now I don't want to lose any length, missy," Queenie admonishes as I grab my nail file. "I've already broken one nail, so I don't need you filing the rest of them down to stubs."

I'm not surprised she's territorial about her claws. She's got a fantastic set, so long and strong I almost took them for acrylics, with the kind of soft cuticles that are moisturized regularly. Having three grandchildren to do her bidding ensures she rarely has to lift a finger.

"It's Tori, and don't you worry. I've got a hack for splits like this."

I dig around the travel case until I find tweezers, a pair of miniature scissors, and—of course—my secret weapon.

"A coffee filter? Now what in the world are you going to do with that? What kind of manicure business are you running, young lady—"

I shush her, and to my amazement, she listens for once. Now that I've got her full attention, I can do my job with mine. After each nail is properly buffed and given a base coat, I cut out a piece of the coffee filter that fits Queenie's index finger and apply it over where it's cracked. Another base coat and we're back in business. I shake the purple polish, ready to finish out the manicure as usual.

"That's a neat little trick you got there, Miss Tori." Queenie admires my handiwork after I apply two coats of the vibrant violet. I revel in the validation of satisfying another customer but also in the petty joy of proving someone wrong. "I need to order more coffee filters for times like these."

I give her a handful from the ones in my bag. "These should be more than enough to get your emergency kit started. Manicure's on the house, in exchange for keeping me fed."

I'm about to don my finger rings, feeling naked without them, when Queenie takes my hands in hers and gives them a grandmotherly pat. "Thank you, dear. You saved the day. I can see why Vahe has taken a liking to you."

I rip my hands from her grasp as if touching a hot stove. "Liking? We just met!"

Queenie shrugs. "I've seen that boy helping behind the counter since he could reach the register, and I've never seen him teach someone his own neat, little trick."

Recognition dawns. "The scream fest I had earlier? I was just having a shit morning—no thanks to you, if I'm being honest—"

"None taken." She chuckles, admiring how her nails glitter in the sunlight. "Now that I've got these, I'll leave the sign installation to my little esh." She squints, a mischievous twinkle in her eye. "You know, Miss Tori, if you're looking for an in with my grandson, it would help to learn Armenian terms of endearment. He'd be tickled pink if you called him that."

I'm torn between embarrassment and curiosity. On one hand, I should be insisting she's got the wrong idea and there won't be any matchmaking going on here. That as soon as I complete my mission and pick up my repaired vehicle, they'll never see my face again. But on the other hand, I want to know what esh means . . . because I like learning new languages, and not just in case an opportunity to use it presents itself.

Queenie packs up her things and calls for Mari and Anush before I can ask her to translate. The morning rush subsided during her manicure, so she waves goodbyes to the few remaining regulars while throwing her bag over her shoulder. By the time Vahe reappears, she's halfway out the door, arguing with Mari about which route back to the Grapevines is the fastest.

"And thank you, Miss Tori." She turns around abruptly, catching the door before it shuts in her face. "I must say my nails have never looked better. I'll be in touch when they need a refresh."

Oh no, she must have memory issues. I try to explain that I don't live in Fresno when she cuts me off.

"Just leave your number with Vahe. I have a feeling you'll be back. Bye-bye for now!" With a sly wink, Queenie's gone, the door chime echoing in my ears as I attempt to make sense of what just happened. Did I become this lady's personal manicurist?

I look back at Vahe. "Are you actually related, or does she simply collect people who can do things for her and hold them hostage?"

Vahe laughs heartily, playfully grabbing me by the shoulder. "The answer's both, but take it as a compliment. She doesn't give anyone the time of day unless she really likes them. You must have made quite the impression."

"Uh-huh." I'm too distracted by the warm roughness where his hand meets the base of my neck. I need to schedule a night out cruising for dudes with Glen and Som. I'm so pent up that the thought of Vahe gripping the sides of my windpipe is making an impression in my underwear.

Vahe catches me, visibly uncomfortable, and removes his hand with a jolt. "Sorry—it's just an old habit, I promise. I've got a big family, so other than cooking, physical touch is our thing. It's a never-ending stream of bear hugs and cheek kisses and slaps on the back."

Images flash in the most depressing montage. Tugging on my mom's leg and being shooed away with an empty beer bottle. Pretending to be sick so I could spend "Donuts with Dad" day with the school nurse. Evenings alone when I should have been tucked into bed but instead I'm watching *The Brady Bunch* on Nick at Nite, wondering what it must be like to have that many people in one house.

"It sounds nice." I cough, overcome with more emotion than I expected. Vahe gives me a sympathetic smile, and I want to retch my painful past up like spoiled seafood so everyone would stop looking at me like damaged goods. "I mean, if you're into that kind of lovey-dovey crap. Maybe it'll grow on me."

Vahe grins, victorious. "Give it enough time, and Queenie will declare you an honorary Derderian, I'm sure of it. There's a reason we call her a hurricane—she storms into your life and there's nothing you can do but take shelter until her path changes course."

No kidding. As a member of Alex's glam fam and now a bridesmaid in Tania's wedding party, I'm used to a constant whirlwind of activity, but somehow these few hours at Dikran's Deli have been more destabilizing. Dikran Derderian. I repeat the surname to make sure I've got the pronunciation right, realizing it's the first time I've heard it. I get this feeling that the longer I stay here, the more I'll learn—about Hurricane Queenie and her frazzled family, but also about myself.

It's just a spark—this urge to be adopted into another collective of kooky characters. I may be overcompensating because my friends are partnering up and moving on with their lives. If I'm going to feel like leftover scraps, I might as well papier-mâché myself into a new crew. Not this one, to be clear, but I'm a long way from home, and practicing on the Derderians will have to do.

"Sounds like everybody has nicknames for each other," I muse as Vahe grabs some paperwork off the counter and motions for me to pull up one of the stools. "Right, little esh?"

"What did you call me?"

At first, I think I've pronounced the word wrong, and he doesn't know what I'm saying. But then the eerie quiet hits me. The last customers straggling between breakfast and lunch have abruptly paused their conversations. It's so silent you can hear the hum of the refrigerator.

"Who taught you that?" Vahe says sternly, crossing his arms.

Oh no, what have I said? I throw my hands up, fidgeting on my stool as if it's a bed of spikes. "It was Queenie—she said it was a term of endearment. Maybe I misheard her, I don't even know what it means—"

My backtracking is interrupted by Vahe's boisterous, deep laughter. He doubles over, hands on his knees, while the rest of the room joins in. And that's when I know I've been conned.

"Okay, I get it. Har har. Is esh even a real word, or did Queenie make it up?"

Vahe wipes tears of joy from the corners of his eyes. "It's real alright. That's why it's so funny. We've been lobbing that at each other for as long as I can remember speaking."

He pauses for dramatic effect, and I want to scream at him to let me in on the joke. "You just called me a jackass."

~

A LIST of things Tori Townsend needs more than a man (in no particular order)

1. A BART route that goes all the way from San Francisco to San Jose without forcing a Caltrain transfer halfway through
2. A societal agreement that any tip less than 20 percent is cheap because it isn't fucking 1982 anymore
3. Durable, healthy nail care that doesn't require toxic chemicals or sticking your hands in mini tanning beds
4. For the first comment after I tell someone I play jazz on the side not to be, "Oh, I love *La La Land*!"
5. The elimination of bridal parties because we're all adults and can stand at an altar without chaperones
6. For everyone to get on board with payment apps so I never have to wait fifteen minutes for another Susan to dig around her gigantic purse for spare change
7. Vaginal dentata, but like retractable, so I can bite off the dick attached to anybody who tries to stealth me from behind
8. The unconditional love of parents who regularly went to therapy so I wouldn't have to
9. The ability to magically teleport a Mission burrito anywhere in the world
10. A swift punch in the tits

chapter
six

"You and Queenie call each other jackasses?"

Vahe grins from ear to ear. "I'm Little Esh, and she's Big Esh. I'm a foot-and-a-half taller than her, but it's more about seniority than size. If we're talking personality, Queenie is big all the way."

"She must be so pleased with herself." I can see her cackling at her own neat little trick on the way to her Friendsgiving party, delighted to gossip about the grumpy goth girl who can't help but ogle her grandson's tight ass every time he walks away. Not that I'd ever admit it.

With Vahe's family off our backs and the crowd of customers finally dispersed, it's just the two of us as the staff in the back prepares for the lunch shift. The weather hasn't warmed up that much, but all of a sudden it's stifling as we're left alone. I'm about to whip out my phone to take notes for Tania as we wrap up the catering details, but Vahe motions toward the door. "You want to take a quick walk?"

Objections pile up in my mind—we've already suffered enough distractions, this is our moment to get real work done, you can't leave your team hanging—but that's not what I spit out first. "In this ghost town? And look at what, exactly?"

Vahe hangs his apron on the coat rack by the door, exchanging it for a faded denim jacket. "Oh, I see. Not the scenic route you had in mind?" He doesn't bother waiting for my agreement, just strides outside, leaving me to jump off the stool to catch up. He locks the entrance, flips the open sign to closed, and leads the way, past the industrial park of auto shops.

Tiny, dilapidated homes flank both sides of M Street, each a unique color and architectural style. Most are weathered white with picket fences, others are modern matte black surrounded by cast-iron, and the occasional quaint and quirky house pops with royal blue. As much as I enjoy the sound of Vahe's breath filling his massive chest, it's too quiet here. If I stayed too long, all the empty space and silence would suffocate me.

When we walk underneath the freeway, though, it's like we've entered a different zone. More businesses line the sidewalk, cars are parked along the curbs, and while it's not busy enough to be bustling, the neighborhood is more inhabited than I gave it credit for when we left the deli.

We arrive at the corner of M and Ventura, and it's not the national hotel chain or the full-blown convention center that stops me in my tracks. It's the historic church in red brick and white trim, symmetrically designed with stained-glass windows. A crimson door stands below an arch that reads HOLY CROSS ARMENIAN APOSTOLIC CHURCH, in English underneath Armenian script.

"Where are we?" Places of worship don't usually wow me, as the only higher powers I believe in are acetone and a good moisturizer. But Vahe intuits that I'm not asking about the letters on the church doors.

"We're in the heart of Old Armenian Town. In 1874, the first Armenian that arrived in California settled here, in what's now downtown Fresno. We came highly educated and entrepreneurial, establishing businesses, newspapers, religious and political organizations. And by the 1930s, we owned seventy percent of the produce in this area, feeding the nation with our farms. Despite what the genocide took from us, we gave back so much more. So maybe before you call this a ghost town, you should learn about the spirits that still live here."

That shuts me up. I hang my head, silently apologetic. Having grown up in New York City, where there's a large Armenian population, I'm familiar with the basic facts of the genocide: 1915–1923, 1.5 million people massacred by the Ottoman Turks, atrocities that Turkey still has yet to recognize a century later. But it was always framed to me as horrors of the past, a black spot in human history. I never equated the decline of a once-thriving community with the lingering effects of ancestral trauma as the diaspora dispersed and assimilated.

Vahe gives the sign of the cross, right to left in the Orthodox tradition, and I expect him to drag me into the church for a much-deserved smiting. That is, until he collapses in laughter. "You know, I'm not spiritual, but I'd pretend to be Hot Priest just to pull your chain like that again. Your face!" He lets out a breath. "I mean, everything I said is true, but I'm no Armenian scholar. I just run a deli in a downtown that's begging to be revitalized, and I don't appreciate outsiders making snap judgments. Got it?"

I don't know what it says about my feminism that a spark of electricity went straight to my downstairs as soon as Vahe asserted his boundaries, but there's something about a man who stays true to his identity and stands in his convictions, regardless of the ridicule that may come from it. Yet again, I should apologize for instigating, but I'm too preoccupied with a more intriguing nugget of information. "You watched *Fleabag*? Wouldn't have pegged you for a Phoebe Waller-Bridge fan."

Vahe waves his hands down his flannel shirt underneath his Canadian tuxedo. "Because I dress like I should be driving a tractor? Phoebe, Kristen Stewart, Aubrey Plaza—what can I say? I have a type. I guess I'm a sucker for pale, dark-haired smart-mouths with deadpan humor." He stares pointedly at me as if I won't recognize the similarities, and I break out into a goofy grin. There goes my cool girl persona. "Plus, it was my ex's favorite show, and I wasn't above watching that sexy sacrilege for research purposes."

Nope, definitely can't be cool when my whole body is heating up. It's not the most progressive thing for a dude to admit he only humored his partner so he could get laid, but damn it for wanting a place in that line. I may not believe in hell, but if I keep imagining Vahe in a clerical collar, that's exactly where I'll end up.

Vahe weaves us around Old Armenian Town, pointing out cultural landmarks, like the bust of famed author and playwright William Saroyan in front of the theater named after him. But I can't absorb the history when I'm distracted by the mention of his ex. Who was she, and how much did she look like me? How long did they date, and why did they break up? And, most importantly, is he seeing anybody now?

Stop it. I'm not going down that rabbit hole. There's no reason to care about the love life of a burly baker I'll never see again. The only relationship I should be focused on is Tania's, because I came here to a run an errand, and it's long past time I cross this task off her to-do list.

"Alright, I don't mean to cut this walking tour short," I say as we approach a small park next to Fresno's courthouse. "But we need to talk catering for Tania's wedding. She runs this bigwig marketing agency, so she's used to calling the shots. She will put my head on a pike if I come back empty-handed."

Vahe chuckles. "I'm not surprised to hear she runs her

own business now. She's got a big heart, but that bossy streak of hers earned her the nickname Tyrant Tania."

My eyes pop. "Wait a minute—you know her?"

"Yeah, we go way back. We went to the same elementary and high schools. Didn't run around in the same social circles, but we lived within the same square mile and rode the bus together, so we were technically neighbors. Never would have guessed in a million years she'd be marrying an athlete though. She couldn't even handle carrying the books she reads, so she pulled around a rolling backpack, bullies be damned."

I can't even enjoy these flashbacks between childhood friends because I'm still replaying Tania's desperate pleas for help. "Why the hell didn't she mention your history before sending me on this godforsaken goose chase? She made it sound like this narrow window of opportunity would close for good if she didn't book the catering contract today."

Vahe shrugs. "Don't get me wrong. It's already mid-November. The holidays are around the corner, and the deli gets backlogged with orders fast. Tania's right not to procrastinate any further, especially since she's tying the knot in three months. She and her family are longtime customers, and she's Hye too, so she would be aware of our busy season."

"High?" I repeat, flummoxed. "I would hope so. The only explanation for this nonsensical turn of events is that she's more stoned than the rocks that fiancé of hers free solos."

It takes Vahe a second to put two and two together before he dissolves into another fit of laughter. "H-Y-E," he spells between breaths. "It's Armenian for being Armenian because we call the motherland Hayastan. You would think with the sheer number of times that miscommunication has happened I would anticipate it better, but it gets me every time." He wipes tears of joy from the corners of his eyes while I roll my own.

"I'm glad this non-Hye has brought you such amusement,

but forgive me if I'm not in the mood. Like you said, we're in a time crunch." I stride back toward Dikran's Deli, but Vahe's legs are so long he catches up no matter how fast I mall-walk.

"Hold up. I'm not laughing at your expense, but I can't have you leave on a bad note. Let me make it up to you. We'll take care of the catering paperwork while I feed you a hearty lunch of shish kebab and the butteriest pilaf you've had in your life—on the house. How's that sound?"

I want to tell him where he can shove his kebab skewers, but my stomach betrays me with a deep, rolling growl. All that self-righteous anger has got me hungry again. I refuse to admit Vahe's right, but it doesn't matter. The way his eyes twinkle is proof he knows he's won.

"It's odar, by the way," he says, keeping pace with my slower steps. "For non-Armenians. I must say you're the most memorable odar I've ever met, Tori."

I smile, even if the compliment is only insurance against impalement. "The odar and the esh. It has a nice ring to it."

Vahe practically shines from within at the casual comment. Given how cheery the glam fam is, I'm used to overly positive people. But there's something different about how I gravitate toward Vahe's light. Am I soaking up his rays like a sunbather on vacation or a moth to a flame? Only time will tell if I'm about to get burned, and we don't have much of it left.

I return to our previous conversation to kill time on our walk back. "If you and Tania grew up together, why didn't you run in the same social circles?"

Vahe chuckles to himself as we make our way underneath the freeway again. "That's not a difficult mystery to solve. Tania was Miss Goody-Two-Shoes, and I was the rebel without a cause. I always knew Dikran's Deli was my destiny, so I didn't apply myself like she did. She probably wrote me off as a knucklehead." He considers the question more carefully. "We had a handful of classes together in high school, and we were always friendly, but I was known for being a bit of a ladies' man back then. She liked living vicariously through my sexual escapades and even suggested girls I should ask out, but I wouldn't be surprised if she steered clear to preserve her pristine image."

So much to unpack in that revelation. As someone familiar with who Tania is today rather than who she was as a teenager, I know people can change dramatically with time. After all, Tania must have a rebellious streak of her own to abruptly quit her cushy C-suite position to start her own marketing agency. Not to mention, end up engaged to a rock climber who defies death on a daily basis.

But what if old habits die hard? It's no secret I've also racked up more than a few notches on my bedpost. What if Tania knew exactly what she was doing when she sent me on this mission, because she can't help playing matchmaker? If that's the case, she must be off her rocker if she thinks I'm going to fall for Baker Bro. Even if I'm the teensiest bit curious to hear about these escapades.

"Are you still a ladies' man? Is that why you gave me the grand tour of a city that was featured on not one, but two episodes of *Gangland*?"

Vahe mocks clutching his chest at my verbal stabbing. "Hey, roll that tape, Townsend. Because that's tied with your precious San Francisco." He leans closer as we turn the corner, Dikran's Deli in sight. "As for your question, let's just say there's more than one reason why I'm rated five stars."

He runs his fingers along the underside of my arm, which despite being covered by a band hoodie feels scorched by wildfire. Holy shit, I can only imagine how my bare skin would react to his touch. Not that it would happen. Not when this pit stop has already resulted in enough delays.

"Welp," I gulp, yanking my arm away, "it doesn't matter

what your ranking is on the OpenTable of one-night stands. I don't run around with fuckboys from Fresno."

I'm about to enter the deli to grab my nail supplies and take my chances with Willis the wacko-mechanic, when Vahe blocks me from opening the door. "Sounds like you only take issue with my residence, not my reputation. So let me convince you of both."

I try to maneuver around him. "You're never going to convince me that suburban hellscapes like this aren't where dreams go to die."

I'm not sure why I'm laying the venom on thick, especially after our objectively nice outing in Old Armenian Town. I don't waste my time insulting cities I've never visited before. Why am I antagonizing a stranger for not only where he was born and raised, but also where four generations of his family planted roots after escaping ancestral atrocities?

Vahe smiles, refusing to take the bait. "Talk nonsense all you want, but what I don't hear are doubts that I'd give you a guaranteed good time."

Holding the door closed with one hand, he leans danger-ously close to my face, which I bet is turning as red as the awning above us fluttering in the fall breeze. "So let's put money where our mouths are."

Oh god, that mouth. Plump lips nestled between a dark, well-defined beard I want to rake my hands through. A mouth that's hovering inches above mine, promising a kiss like a threat. Barbs bubble up my throat, but I close my eyes and await my fate. What harm is there in letting him win this round?

Vahe chuckles softly. "My, my, let's not get ahead of ourselves." He pulls back with a smirk. "But I appreciate your enthusiasm for the competition."

I balk, mortified he caught me anticipating his mouth on mine and ready to exact revenge for leaving me hanging. If he wants to place a wager, then I'll do whatever I can to crush his spirit.

"Get to the point, little esh. Because if I wanted to walk in circles, I'd keep looping around that dump you call a downtown."

"That's the kind of energy I'm talking about." Vahe rubs his palms together in delight. "Sure, Fresno might not be the quaint small town of a Hallmark romance, but let's be real— SF isn't some utopia either. So how about we put them to the test? City versus not-quite-country. Crowded capital of coastal elites versus the breadbasket of the entire world. How about it?"

My mind whirs at the nonsensical notion. It's such a subjective contest that I can't fathom how we'd pit two vastly different places against each other. It's not even comparing apples to oranges—more like apples to mimosas. Vahe's representing a bland, mediocre Red Delicious that's anything but, and I'm holding a crystal glass of Dom Perignon with a splash of freshly squeezed fun that brings the party to every weekend brunch.

I grin like a Cheshire Cat. There's nothing I love more than judging things by arbitrary standards. "It's not a fair contest, but I'll play along. How would we make our cases?"

He gives the question some thought. "I usually don't need more than one night to wow a woman . . ." he says, pausing while I mock-hurl, "but backyards are a lot bigger than bedrooms. How about we spend one weekend in each city? Friday night to Sunday. We'll plan the most amazing forty-eight hours we can imagine, highlighting the best of what our homes have to offer."

I'm running through my mental list of San Francisco's most exciting events and attractions, ready for the challenge. "But we clearly have conflicts of interest. How are we going to objectively evaluate each city?"

"I don't know about you, Tori, but I conduct myself with integrity." Another smirk from him, another eye roll from me. "This isn't going to be some boring ranking of the best place to live by sad, stuffy criteria like the unemployment rate and the quality of the school districts. This is about something much more important—the vibes. But if you're so concerned about bias, we can hold ourselves to the highest standard in my business: the Michelin guide."

I tilt my head, perplexed by what restaurants have to do with comparing residences. "I'm not following."

Vahe holds up three fingers. "The official criteria for Michelin stars is more nuanced, but I like to break them down by the three C's. One star is awarded for the cuisine—its ingredients, how they're constructed, the flavors they evoke. Two stars are for culture, when an establishment is celebrated for its personality as much as its prep. You're only given three stars if you have the cool factor, when you're destined to go down in history as a legend at the top of their game."

I nod. "Cuisine, culture, and the cool factor. Got it. Stripping down countless dimensions to what makes a truly stellar scene: arts, entertainment, and, of course, food. I can get on board with that. When are we carving this competition into our busy schedules?"

Vahe pulls out his phone, tapping through his calendar. "Naturally, I propose this logistical behemoth during Dikran's busiest season. But in a couple of weeks, the deli closes for Thanksgiving weekend, so you could come back down then. It would be the perfect time for a meal tasting, so bring Tania and the wedding party. That way I can impress your friends and prove without a doubt that I deserve to come out on top."

Setting Vahe's sky-high confidence aside, it's not a bad idea. As a bridesmaid, I'm already required to tag along to Tania's pre-wedding events and errands. And if Tania was sneakily plotting our introduction all along, then she'll be totally on board with anything that keeps us in close proximity. Now that I think about it, I should set the right expectations, so neither Hye considers this as anything more than a friendly competition.

"I don't know what kind of games you play with the ladies," I say, briskly entering the deli and gathering my stuff, "but let me be clear. These weekend rounds aren't dates. Regardless of which city wins, neither of us intends to relocate, so let's not pretend anything romantic is going to happen."

My tone is sterner than I'd like, and my back is turned so I don't have to face him. It's not because I'm angry. I'm excited to play tourist for once, to see both my city and Vahe's through his eyes. But bad things happen when I put my hopes in people who will inevitably leave.

"Tori."

His voice is calm, playful even. I slowly meet his gaze, trying not to stare at his bulging arms that could pop watermelons like balloons.

"As heavenly as my wedding cakes are," he says, "I'm not planning on getting hitched anytime soon. Don't get it twisted —I'm the coolest uncle who never fails to bribe my sisters' kids with sweets, but the deli's my baby. Nothing wrong with the picket fence and two-point-five children, but I'm thirty-five. Between living in a city where everyone settles down after graduation—college, if you're lucky—and being pressured by a stubborn Armenian family who considers singledom a tragic curse, if that life path was meant for me, it would have happened by now. If anyone was going to understand when I say life keeps me plenty busy, I think it would be a Ms. Independent type like you."

I should be offended that Vahe's taken one look at me and written me off as a man-hating spinster, but he hit the nail on my half-shaved head. I'm sure there are jazz-playing, nail-painting punks out there going to parent-teacher conferences, but I can't entertain that alternate universe for myself with a straight face.

Raising an eyebrow, I stare him down. "Life keeps you busy, or that long line of lovers, Baker Bro?"

He looks pleased with himself. "Más o menos. Por qué no los dos?" At my bewilderment, he laughs. "What, you're surprised I'm trilingual? I work in food service in a city that's fifty percent Hispanic. Or are you just pissed I'm more cultured than you?"

I bristle at the thought. I did not spend the early years of my career in New York nail salons to be one-upped by a dude whose city's airport is so small I question its international status. "Mình sẽ không để anh ta làm vậy."

He doesn't have to understand Vietnamese to know I've insulted him, but it doesn't deter him in the slightest. "You seem to care quite a bit about my extracurricular activities. What does it matter if that line circles the block a few times? You said it yourself there won't be anything romantic between us. If what we're doing is just a game, then what's the harm in playing?"

Every word out of that tempting mouth is as smooth as butter, like he's equally intimate with seducing women as making phyllo dough from scratch. His confidence isn't over-compensation. He'd pass a lie detector test with flying colors, because he truly believes he'll win this competition . . . and whatever we wager.

I jut out my chin, defiant. "What are we playing for? The prize has to be large enough for me to even bother."

Another knowing smile. "Oh, it's large enough, alright," he taunts. My hands are full with my bag and travel case with all my nail equipment, but I'm about to drop everything at the deli entrance and beat him to death with the coat rack.

Vahe takes a step back. "Kidding! But I mean it. If we're

going to travel two hundred miles to spend a weekend with each other, then we should raise the stakes. So here's my best offer. If I lose and you convince me San Francisco is indeed the superior city, you can tell Tania that Dikran's Deli will cater her entire wedding for free. Hors d'oeuvres, starters, entrees, wedding cake, and Armenian desserts on the house. How's that sound?"

Take me back to Holy Cross Church because I'm witnessing a miracle. I may be nowhere close to walking down an aisle, but I know that weddings are fucking expensive, and catering is typically the most exorbitant part. Between Tania's colleagues and Nolan's rock-climbing buddies, their guest list has ballooned to two hundred people. That's thousands of dollars Vahe is putting on the line.

Does he even have the authority to place a bet that big? I'm not sure how Dikran's Deli is managed, but it's a family business, so his family must have some say. Especially Mari, who balances the books. This wager would throw those books off-balance immediately. It's not like Vahe can sneak a pro-bono booking of that size past her. Which means he's writing a check his ass can't cash, or he's so sure he's going to beat me that he doesn't care what's at stake. Either way, I can't wait to tell Tania every bite at her wedding will be comped, thanks to me, because I've got this challenge in the bag.

"I say you got yourself a deal, little esh." I rearrange my stuff so I can stick out my hand, but he hesitates to shake it.

"And what will I get when I win?" he says softly, emphasizing the *when* to make it abundantly clear that there isn't an *if*.

I open my mouth to correct him, but the words die in my throat when Vahe lifts my outstretched hand to press his lips to my palm. This isn't a chaste peck on the knuckles like we're in some period drama. He's kissing the sensitive skin in a way I can only describe as sensual. In my line of work, it's natural to cradle someone's hands in my own. I do it without thinking so hand-holding has never got me going. But when Vahe's tongue flicks against my heart line, my actual organ pounds so hard I'm afraid it's going to send me into cardiac arrest.

I should clench my fist and punch this presumptuous fucker right in the face. Sure, I've had the most intriguing morning of my life. Vahe has spent the last few hours plying me with delicious food and rich coffee I won't be able to find anywhere else. And then there was the one-man walking tour around downtown and the screaming stress release prior. But just because Vahe has anticipated my needs before I can, that doesn't make us affectionate. I had no idea he existed when I woke up. He may see me as a gothic Good Samaritan with a knack for manicures and mollifying senior citizens, but he doesn't know a single real thing about me. That my dad's in and out of jail so frequently he might as well be trapped in a revolving door. That my mom needed the next drink more than a functioning liver and daughter. That no matter how hard I worked to claw my way out of poverty and make something of myself, it will never relieve me of the fear that I'll be orphaned by everyone I love.

We're the very definition of strangers, and here he is, dangerously close to melting me into a puddle on the linoleum. Before I can stop myself, my remaining common-sense escapes with my reply.

"I'll sleep with you."

Vahe drops my hand in surprise, as if he never expected his Casanova act to actually work. "What?"

Take it back, Tori. Go grab some pots and pans and chase him off like the ravenous dog he is. But no matter how much I want to yell obscenities and demand that he scram, I'm caught between *I can't* and *I won't*. Torn in two by my lust and pride.

"Are you sure?" Vahe cautions, eyes narrowed. "Because I was thinking a lifetime's supply of nail polish for Queenie or even a sincere 'Vahe Derderian is an amazing human-slash-genius' would do the trick."

I chuckle at the *Brooklyn Nine-Nine* reference, in no small part because I've received my share of comparisons to tough-as-nails detective Rosa Diaz. If my favorite badass on television never backs down from a challenge, then I sure as hell won't either.

"I've never been so sure of anything in my life," I declare, squaring off with Vahe. "You're putting your money where your mouth is, so I'll do the same." I curl an adorned claw, gesturing Vahe to drop his head closer as if I'm sharing a juicy secret. "If the sheer number of men I have pining over me is any proof, it's my mouth that's priceless."

Vahe goes red so hard, and the stifling heat wafting from the kitchen ovens has nothing to do with it. That's right. You're not the only person who could teach a masterclass on seduction.

Two enter a battle of wits and willpower. One will be crowned the victor—and that someone is me.

Game on.

***GLAM FAM GROUP* chat on Sunday, November 12, at 3:17 p.m.**

ALEX

Remind me who's hosting Glam Fam Friendsgiving this year? Som, is it your turn?

SOM

No, I hosted two years ago, remember? I made all my childhood favorites. Green curry, papaya salad, and basil chicken with crispy fried eggs. Damn, now I'm hungry . . .

TORI

It's my turn! Get ready for delicious NYC deli classics: pastrami on rye, bagels with lox, and the quintessential bacon, egg, and cheese.

CASEY

You sure you don't want us to bring a turkey?

ALEX

You know Tori's allergic to anything basic.

TORI

If turkey was good, we'd have it more than once a year. You'll have to wait your turn for your colonizer fare.

GLEN

Hey now. We Brits are the ultimate colonizers, and I'd much rather have beans on toast.

SOM

I say we let Alex host next year. Not because I like white meat (unless we're talking about Tom Holland lol), but then her Michelin-starred chefs can cook us anything we want.

GLEN

Fancy beans on toast it is, then!

chapter
seven

"Alright, I'll concede," Casey says, gesturing to the pile of plates we've practically licked clean. "This may not be a conventional Thanksgiving meal, but I did not miss the turkey."

Alex, the other former Southern belle in our friend group, nods in agreement. "We know you love nothing more to hate on anything *basic*"—she whisper-shouts the word as if it's a slur—"but this New York smorgasbord gives my family's world-famous mashed potatoes a run for their money."

I hold back a scoff. I've yet to see Alex or her billionaire parents attempt to cook a meal that didn't end with an intervention from the fire department. Rather than quibble about the fleet of Le Cordon Bleu–trained chefs on their payroll, I raise my wine glass. It's hard for people to admit you don't have to follow traditions for the sake of them. "Why thank you. I know hosts are supposed to be humble about their cooking, but I fucking crushed it."

My only complaint about my mouth-watering pastrami sandwiches is that Vahe isn't here to drool over them. Our game hasn't started yet, and I'm already raring to win him over with everything in my life.

"You really did," Tania agrees, jumping up to clear the table. Since we're celebrating our Friendsgiving the weekend before the actual holiday, she decided to join us and use the time with the glam fam to find the perfect bridesmaid attire for us. I'm not a fan of dresses, but Casey outdid herself with the final selection: a velvet emerald gown with long sleeves, a flatteringly deep V-neck, and a high slit. It's a statement piece that's both hella sexy and warm enough for a winter wedding in Yosemite.

"Don't you dare," I warn, swatting Tania's hand away from the dishes. No matter how many times I insist she's a guest, she is not comfortable being the center of attention. Even on her big day, she'll be desperately looking for ways to be useful.

As roommates, Som and Glen, however, have no problem letting me call the shots in our apartment. You don't need a chore chart when you have the formidable personality of a drill sergeant. I direct them to soak the dishes in the sink while I usher everyone else into the living room to finish off the expensive Napa cabernet that Tania brought.

"When it's my turn to host Friendsgiving," Glen says as we settle into the mismatched seating we found at the most eclectic boutique shops around the city, "I'll need to bring my A-game and show you Yankees what you're missing across the pond. Leave it to Tori to turn everything into a competition."

I let out a loud snort without thinking. They have no idea how true that is. Everyone focuses on me, wondering what I find so funny.

It's not that I can't segue the conversation. I'm the most private person in the glam fam, and I have no problem taking a secret to the grave if I have to.

But what if I don't want to? What if I've been obsessively thinking about Vahe Derderian these past eight days since we parted, and if I don't talk about him to my best friends, I'll explode?

I'm not a giddy schoolgirl with a crush. It's just that this wager directly affects Tania's wedding, and they deserve to know about it.

"So, the thing is . . ." I spill my guts, summarizing my trip to Dikran's Deli and explaining the terms of our bet—save for the part where I said I'll sleep with Vahe if he wins. It's never going to happen, so it's none of their concern.

I expect them to demand details about the Michelin-inspired criteria or brainstorm spots in San Francisco that are sure to come out on top. But who am I kidding? By the time I stop talking, the glam fam is kicking their feet and squealing with delight, only one thing on their minds.

"Our little man-eater has a date?" Som screeches, launching off the sofa to grab a bottle of champagne to celebrate.

Tania takes a flute with a knowing glance. "I'm not sure what's more delicious—the meal we just ate or the fact that you and Vahe hit it off in spectacular fashion."

I should give Tania a much-deserved piece of my mind for conveniently omitting that Vahe was a childhood friend of hers. From the smug look on her face, she's about as shameless about her unsolicited matchmaking as Alex is about hawking her staff's fine-dining courses as old family recipes.

"Let me make this clear. There's a zero-percent chance of anything happening between me and Vahe, no matter how tasty his goods are. His baked goods, I mean."

She tips her head back, taking a long sip of the sparkling wine. "Mmhmm. Which is why you've planned a weekend-long date."

"It's not a date. It's a competition between regional rivals. One I'm only participating in so you can save major bucks on this shindig, by the way." The plus side of Tania having the chance of coming in significantly under budget is that she's too thrilled to ask any follow-up questions.

"And I'll be forever in your debt if you win this bizarre contest, you know that." Tania takes another sip. "But you know what would make me even happier? If you opened up your heart the tiniest crack and let an absolute gem of a guy like Vahe in."

I cross my arms. "You sure you're talking about my heart and not a completely different body part?"

It's Tania's turn to snort, sending champagne bubbles up her nose and tears out the sides of her eyes. While I was prepping the Friendsgiving feast, Som did a wedding makeup trial on Tania, and now we have evidence that her mascara application will withstand the waterworks. "Phew!" she exhales as her laughter subsides, dabbing her face dry with a tissue Som shoves in her direction. "Give a woman a heads up, will ya, before you tell a joke, Tori. A wit that sharp should be considered a weapon of mass destruction. As for which void Vahe has a better chance of filling, I'm sure he'll take whatever he can get, but something's different this time." She pauses, as if flashing back to high school. "When I consider how much of a playboy he's been, let me tell you—not once has he planned forty-eight hours so elaborately. He must really want to impress you."

It's sweet how adamant Tania is that Vahe is genuinely infatuated with me. I don't have the heart to tell her he hasn't abandoned his rakish ways, if his enthusiasm for my wager is any indicator. But if I'm competing to make a quick buck, I can't take it personally if he's doing the same for a quick lay. Fresno can't hold a candle to San Francisco, so I'll cash his blank check on Tania's behalf and be on my merry way. An amusing couple of weekends, and it will be over before we know it.

"I pity him, really," I reply. "He's going to lose by epic

proportions. Because what's the best his hometown has to offer that the Bay doesn't already have? Other than real estate that doesn't cost a million dollars, I'm coming up short."

I can tell from the uncomfortable glances coming from Alex and the glam fam that I've put my foot in my mouth. That's when it dawns on me. I'm not just shitting on Vahe's hometown, but Tania's too. My mind races to walk back my statement, but Tania speaks first.

"Look, I get it," she concedes, "I lived on the outskirts of Fresno for more than half my life, so I know how bored I was in my tiny town. They call it 'brain drain' because anyone with half of one gets the hell out as soon as they can. Escape to greener pastures where they can benefit from cleaner air, higher-paying jobs, and everything they could possibly need within walking distance."

She sets her champagne flute on the coffee table. "But here I am, eating my words. After a decade of living in a city I thought I'd never leave, I swapped Oakland for Oakhurst. I've retreated further into the middle of nowhere. At least Fresno has a Whole Foods!"

I gape at her in mild horror. If that's her new definition of civilization, then she's not selling me on her decision to relocate. Tania's home is only fifty miles from Dikran's Deli, but it might as well be a wilderness wasteland given the difficulties of accessing basic amenities.

"Don't give me that look, Tori," Tania says, shaking her finger. "It will make me root for Vahe just so he can wipe the superiority complex off your face. I'd give up Lyft and Door-Dash all over again, in a heartbeat. Because I have the one thing you can't order via mobile app."

"A moment of zen?"

Tania ignores my wisecrack. "*Love*. The kind of love that has you quitting your job and living in a van, so you don't have to spend one more minute of this offensively short life apart. Sue me for wanting that same love for you."

If a stranger were to eavesdrop on us, they'd assume Tania's being dramatic, but she means every word literally. When Nolan free-soloed a skyscraper to propose after only six weeks of dating, I thought she lost her ever-loving mind when she said yes. I can't imagine temporarily living the van life or closing on a house in the backcountry like Tania did, but I can respect her decision. Why can't she show me the same courtesy when I tell her Vahe's staying in the friend zone?

By now the glam fam has moved on to discussing the latest reality TV drama, so they're not paying attention to our conversation. At least they know to mind their own business, even if Tania hasn't taken the hint herself.

I don't blame her. She's not the first bride to gush about the life-fulfilling properties of tru wuv and mawage, as *The Princess Bride* put it. I'm just uninterested in getting caught in the crossfire, dodging unsolicited dating advice like shrapnel. Why don't Glen and Som get the same third degree? They're bigger man-eaters than I am—and I say that with envy because leaving a trail of broken hearts in your wake takes a special power. But because they're gay and trans respectively, they're not expected to settle down as soon as possible.

As satisfying as it would be to unload a feminist diatribe on Tania about how I can be a complete and whole person without a significant other, thank you very much, I simply don't have the energy. For once, I'm walking away from an argument instead of into one. I tell myself it's because I want to win thousands of dollars and be the MVP of this bridal party, but the butterflies in my stomach betray my true intentions.

I'd rather die than admit it out loud, but I'm excited to see my little esh again.

My? Whoa there, let's not get carried away.

VAHE

Would it be breaking the rules of our wager
if I convinced the bride to hand over your
phone number?

TORI

I guess you can't break the rules if we
didn't establish any in the first place. So
permission granted.

VAHE

You're right. We should lay down the law
when it comes to long distance
communication. Like don't send me six
texts in a row when one paragraph will do.

TORI

I'm with you on that one. My friend Som
does that constantly, and it drives me nuts.
I'll add: don't call me without texting to see
if I'm free first. And no dick pics, obviously.

VAHE

. . . *deletes text* You drive a hard bargain,
but fair enough. What about asking my
opponent what she's wearing?

TORI

Any ridiculous question will be met with an
even more ridiculous answer. I'm wearing a
wetsuit with a top hat and tutu. Does that
get you going?

VAHE

It would if I wasn't wearing the same thing.
You're trying to steal my thunder.

TORI

How selfish of me. Let me change into
something else.

VAHE

Let me guess. A powdered wig, puffer
jacket, and dinosaur slippers?

TORI

I was thinking your chef's apron with
nothing underneath.

VAHE

. . . Well played.

chapter
eight

With the end of daylight savings time earlier this month, the sun's been going down around five o'clock. I have no idea what Vahe has planned, but the one hint he gave was to show up while the light was still on our side.

I park in front of Dikran's Deli at the peak of golden hour, and find Vahe standing outside the entrance. At first, I'm confused as to why the restaurant is closed, until I remember it's the day after Thanksgiving and this weekend is one of the few his family doesn't work. Vahe is spending his precious vacation time hyping up a city that was 126th on a recent list of happiest places to live. Out of 182. Seventy percent of the country was rated better, but here he is, thinking he has a legit chance of winning this wager. Sucker.

"Ready to get this party started?" he enthuses, shaking his car keys above my head. We walk around the back where an old, white Chevy pickup is waiting, lowered as close to the ground as it can get. His choice of truck should be obnoxious, but when I jump in the cab and breathe in the blend of leather and gasoline, I'm oddly comforted. This is the kind of beat-up vehicle I would have lost my virginity in, had I not been raised in a walkable city.

"Why not?" I say. "Let's proceed with the grand tour. Can't be that much to see, right? We should be done in, say, twenty minutes?"

"Says the resident on the tip of a peninsula that's only seven miles long by seven miles wide." Vahe starts the engine with a smile that's just as revved up. As I expected, my razzing doesn't dampen his spirits in the slightest. If anything, he welcomes it in the name of friendly competition, and my instinct is correct—we've both done our research. I adjust restlessly in my seat, brainstorming regional insults to save for later. We haven't even started, and I can't imagine anything more fun than negging a hot guy's hometown—with his own enthusiastic consent.

Vahe's right. Fresno has over double the square mileage of San Francisco, so I'm expecting a bit of a drive to wherever we need to go. But five minutes later, he parks a few blocks past the park we visited last time near the courthouse.

"We're here?" I ask in confusion, unbuckling my seatbelt.

Vahe exits the vehicle in a rush, all so he can open the passenger door for me. It's too much of a date-like gesture, so I blow it off the only way I know how—with more jokes at his city's expense. "Why thank you, kind sir. Will you be my bodyguard for the evening? I heard the crime rate's atrocious around here."

"You know it. Because the first activity for team FresYes is an urban safari where you can witness one of the dangerous sights that has folks on NextDoor clutching their pearls."

"Oooh, a meth lab? Is the cartel in town? No, you got me tickets to a cock fight!"

He grins. "Even better—graffiti."

From the way Vahe's parked his truck diagonally on the street, I can only see an empty plot of dirt, with nothing but a couple of barren trees and a few patches of dead grass. But then he swings his arm to point in the opposite direction, and the epic sight smacks me right in the face. "Whoa."

We quickly cross the road, barely checking for oncoming traffic as this burst of shape and color draws us in. On the side of a large warehouse with the insignia STANISLAUS STUDIOS is one of the boldest, most psychedelic murals I've ever seen.

I crane my neck up to take in a large chimpanzee head, its brain exposed like the center of a sunflower, surrounded by floating eyeballs and fluffy clouds. "As a loud and proud urban dweller," I say, "I like to think of myself as a graffiti connoisseur, but you have clearly undersold this."

At the end of the building, a giant bumblebee with a human face dukes it out with an electric blue praying mantis. We walk around the corner where the mural continues, a surreal display of more fantastical creatures—a horned rabbit here, a flaming phoenix there—followed by an industrial garage with the most vibrant red rose painted on the door.

"We're standing in the heart of the Mural District," Vahe explains. "Every first Thursday, dozens of studios like this one open their doors for Fresno's ArtHop. It's an awesome tradition for the community to appreciate their exhibits and support local artists. In fact, most of the home decor I've collected over the years are pieces made by the friends I've met here. I think that's pretty cool."

"It *is* pretty cool," I agree, standing back so I can take the scene in fully. "It's a shame I'm missing out. On the ArtHop, I mean." Can't have Vahe thinking I'm disappointed about not being invited back to his place, getting up close and personal with his most prized possessions.

He smiles, steering me away from Stanislaus Studios and around the block, where every vertical surface is covered with street art. It takes me back to the outdoor galleries of San Francisco's Mission District, down Twenty-Fourth Street and through Balmy Alley, where you can honor the cultural heritage of the Latin American artists and activists who refused to be stamped out by the city's unrelenting gentrification. I can't speak to their lived experiences, but here with Vahe, I'm amazed by his instinctive ability to make me feel like I'm home.

We walk around leisurely, enjoying the way the setting sun cascades over each wall in a warm glow. Our shoulders and the tips of our fingers are mere inches from touching, but despite wondering how my hand would feel in his, I don't dare to make the first move. That would be a very date-like thing to do, and this stroll through the Mural District isn't that. So.

"It's an acquired taste, for sure," he hedges, unsure how to interpret my silence, "but if anyone could appreciate something like this, it would be an edgy badass like you."

He motions to my monochromatic outfit: a black body-suit paired with matching jeans, knee-high platform combat boots, and leather jacket. The only seasonal addition I've added is a beanie to keep my half-shaved head cozy in the November chill. It's such a standard uniform that I never consider what other people think of it, and Vahe's observation unnerves me. He's paying me a compliment, but I can't let it sink in. If I take his words seriously, then I'm one step closer to taking him—and possibly *us*—seriously.

"Yeah, well, with this riveting nightlife, you probably think staying up past curfew is edgy and badass, so what do you know?"

A flash of pain crosses his eyes before he recovers with a slight smile. If he wants to say something, he's holding back. Maybe because he can't argue with the reason why I'm here. And it's for the love of the game, not actual love.

I resist every urge to take back my words, but they've already done their damage. Vahe's put a healthy distance between us, because everything that comes out of my mouth is not healthy. I'm not sure how to function around Vahe without resorting to insincerities and jokes. But I won't be getting to the bottom of it anytime soon—not when he's leading the way back toward the truck.

Vahe opens my door with a flourish, inviting me to climb into the cab. "Then it's a good thing we've only just begun." Once I'm inside, he leans over to grab my seatbelt, and I hold my breath, flustered by the breach of my personal space. As he pulls the strap across my lap, there's no fumbling around with the buckle. He lines it up on the first attempt, securing it with a decisive click. Heat rises to my cheeks as I imagine what else he could insert without assistance.

My face must give away my inappropriate thoughts because Vahe hovers over me with a smirk, enjoying me squirm underneath him. "Hope you got a jolt of caffeine before you arrived," he murmurs, "because I can go all . . . night . . . long."

Every time Vahe speaks low and slow, he draws me in—a punishment for pushing him away. When I think he's going to put me out of my misery and seize my lips in a passionate kiss, he slams the truck door in my face.

It doesn't take a genius to see the power dynamics at play. While I hide behind verbal jabs, Vahe's armor is his charm. I'm barbed wire, and he's bedroom eyes. The frigid bitch and the fuckboy.

And if I don't take charge of this tug of war, I'm going to lose my shirt—and my pants.

∼

UPDATED *voicemail message for Dikran's Deli on Wednesday, November 22, at 5:30 p.m.*

. . .

HI THERE, you've reached Dikran's Deli, this is Queenie. We are currently closed for Thanksgiving weekend. Yes, you heard what I said. The whole weekend. Friday, Saturday, and Sunday. I have been up to my eyeballs in orders preparing for this holiday, so if you haven't picked yours up by now, you're what my father would call shit out of luck.

Contrary to unpopular belief, we are not a supermarket and do not offer Thanksgiving feasts on-demand. I can't imagine why anyone would procrastinate until the last minute and settle for eating instant mashed potatoes wrapped in cellophane, but I'm not you. I don't live your life. What I do know is that we're closed this weekend.

But, Queenie, you say—it's an emergency! Do you hear the words coming out of your mouth? A full-course meal with fifteen different sides is not an emergency. I know our souboreg is the best, but trust me, you will survive without it. Barely, but maybe it will motivate you to plan better next time.

Speaking of emergencies, can you believe I almost died falling off a ladder recently? I won't bore you with the details, but I got to say my grandson Vahe's new lady friend is a real firecracker. Reminds me of me when I was her age. Anyway, Vahe will be cooking for her this weekend—not you. We will be closed. If you're calling for any other reason, leave a message after the beep. [*beep*]

Ten minutes later, after a straight shot down Van Ness Avenue—which had me doing a double take since San Francisco has a street with the same name—we arrive at our next destination. By now the sun has set, and as I exit the truck, I search for any clues as to where we've ended up. Unlike the industrial aesthetic of the Mural District, everything here is lush and green, from the Italian cypress trees lining the perimeter like regal columns to rows upon rows of plant life beyond the parking lot.

"Is this a nursery?" I wonder aloud, as if the sight beyond the white-trimmed awning wasn't evidence enough. Between the aisles of potted greenery and the handful of flatbed carts, it's like we entered through the back of a Home Depot. Out of all the places that could have been on the itinerary, this would never have been my first guess.

I'm waiting for the other shoe to drop, for Vahe to turn around in a fit of laughter and declare I've been punked. Instead, he taps his nose mysteriously and leads me past a stone fountain. We walk down a gravel path, which is lit by iron lamps hanging from shepherd's hook posts. It dead-ends at a tall wooden fence, its white paint glowing against the dark void of the night surrounding us. Surely, this is when the jig is up, and Vahe comes clean about his elaborate joke.

And yet when he lifts his arm, it's not to slap me on the back and exclaim how gullible I am, but to rap on the fence with a quick knock. A hidden door swings open, and a blonde woman in chic denim overalls comes into view.

"Chrysanthemum," Vahe says with confidence, as if it's a normal thing to tell a complete stranger. But if this woman works here, it might be. It's six o'clock on a Friday night and the place looks deserted, but perhaps he needs some fresh flowers to . . . make the deli more inviting?

"Welcome to Bloom & Brew, Vahe, party of two!" the woman chirps. "Right this way." She opens the door fully, revealing a hidden wonderland. A gazebo-inspired structure, so massive it could pass off as a tent during Oktoberfest, is draped in string lighting. Throngs of people are seated at wooden picnic benches, both large and small, filling the air with boisterous camaraderie.

Recognition dawns. "It's a bar," I blurt out lamely as our hostess steers us toward a more private bench to the side, where a pianist is playing.

"It's both a nursery *and* a bar," Vahe clarifies proudly. "The only place I know of around here that has a beer garden within an actual garden. Ingenious, right?"

I know he's referring to the venue, but I have to give the credit to Vahe. If anything has kept me on my toes all evening, it's him.

The hostess shows us the QR code for ordering food and drinks before returning to her post as botanical speakeasy security. After a few minutes of negotiation, we settle on the south of the border special, which pairs a basket of carne asada loaded fries with two Mexican beers.

"Cheers." Vahe clinks my glass. "Figured if I was going to pull out all the stops and truly surprise you, I had to bring you here. San Francisco's not the only metro with award-winning spots that you need a password to enter. And Bloom & Brew has the one thing that's extremely hard to come by in the Bay."

I select a crispy fry coated in guac, sour cream, and nacho cheese. "Grow rooms for greenery other than cannabis?"

"Nope." Vahe snatches the fry out of my hand and into his mouth with a victorious grin. "Space. Glorious space." He stretches out his arms to make his point, then licks the remnant sauce off his fingertips. I make the mistake of staring a little too long, fantasizing about where else he could flick his tongue, and he winks to rub in the fact that he's caught me in the act.

Resisting the urge to hide under the picnic table, I push back. "Most people don't require acres of space. No need for heavy machinery or a toolshed when there's no grass to mow or pools to clean. Everybody loves to throw our tiny apartments in our faces, but we're too busy having a blast in a city where there's more to do than pack a McMansion with enough kids to create your own youth basketball team."

Vahe laughs heartily. "Okay, you got me there. With six nieces and nephews, I know I don't want that kind of chaos in my life 24-7, but I appreciate having a big backyard to rent the occasional bouncy house for their birthdays. I don't care how old you are—a bouncy house fucking slaps."

I grin, imagining what it would be like to jump around in an inflatable castle, dressed in a tutu like a princess. It could have been fun to celebrate with the few school friends I made, our hands sticky from pizza grease and confetti cake. But I can't even recall their names, let alone a moment when my mother had money to spare after draining her bank account for her own vices. My birthdays passed by like any other day because they didn't matter and neither did I.

Vahe must have seen my face fall, because he immediately orders us more drinks and returns the conversation into safer territory. "So is a beer garden like this not good enough for you and your celebrity friends?"

Celebrity? Has he been talking to Tania? I thought Alex stopped her from running her mouth years ago, shutting her down the only way a marketer like Tania can understand: making her sign an airtight NDA.

"I'm not revealing industry secrets, Tori," he explains, whipping out his phone. "Your profile is public."

I gasp. Not because he's showing me my own social media photos, behind the scenes at Alex's various fashion shows and publicity events. I'm so used to being her aesthetician that I forget a typical Tuesday for me would be the opportunity of a lifetime to somebody else.

I'm shocked because Vahe's admitted a cardinal sin. "You've been lurking this whole time, and you don't even give me the courtesy of a follow? Hella rude." I act like he's been spying on my innermost thoughts when he's only known me for two weeks and the most riveting content I've posted is the nail art I did for the Met Gala. Still, it would have been nice to get a reciprocal peek into Vahe's life.

"Done. See?" He points to the confirmation. "I would apologize, but then I wouldn't have heard you say 'hella,' and I got to admit, that's cute."

I make a face of disgust, sticking my tongue out like I'm dry heaving.

"Pardon me," Vahe mock-apologizes, "is that too basic of a compliment for you and your haute couture crowd?"

I shake my head with conviction. "To me, everything's fucking basic. But that doesn't bother my friends in the slightest. Nine times out of ten, Casey's drinking a syrupy iced coffee from some soulless chain. Alex is fondly referred to as Princess, and Tania couldn't resist reserving Valentine's Day as her wedding date. Every one of them would be tickled pink if they were called cute underneath some string lights in a gazebo beer garden."

"So they would approve of my nightlife selection?"

"Oh yeah. They'd want this place to lean even harder into the twee aesthetic." I wave my hands to paint the picture. "An over-the-top flower wall in that corner, decked out with a derivative neon sign that says something like *In My Bloom Era*. A VIP section for luxury picnic parties and bottomless brunch. And, of course, try-hard themed cocktails with mildly provocative names like Orgasmic Orchid and Sex on the Peach."

Vahe nods, impressed. "Damn, with that vivid reimagining, it doesn't sound half bad. You should be in charge of bringing Dikran's Deli into this century. Your puns alone would have customers begging to try our menu." He sips the foam off his latest beer, studying me. "But I'm guessing that's not where you're most comfortable."

"Tania's the marketing expert, not me. While she and the glam fam would be deliberating which of the three hundred photos they'd take deserve to go on the grid, I'd be on that stage, in my own world." I nod to the piano, which is silent at the moment as the pianist takes a break.

I don't mention that most of my life I only had musical notes to keep me company. I held on to my silly sixth-grade recorder well until my teens until I could pool together enough paychecks to buy my first keyboard. Too poor for extracurriculars, I was entirely self-taught. After-school was for shifts at salons with questionable labor practices, rather than band practice. Nowadays, you can watch tutorials online, but I convinced the flute girls to photocopy their sheet music by bribing them with makeup I stole from the drugstore. The scores didn't always translate to other instruments, but I made do. Now between painting nails and playing the piano, the only time my fingers aren't flying are when I'm sleeping.

"You should be." Vahe startles me out of my flashback. "Up there. Kicking ass." He interrupts my instinctive refusal. "Yeah, yeah, I see that look. You may think I'm ludicrous for suggesting it, but I've planned this whole weekend to show you my world, and it's only fair that I get the tiniest glimpse into yours."

He got more than a glimpse while cyberstalking me for weeks, but that's not my biggest concern. "I can't barge into someone else's gig, Vahe. That's literally taking food out of another person's mouth."

Vahe shrugs. "He doesn't look like he's hungry."

I'm about to rip him a new asshole for making assumptions about who's a starving artist, when I see the pianist off to the side of the stage, taking a hefty bite of a hamburger.

"Now's as good a time as any," Vahe declares, abruptly standing and striding over to the musician, still mid-bite, before I can stop him. I freeze, eyes wide, as Vahe negotiates on my behalf. He points to me, and I want to sink through the picnic table until I'm six feet down, buried alive. I don't have time to die of embarrassment, because within seconds, Vahe's giving me a thumbs-up and a goofy grin.

I guess the show must go on. But I'm not going to carry it alone.

"Sit," I hiss, pointing at Vahe, then the piano bench. He mirrors my deer-in-headlights expression, eyeballs darting for the exits. "If you're going to rope me into this performance, you're going to learn a thing or two."

Defeated at his own game, Vahe takes a seat next to me as I crack my knuckles. "Alright, little esh, what will it be? What's your jukebox request?"

He draws a blank. People always react the same to that question, when every single song you love disappears from your brain the moment you need to recall them the most. "I, uh, like the '90s, I guess?" he blurts out lamely.

I consider a decade of options, before landing on the perfect one. "Okay, you're going to put your hand here," I say, pointing to the keys. "Index finger on E-flat, middle finger on B-flat. Yep, right there."

Vahe raises an eyebrow, fingers dangling above the keys. "Now what?"

"Press them like a little jab—ba-dum!"

He taps the keys, the sound ringing out hesitantly.

"Great, now slide down and hit G and B-flat, same fingers. Quick and punchy. Ba-dum again."

He follows my instruction, glancing at me for reassurance. "So jab, then slide?"

"Exactly. Now, combine the two. Over and over, like a heartbeat. Trust me, it'll make sense."

He gives it a go, clumsy but determined, beaming from the simple joy of playing his first notes. It feels good to show a newbie the ropes—even if I have to hold back a laugh from what comes next.

"There you go! Now before it's your turn, I get it started with this." I bring Vahe's piece in after mine, so the riff comes together in a peppy doooo-do-do-do-ba-dum-ba-dum. We repeat the sequence several more times until the rhythm is seamless, and Vahe's face falls in recognition. "Come on," I tease. "You know this song."

He refuses to indulge me, so I exclaim MC Hammer's famous line, "Can't touch this!" His annoyance almost makes me regret trolling him, since he indeed can't touch this unless he wins our wager. But nobody can stay mad during this song.

I play the rest of it until Vahe's smile comes sneaking back, and he starts singing along with me. At one point, he jumps up from the bench to bust out his best hammer dance, and the crowd goes wild, hooting and hollering. I lose all of my performance composure and laugh harder than I have in forever. Between prepping for Tania's wedding and maintaining a breakneck pace of client bookings and piano gigs, I can't remember the last time I goofed off for the sake of it.

When the song fades into silence and Vahe takes a bow, I'm not ready for this moment to end. Most of the guys I take home from the jazz club pull the same move, demanding I wrap up my set so we can start the real show back at their places. But Vahe isn't in a rush to complete a transaction. He simply rejoins me on the bench and nudges my elbow. "What else you got?"

Some unoriginal loser in the back shouts at me to play "Wonderwall," but I disregard him, rolling into other chart-topping '90s hits. First, the equally ridiculous classics like "Ice Ice Baby" and "Baby Got Back." But the longer Vahe hovers, leaning closer, the more romantic the ballads get. Before I know it, I'm reliving every middle school dance with slow songs from Savage Garden and K-Ci & JoJo. None of these are particularly hard to play, but I find myself fumbling a few keys, especially when Vahe starts whisper-singing in my ear.

"This is supposed to be an instrumental performance," I hiss, sharper than I intended. I'd give him a playful sock in the shoulder, but then my hands would have to stop what they're doing and disrupt everyone else's evening. And yet, if I leave Vahe to his own devices, I fear he'll disrupt my evening—in the most handsy way possible.

Vahe closes in, sliding down the bench until he's an inch away from my right side. "You were the one who made the rules, Tori. Apparently, I can't touch this, but that rule goes both ways."

I bristle at his response. "That's entirely the point."

"Is it? You sure you're not regretting your decision?" He breathes each word down the back of my neck. I can feel every syllable as it lands on my skin, which immediately prickles with goosebumps. I know the juvenile game he's playing—like we're two kids in the backseat during a long road trip—but he's on expert mode and my resolve is rapidly waning.

Up this close, all I can smell is his freshly laundered flannel and the kind of lady-bait cologne that I bet killed in college. It's just a guess, but I can picture it vividly: Vahe with a piecey faux-hawk and a wardrobe full of Ed Hardy. Teenage Tori would have known exactly what kind of trouble she'd be getting herself into, and she still would have fucked him in his pickup truck. The problem, however, is I'm seriously considering making the same mistake now.

"God, what a cliché I'd be." The words tumble out of me so quietly I wonder if I've even said them aloud, but considering how Vahe stiffens and relinquishes my personal space, it's apparent I did.

He stands up, muttering something about tipping the pianist for his time. I stop playing mid-song, feeling adrift. I'm flustered in his presence, but even more so when I'm not.

"Meet me at the truck," he insists. "I'll be there in a few."

Vahe pulls out his wallet and walks off the stage to where tonight's paid entertainment is enjoying the longest break of his career, scrolling his phone with one hand and taking drags from a cigarette with the other.

The walk past the hidden beer garden and through the nursery is so much longer on my own. I shiver, but it's not because I've left the radius of the heat lamps. I don't want this night to be over, but I keep putting my foot in my mouth and ruining the moment. Why? What is wrong with me?

If I concede, even to myself, that the moment I'm ruining is heading a romantic direction then I'll be admitting defeat. There would be no reason to continue the competition because I'd be handing my only bargaining chip to Vahe on a silver platter. Sure, the whole concept of this contest could be his flimsy excuse to date me. But if nothing happens between us, I can keep up the pretense that we've found an amusing way to pass the time while planning our mutual friend's wedding.

I wait outside Vahe's truck, kicking the loose gravel, until I see him approach with an impressive bouquet, walking down the nursery path like a blushing bride without a veil.

"Did Tania order a floral trial run for pickup?" I ask, confused.

Vahe shakes his head exasperatedly, handing the bouquet to me. "Consider this a peace offering. I can sense when I'm coming on too strong, so this is proof I have zero intention of being anything other than a consummate gentleman." He chuckles at my skepticism. "Don't get me wrong—I'd have no problem being on my worst behavior if you were game, but I prefer to be the fuckboy of your dreams, not your nightmares. So I will delay gratification until I'm the uncontested victor. I'm not interested in winning by pushing your buttons, no matter how much I enjoy it."

I inhale the floral notes, relieved that my boundaries will be left intact, even if Vahe's gesture is a bit gauche. No one's bought me flowers since high school prom, and that dude's name has been buried in the graveyard of my mind, like every other man to wander in and out of my life.

Then something intriguing catches my eye. Tubular stems, adorned with crimson veins to attract unsuspecting prey, jut out between the greenery and blush roses. "These are pitcher plants."

Vahe flashes a mischievous smile. "Just a reminder that even something as cliché as gifting flowers on a first date can manage to surprise you. Remember that the next time you want to swallow me whole like an insect."

So many objections bubble up to my lips: that this isn't a date, that I wasn't calling *him* a cliché, that, technically, pitcher plants eat their prey by drowning them in a pool of digestive enzymes. But by giving me a carnivorous bouquet, Vahe's made his point.

Don't let my man-eating ways get in the way of a good time.

GLAM FAM GROUP* chat on *Friday, November 24, at 9:08 p.m.

TORI

Alright, everybody, listen up. This is your final reminder that the meal tasting will start at 6 p.m. tomorrow. That means be at Dikran's Deli at 6 p.m., not text me "on my way, traffic is like hella crazy omg" at 6 p.m.

SOM

You can just @ me next time, betch.

CASEY

If the fake lash fits . . .

GLEN

Don't worry. I'll shove Som into the boot of my car if I have to. We'll pick up the blondies at Alex's.

TORI

Wait, wait, wait—you're driving all the way from the Bay? Why wouldn't you just take the jet to Fresno airport?

ALEX

We would, but Princess Alex Air got added to that celebrity flight tracker. My PR team wants me to cut down on trips shorter than 200 miles, so I look less entitled.

TORI

You have a private jet named after you . . . whatever, props on doing your part for the planet, I guess. Make sure to leave by no later than 3 p.m. to give yourself enough time.

ALEX

You got it Plus, a road trip will be fun! My chefs have packed the absolute best snacks.

SOM

I'd say, "and none for Tori Townsend," but you got us beat. That hot baker of yours is the ultimate snack.

GLEN

A snack attack

CASEY

A snack and a half

ALEX

Snack-tacular

GLEN

2 snack, 2 furious

TORI

Sighhhhhhh . . .

chapter
ten

The next morning when I wake up, all early signs indicate that it should be a great day. I avoided getting head-splittingly hungover from our beer garden antics. My carnivorous bouquet greets me cheerfully on the small desk in my hotel room, secure in the vase I requested from the front desk.

But there is one problem: I'm horny as fuck.

I briefly consider jerking off but decide to pass—and not just because I made the amateur mistake of forgetting to pack my bullet vibe. When only one remedy will do, and he's decided to respect my boundaries, anything else is a poor substitute.

Instead, I jump in the shower, not bothering to wait until the water warms up. If a cold shock can careen dudes' sex drives into the ditch, then it's good enough for me.

Vahe's plan today is twofold: showcase the best of Fresno's Armenian food while conducting a meal tasting for the bridal party. I understand the benefits of feeding two birds with one scone—the tasting is a critical component of wedding planning, after all, and with Dikran's Deli closed for the Thanksgiving weekend, we won't have to worry about catering to other customers.

But, for once, I wish I had the buffer of incessant distraction. I'm afraid without anyone barging in, our business will rapidly devolve into pleasure if we're left to our own devices. In a desperate series of texts last night to the bridal group chat, I begged everybody to join us for the cooking. The glam fam tends to be agents of chaos wherever they go, and I know it would be infinitely easier to keep my hands to myself if they were making the day all about themselves. But nobody budged.

They're way too eager to play matchmaker. It's obvious they're ready to plan another wedding before Tania's marriage contract is even signed.

Joke's on them. Because now I'm refusing to entertain a fling with Vahe, let alone a real relationship, out of spite. I can't fall madly in love if I stay mad.

After the quickest shower I can stand under a frigid waterfall, I check my phone for the time. Vahe sent a good morning text with a reminder to dress cool and comfortable since we'll be on our feet in a hot kitchen all day.

I grin, donning a pair of distressed, low-waisted gray jeans and a burgundy top that reveals plenty of midriff. The only thing I love more than showing some skin to drive a guy wild is having a sweltering environment as a foolproof excuse to fall back on. Oh, you thought I dressed this way for you, Vahe? My dude in christ, sorry, it's a billion degrees in here, and it's not my fault my hot-ass body is breaking the thermostat.

Vahe may want me to take the man-eating down a notch, but if he's going to be in his element, muscles bulging underneath his apron, then I need my wits about me. I complete the look with the vampiest makeup I can get away with while the sun's still out, painting on a sharp cat eye and a wine-stained lip like armor. Vahe was crystal clear that he wouldn't make any moves on me, but that doesn't mean I can't torture him just to see how long his resolve can last.

My more evolved self would call my behavior juvenile. It would tell me I'm obsessed with a game of cat-and-mouse, playing with a man's emotions like I'm hunting for my next meal, because it keeps me in control without the pesky problem of forming genuine connections.

And to that evolved self, I say fuck off. I've willingly entered a battle between cities with a baker shaped like a tree trunk. Nothing about this arrangement makes sense. Might as well have some childish fun while it lasts.

I grab my bag and exit the lobby. Because I'm used to having everything within walking distance, the thought of driving a mere half mile to Dikran's Deli seems ridiculous. But as much as I'd like to blame my jogging pace on the chill of wearing a crop-top in late November, I'm looking forward to seeing Vahe. Our first date was less than twelve hours ago, and I'm already itching to be back in his presence again.

Ahem, not a date. If I keep misspeaking in my own mind, who knows what's going on in Vahe's? I can't let him get the wrong idea. For a competition like this, it makes more sense to call them rounds. According to the Michelin-starred criteria we agreed upon, last night's round was all about culture. He managed to surprise me with a district dedicated to street art and a secret beer garden within a nursery, so I'd say—not even begrudgingly—that he's up one point.

And if the aromas wafting from the bakery are any indicator, today's cuisine round is going to be a slam dunk.

The door chimes behind me, and Vahe perks up from pouring two mugs of coffee. "Hey, hey! Look who came back. I was afraid you'd be halfway to San Francisco by now."

He offers me the drink, beaming with the bold confidence that knew I wasn't going anywhere, and I accept it with the same smile. It's not a facial expression I'm used to, and if I'm not careful, my muscles are going to end up sore. But I can't help it—he's more of a pick-me-up than any caffeinated beverage.

Vahe scans me from head to toe, settling on the tattoo peeking out from my crop top. I can see the rainbow beach ball of death spinning in his brain. He either doesn't know how to interpret the dotted line of ink around my underbust or he's too busy imagining running his hands along the sliver of skin.

We lock eyes, taking hearty swigs from our mugs. Let's get the obvious out of the way—I'm not the only one who looks damn *good*. Vahe clearly watched *The Bear* and thought to himself, fuck that noise. Because instead of dressing like a cretin who takes bumps of coke when nobody's looking, he's sporting a crisp work shirt and slim-fit pants under a navy apron with leather detailing. Even though Dikran's Deli isn't expecting any customers, he's put the same level of effort into his appearance as he did last night, smoothing his wavy hair with pomade and keeping his salt-and-pepper beard sharp and trimmed. He's elevated without being overdone, and it hits me hard that this fuckboy is a fuck*man* in every sense of the word.

Coffee goes down the wrong tube, and my coughing shakes us out of our mutual ogle fest. "So, uh, what's on the agenda today, chef?"

Vahe sets his mug down on the counter and claps his hands together. "Well, sous-chef, we've got an ambitious menu to prepare for the tasting tonight. Our sarma and cheese boregs to start, followed by our mains of chicken and shish kebab with pilaf and Armenian cucumber salad. Dessert, of course, will be our famous paklava."

My finger raises instinctively to throw in Tania's ubiquitous reminder, and Vahe anticipates what I'm going to say. "And, yes, I've already considered how to make everything vegan-friendly. What kind of award-winning establishment do you think I'm running here?"

I'm ready to crack a smart-aleck remark when a timer goes off. "But first," he says, "breakfast!" He turns on his heel to pull out a familiar sight from the kitchen.

"Choreg!" The name rolls off my tongue, already salivating with delight. I'm not ashamed to admit that I searched high and low for a worthy substitute in the city but came up short.

Vahe gives me the rundown of what he's prepared ahead of time while I hoover up bite after scrumptious bite of buttery, flaky goodness. The pastries lull me into a state of pure bliss, and before I know it, I've eaten five of them.

A tap on my shoulder jolts me out of my trance. "I'm sorry. I'll stop!"

Vahe chuckles, tossing a matching apron over my head. "Hey, don't let me get in the way of a good time." He steps closer to adjust the straps, and I will my heart to slow down so he can't feel it pounding as his fingers graze my chest. His voice drops an octave lower. "I don't ever want you to stop indulging yourself. Life is short, and moderation is bullshit."

I laugh, while Vahe gently guides my hips, turning me around and away from him. He must be taking advantage of my choreg-induced stupor to place his hands along the waistband on my jeans without fearing violent retribution. And yet, I let him.

He traces the exposed sliver of skin before tying the straps into a neat bow. "Can't have you getting dirty," he whispers in my ear, moving my hair to the side so he can tighten the strap around my neck. My breath catches in my throat as I imagine the dirtiest scene imaginable: Vahe ripping off my clothes and bending me over the counter, driving himself into me over and over again as he grips the side of my neck with one hand and twists my hair taut with the other. I wouldn't even care about being head-first in scattered choreg crumbs. I'd be so busy screaming that Willis the kooky mechanic next door would burst in, convinced we were being robbed at gunpoint.

That's when I know, deep down in my bones, especially in the pelvic region, that if Vahe touches his lips to my neck, it's game over. My back arches, daring him to make the first move, but it brushes blank space instead of Vahe's apron-covered abs.

I turn around to see Vahe leaning against the counter, a smug smile across his face. He knows the effect he has and takes as much pleasure taunting me as I do him. "Ready to get started?"

"Born ready, Baker Bro." I gulp down the last of my coffee and remove my claws, shoving them down into my pocket, prepared to get messy. "Let's do this."

Vahe leads me into the back for my first up-close look into the industrial kitchen. It's already warm thanks to multiple preheated ovens, and overhead vents keep the air circulating. As someone used to sterile environments, I appreciate how clean the workspaces are, all gleaming stainless steel and spotless surfaces.

"I can't take credit for this," he explains, noticing my impressed expression. "Queenie went out of her way to tell the deep cleaners I was opening for you today, so they went the extra mile. It was embarrassing and highly unnecessary, but I must say they did a fantastic job. I could eat off these floors."

I don't know what's more adorable—that my arrival is considered a special occasion or that Queenie's enlisting strangers in her matchmaking schemes. I shouldn't appreciate her meddling, but the idea of anyone going above and beyond for me makes me shine brighter than these sparkling kitchen appliances.

Vahe pulls out several containers from the refrigerator and sets them on our workstation in the center of the kitchen. "Technically, I could have prepped most of these dishes in advance and left the assembly for today, but where's the fun in that?" Spices galore are already waiting in small glass bowls. "Plus, I can't have you return home without making classic Armenian dishes from scratch. The aroma of pilaf alone is therapeutic, and eating it fresh off the stovetop should be approved as a mood stabilizer, because it's never failed to cheer me up."

My mouth waters at the thought, and I'm practically bouncing in my boots in anticipation. Everyone's relationship with food is complicated, but for most of my life, it was simply a necessity. I don't know what it's like to have a functional family that ate a homecooked dinner and went around the table to talk about their days. As soon as I could open a can of store-brand soup or microwave a frozen meal, that's what I was left to do while my mom was out, doing temp jobs when she was sober enough to work or on the hunt for a bar she wasn't already banned from when she wasn't.

Vahe must sense I'm not enjoying my walk down memory lane because he pulls me back into the present, handing me herbs and vegetables to chop: onions, peppers, parsley, garlic, fresh dill, and mint. "So, what are your favorite comfort foods to make?"

I grimace. The phrase 'comfort food' has always been an oxymoron to me. "There's no point cooking when you live in a culinary mecca like San Francisco. I could eat out every meal for the rest of my life and only make a dent in all the city has to offer."

"Is that so?" he says with a twinkle in his eye. "How's the choreg up there?"

There's that smugness again. Has he learned about my failed search from Tania?

Sure, there's no shortage of Mediterranean and Middle Eastern restaurants if you've got a hankering for hummus.

Greek, Persian, Syrian, Turkish—an eclectic blend of influences across the region—but no establishment can compete with the great Vahe Derderian. Not that I need to give him the satisfaction by admitting it.

"I'm starting to understand why Queenie calls you a little jackass." I bring a knife down a bit too forcefully on a bell pepper, sending it flying.

Vahe laughs, diving into tales of the matriarch's unmatched attitude, and we get into a rhythm. After the veggies are finely chopped, he teaches me how to blanch grape leaves in boiling water. He seasons minced beef and lamb for the carnivores, as well as a vegan mixture of lentils, chickpeas, and red kidney beans. The veggies are added to both fillings, which are mixed with tomato paste, bulgur wheat, and a few pinches of coriander and other spices. Then begins the long yet soothingly repetitive process that I'm familiar with whenever Som makes kanom jeeb: the stuffing.

"Whoa there, city girl." Vahe stops folding the phyllo dough for the cheese boregs, covering them with a damp towel. "This isn't one of those 'go big or go home' situations. Grape leaves are fragile, so you only need a tablespoon or so of filling, max."

I try to keep Vahe from interfering, but my hands are covered in raw meat, and I don't want to spread bacteria everywhere by flailing them around. He comes up behind me and removes part of the dollop I've got scooped in front of me.

"Hey, now. I don't need your assistance. You're not the only one who works with their hands. I'm perfectly capable of completing this task on my own." My aggressive tone is undermined by the fact that my hair keeps falling into my eyes, and I have to blow it away from my face every few seconds lest it get contaminated by uncooked beef. If I had tied it up in a braid before I left the hotel, I could look as competent as I sound.

"Alright, Ms. Independent, chill. If you keep flapping around like that, I'll need to bleach the whole kitchen to prevent an E.coli outbreak." In one smooth motion, he takes a bobby pin out of his apron pocket and secures the loosest strands. Did he pull off the whole hair-tuck-behind-the-ear trick before I could call him out on it?

Vahe admires the violet streak between his fingers. "You must get countless comments on your appearance, which is why I haven't said anything until now . . ." He bites his lip. "But I can't have you thinking I'm not a fan. Because I am."

I'm taken aback by his candor. He's right about the unsolicited feedback I receive, both critical and creepy. If I'm not fielding remarks about how much prettier I'd look with my natural hair color, I'm dodging body mod fetishists who can only get off from Suicide Girl porn. Some men take one look at my tattoos and steer clear, but a significant percentage mistake them as an invitation to objectify me. What I'm not used to, however, is matter-of-fact appreciation. Vahe wants me to know that he likes what he sees, and he's prepared to leave it at that.

"Me too." I gulp. "I mean, I'm a fan of yours as well." The words come out awkward as hell, but they aren't untrue. The clubs I frequent are typically overrun by emaciated, toxic musician types. But for every young Pete Doherty or Jared Leto lookalike that has stumbled into my life, I've secretly wondered what it would be like to try a boy-next-door on for size. One who pays taxes, owns a headboard, and not only remembers my birthday but also surprises me with the perfect gift. Somebody who could never fathom punching a bartender or getting his license revoked.

Yes, I know my standards are on the floor, but my racing heartbeat is proof that Vahe is raising them in real time.

"I'm glad to hear it." Vahe chuckles softly. "Because we

have a lot of sarma to wrap, and it would be a real drag if you spent the whole time hating my guts."

"I don't hate your . . ." I trail off, distracted by Vahe grabbing a damp washcloth off the counter and wiping the excess filling off my hands. Over the knuckles, across the palms, and in between each finger. The gesture reminds me of when I end a manicure with a hot towel and a slick of lotion, but it's never felt this sensual. Handholding isn't intimate for a nail artist, but Vahe manages to prove me wrong again. And when he wraps his hands around my wrists and massages the tender spots under my thumbs, a sigh escapes my lips.

"You're baiting me," I groan, embarrassed by the effect he's having on me but too blissed out to pull away.

"You make it sound like I'm a medieval torturer, Tori. I'm just giving you permission to do whatever and whoever you want. It doesn't have to be this massive ordeal."

It may be the lustful haze clouding my judgment, but Vahe does make some sense. There's something to be said for delaying gratification just long enough to deliver peak satisfaction rather than holding out so long you are miserable. "I guess indulging in one moment of weakness would take the edge off, so we can refocus on the competition."

Vahe rolls his eyes ever so slightly but doesn't drop my hands. "I won't lecture you that listening to your body isn't a sign of weakness. But if that's what will help you sleep at night, consider this a time-out—a temporary truce from our little game. What's it going to be?"

He doesn't move a muscle. I wish I could say I'm leaning toward him against my will, but Vahe is taking the whole 'ball in your court' thing seriously.

I take the washcloth out of his hand and toss it onto our workstation. "The second I say to back off, you back off."

At this point, most guys would get outraged that their behavior could ever be considered predatory. But Vahe's not offended in the slightest, content to keep his mouth shut and his hands where I can see them.

Placing my palms on his chest, I pull the straps of his apron to bring his face closer to mine. Just one kiss, and we'll get back to cooking as if nothing happened. One meaningless kiss, and that will be that.

"Fine." I let out a breath. "Fuck it."

I briefly hope the food sitting out won't go bad, because the moment my lips land on his, it hits me that the only thing I'll be eating for a while is my words.

❧

A LIST of things Tori Townsend has said "fuck it" about (in no particular order)

1. Not knowing whether the small, brightly colored tablet at the bottom of my bag was a Smarties candy or ecstasy, and eating it anyway
2. Getting all my toes tattooed during an artist's "buy one, get one half off" sale
3. Putting a plane ticket to Europe on credit despite being behind on rent that month
4. Blocking my father's number after he asked for bail money for the fifth time
5. Flashing my tits at a bus of college lacrosse players just to see their jaws drop
6. Getting my first jazz gig by offering to fill in for a sick pianist, even though my only training was YouTube tutorials
7. Moving across the country to work for a social media heiress because she loved my nail art

8. Letting Glen shave off half my hair after he said I
   had a beautifully shaped head
9. Being persuaded into another round of drinks no
   matter how busy I was the next day
10. Hooking up with any man I found remotely
    attractive without a second thought

chapter
eleven

I know I'm a goner the second I make impact. With Vahe's encouragement to stop resisting the inevitable and give into his gravitational pull, we crash hard into each other like two colliding planets. Now that his hands are wrapped around me, how did I ever believe I could escape his orbit?

I'm not one to fetishize gargantuan men. The logistics of hooking up are usually too much of a hassle. But there's at least one benefit of Vahe's abnormal size: his body is *everywhere*. Chest against mine, beard scraping my cheek, hands squeezing my ass, and his—oh god, *wow*—pressed against my jeans. Clearly, it's not just his personality that's larger than life.

Only a few pieces of fabric are keeping us apart, and despite all my previous objections, I desperately want to close the gap. The dam is broken, I'm already soaked, and I've waited long enough. I need a real release.

"Inside me. Now," I demand, untying his apron and throwing it on the pristine kitchen floor.

He smiles. "Said like a confident woman who goes after what she wants." I should be grateful for the compliment, but he blocks my fingers from unzipping his pants, and I groan in frustration.

"Isn't this what you've wanted all along?" I pout. Vahe glares pointedly at me, forcing me to amend my statement. "What *we've* wanted all along."

"Thank you. Trust me, there's nothing I want to do more than tango, but you know what they say about how many people it involves." He attempts to redirect my attention to above the waist, nibbling at my ear, but I'm in no mood to slow down.

"Listen up, little esh. One of my biggest irritations is when I have to reiterate consent. I don't grant it lightly, but when I do, I expect all parties to get on fucking board. If you keep hemming and hawing, I'll change my mind faster than I gorge on choreg. Do you want to roll sarma with blue balls?" A beat of silence passes without objection. "That's right. You don't. You may own a bakery, but I run the bedroom. When I tell you to drop trou, sous-chef, that's an order. Now unzip your pants, bend me over this counter, and fuck me senseless already."

I can tell by the way Vahe's eyes darken that I've finally gotten through his thick skull. With his Casanova-level charm, I bet few women have asserted dominance, and it's lit a fire under his ass.

He pulls down his zipper with glacial slowness, drawing out the anticipation. It's his only form of disobedience because he knows, regardless of who wins the actual competition, I'm the victor this round. "Let the record show you got what you asked for, Tori Townsend."

A shiver runs down my spine at his use of my full name. In this moment, every word sounds like a threat, and when I get a glimpse of what I'm working with, I understand he means it as one. "Why the deer-in-headlights look?" he teases. "You know you can always back out if I'm too much for you to handle."

"No fucking way." Preserving my pride always trumps my desire to walk properly afterward. "This is a contest, remember? If you go easy on me, it's game over. Give me everything you've got."

"In that case, hold on tight." Vahe's wolfish smile is the last thing I see before he whips me around and bends me over the counter. He pulls my jeans down to my ankles, showcasing my ass in just a black G-string. Did I purposely wear it today because I knew Vahe would earn a fast pass to pound town? Perhaps. If push came to shove, I could hike up the straps into a whale tail to taunt him into making a move. Considering how Vahe exhales at the mere sight of my ass, I made the right choice.

I snap out of my self-congratulation when Vahe lands a light slap on one ass cheek. It's just to test my reaction, a taste of what's to come if I'm on board. And fuck *yes*, I am.

"Not even a flinch," he says, impressed. "You ready for something stronger?"

I nod my head. "As you can tell from the tattoos down my legs, I'm no stranger to pain." I scan the counter when the safeword comes to me. "If I say sarma, you'll know to stop."

He chuckles. "You've officially desecrated my favorite appetizer, but sarma it is. Now brace yourself."

I don't have time to grit my teeth before Vahe smacks the air out of me. I gasp, relishing how the impact ripples throughout my body, sending tingles to all the nerve endings in my clit. He evens out the other side, rinsing and repeating several times, until I'm sure my ass is as red as the noses of all the Rudolph decorations infiltrating stores before it's even December.

When I'm so slick my G-string is soaked through, Vahe shows me mercy. He kneels down to kiss my inflamed skin while pushing my legs farther apart. Once I'm wide open for him, he pulls my underwear to the side and runs his tongue from my entrance to my clit, tasting me like I'm more delicious than anything we'll be making today.

I'm rarely eaten out from behind, but without Vahe in my immediate view, it allows me to focus solely on the sensations coursing through me. Most men would take a few hesitant licks before prioritizing their own pleasure, but Vahe circles my clit like it's his civic duty. If anybody knows the importance of preheating the oven, it would be a professional baker.

I'm so relieved we have the deli to ourselves. My moans are so loud they're echoing off the stainless steel. I thrust back against his tongue, again and again, because I can feel it—I'm so, *so* close.

Mouth too full for dirty talk, Vahe doesn't let up. He slips one finger, then another inside me, while sucking on my clit until I can't see straight. Finally, the tightness in my core snaps as he pushes me to my peak and beyond. He holds my legs steady as my climax washes over me, and the second he stands, I collapse onto an empty section of the workstation.

"Five stars," I pant, appreciating the cool metal against my skin.

"That was just the starter. We haven't even gotten to our main dish yet." He stands up and shifts around, reminding me in my blissful haze of the most crucial ingredient.

"Condom!" I blurt out inelegantly, but Vahe's already ahead of me. When I turn my head, he shows off his well-wrapped cock, standing at attention.

"Don't you worry. I would never serve you raw meat."

He grips my shoulder for counterbalance, pinning me down, as he enters me with a half-sigh, half-groan. He's been waiting for this as long as I have.

"*Fuck*, you feel delicious," Vahe exhales, pausing for a beat while I adjust to his impressive size, before slowly withdrawing to the last inch and sliding back in. He's right to call these sensations delicious. Every move he makes mirrors the care he takes while cooking. He snakes his hands up my crop top and underneath my bra, gently kneading my breasts like delicate dough, tweaking my nipples as they rise to greet him. I've fucked enough musicians to know there's something to be said about men who know how to use their hands, but it never occurred to me that I could find sex gods in the back of restaurants.

"They teach you this in culinary school?" I tease, arching my back into him as he picks up the pace.

"Ha, even if I could have afforded to learn pastry-making in Paris, formal training can't compete with hard knocks." Hard, indeed. He slams into me, emphasizing each word. "But you like it rough, don't you?"

My whole body shakes as he impales me like his own personal shish kebab until my moans come out desperate and shrill. "Don't stop," I whine, aching for release before my knees buckle under.

"I'll never do you like that," he reassures, hitting my spot like his life depends on it. "I don't clock out until every customer is satisfied."

He's casually mentioned before that it's not uncommon for him to work sixteen-hour days during the holidays, which is why I'm about to go into cardiac arrest and he's not even winded.

"Now let me finish providing you phenomenal service. One earth-shattering orgasm, coming up." His right hand travels under my G-string and circles my clit, increasing the tempo until I'm boiling over like a pot of scalding water. Another climax overtakes my body, and Vahe holds on tightly to prevent me from wiping out on the kitchen floor. We grip onto each other, his fingers digging into my hips, my pussy pulsing around his cock, until he can't hold out any longer and comes hard with a few final thrusts.

"Damn," I exhale, as Vahe kisses the back of my neck before dismounting. "You sure put the dick in Dikran's Deli."

He laughs heartily as if he rode a rollercoaster and is

coming down from the rush. "You know, you're not that far off. I've been told Armenians may have influenced the English language more than we think. Dikran and Richard both translate to 'strong ruler,' which is probably why any old guy with that name goes by Dick."

"Huh, the more you know. Multiple orgasms and a language lesson—you are a man of many talents, Vahe Derderian."

"And you haven't tasted this sarma yet. Just you wait, Victoria Townsend."

I don't bother correcting him for calling me Victoria. Using our full names sounds even more ludicrous after a mid-morning fuckfest in an industrial kitchen. But it's not just our names that go together perfectly. I'm not one to overvalue a nice, girthy Richard, so to speak, but did I just have the best dick of my life?

∾

GLAM FAM GROUP chat on Saturday, November 25, at 2:48 p.m.

CASEY

Hey, Tori, we know you're busy cooking up a storm, but the glam fam road trip is all systems go. Glen and Som just picked up me and Alex, and we're making great time. See you soon!

SOM

I'm trying really hard not to fill up on snacks, but Alex wasn't lying. The cornucopia her culinary team packed for the ride is bomb.

ALEX

We'll make sure to save some for you!
We've got a little bit of everything: house-
made trail mix, Italian-imported parmesan
crisps, dry-roasted edamame, and these
delectable mini cranberry-orange scones if
Glen doesn't eat them all himself.

CASEY

He's driving so he can't reply, but he says
no promises lol.

SOM

Tori's salty and sweet, so she'd love the
chocolate-covered pretzels.

CASEY

Not the white chocolate though—she hates
it. She once said cookies-and-cream bars
are crafted on a bed of lies.

TORI

And that's still a hill I'm willing to die on.

The cooking takes way longer than we anticipated, thanks to our frequent boning breaks—including a cowgirl quickie after grilling the kebabs and a sexy-as-hell sixty-nine involving leftover sugar syrup from the paklava. But we manage to heat the place up without burning everything down. Miraculously, we complete all the dishes on the wedding menu with a few minutes to spare. By the time the glam fam raps on the door at six o'clock on the dot, I've refreshed my makeup, spritzed on some perfume to mask the after-sex musk, and slipped on my trusty claws.

"Hey, hold up," I hiss, grabbing Vahe's arm before he makes his way to the entrance. "We're keeping this"—I gesture between our two crotches—"wrapped up tighter than our sarma. The last thing I need is our hookup becoming tonight's topic of conversation. The attention should be on Tania and Nolan's sacred union—not on two hopeless pervs who can't keep it in their pants long enough to bake a paklava."

Vahe blinks, crossing his arms in that now familiar way that both intimidates and arouses me with his overpowering biceps. "As proud as I am of my extracurricular activities, I wouldn't betray a woman's trust. A sex partner is still a partner, after all, regardless of how brief the relationship." He leans down to place a kiss on my forehead. "But if anyone forced me to spill the beans, I'd be honored to say I know Tori Townsend in the biblical sense. And I hope she'd say the same."

The ovens have been cooling down for a while now, but my face feels like it's been blasted with heat. I open my mouth to respond, until there are several more knocks on the door in quick succession. We've clearly depleted our guests' patience.

I rush past Vahe to let them in. I'm less concerned about making the glam fam wait and more about avoiding a heartfelt assessment of where the two of us stand. Jeez, we only got redressed a few minutes ago. I want to bask in my post-orgasm glow and enjoy an evening with my best friends, not make any ironclad commitments.

Opening the door, I throw myself into the arms of my immensely fabulous roommate Som Srisati. But when she stiffens in my grasp, I know I've committed a fatal mistake.

"In all the years we've lived together," she says, eyes narrowed, "not once have you ever greeted me with a hug. You're so allergic to physical touch, Tori, that when we first met, I thought you had one of those rare butterfly skin diseases." She leans in to sniff my neck. "Betch, did you put on perfume?"

Shit. I thought it was a good idea to hide the evidence of our escapades, but I might as well have bought a billboard outside the bakery that reads in big, bold letters: I had sex with Vahe Derderian.

Speak of the devil. Vahe enters the deli behind me, waving cheerfully to Tania and Nolan and the rest of the glam fam, who have formed a semicircle around us.

I must be too pale to hide the blush rising to my cheeks. Som's eyeballs ping-pong from me to Vahe and back to me, piecing together the puzzle.

Please, I telepathically plead with the makeup artist. *I'll let you and Glen bleach my eyebrows if you don't state the obvious right now.*

But Som is a diehard fan of *The Real Housewives*. If she gets a whiff of drama, she'll stick her nose where it doesn't belong.

After several more double-takes at Vahe's bodybuilder physique, she throws down the Bravo-level bombshell I desperately wanted to avoid. "Have you two been *fucking*?"

Maybe I wasn't doing such a bad job keeping this secret because everyone's jaws drop simultaneously. Even Nolan, who's usually rock-climbing a route in his head, has directed his attention toward me.

I tug on my talons, itching to flee the crime scene before my friends lock me up in horny jail. "It was just once! Well, not once. Technically, it was a handful of times, but they all happened today, so it's not like it really—"

Everyone can see me scrambling. But when I lock eyes with Vahe, I can't finish my disaster of an explanation. Because however spur-of-the-moment our first hookup may have been, it counts. They all count.

It would be so easy to write off Vahe as the fuckboy from Fresno and lean into the glam fam's objectification of him. Man-eating Tori would let them make as many jokes about his sexual prowess as they wanted before calling off the competition early and never seeing him again.

But I don't want to do that. My entire life has been spent building an emotional fortress to keep deadbeat dudes at a distance, starting with shutting out my own father. As satisfying as it is to paint every man with the same brush, Vahe's more than a hunger-curing hunk. He's his own person, and a hilarious, hella talented one at that. And goddamn it, I hate to admit it, but he's right.

"Alright, listen up, everybody." I shut down their

squawking with a steely tone. "I'm only going to say this once, and no, there won't be any Q&A. Allow me to introduce you to Vahe Derderian. I'm honored to know him in the biblical sense. In any sense, frankly. I'm glad I met him."

I turn back to Vahe for reassurance, and he's smiling so wide I half expect him to pump his fist into the air. Our battle royale may not be on the top of our minds this very moment, but Vahe looks like victory is already his.

The glam fam honors my wishes to drop the questions, simply giving quick hugs and elbow nudges of approval. With that matter settled, we start pushing tables together. The guys focus on plating our first course while Alex and Casey assume the responsibility of making the place settings picture-perfect.

Som waves me to the counter, pulling out a bottle of champagne from her tote bag. "Bring those claws over here, Tori, and help me cut off this foil."

As I slice the wrapper with a flick of my wrist, she leans in to whisper in my ear. "Best believe we're getting more info from you when we're back in the Bay, but we're happy you're happy. It's definitely a step up from the smugness we usually witness."

I playfully shove her shoulder before pouring her a drink. "Watch out, Som. With Vahe and I in the same room, we're smug squared. I bet he never met an 'I told you so' he didn't like."

Tania catches our conversation, pulling me into a tight hug. "We hope Vahe winning you over is his biggest 'I told you so' yet." She winks as I hand her a glass. "You two are so adorable together I'm going to forget that I'm the one getting married."

I pour myself some champagne and gulp it down. From how my body seizes at Tania's words, I know it's not the alcohol's fizz that's burning my throat. I want to grab her arm and tell her to knock it off, that it's way too early for me and Vahe to be talking about holy matrimony.

But before I can insist that Vahe and I are just having fun, she gathers everyone to take their seats. Vahe pulls out my chair opposite Tania and Nolan, while Alex and Casey flank one side and Som and Glen grab the other. "To love!" Tania toasts, giving Nolan a kiss on the cheek. "Not just ours, but to everyone who's lucky enough to experience it. May we cherish it as hard as we're about to chow down. Cheers!"

"Kenadz!" Vahe tips his glass back. As I'm stuck ruminating about our situationship, Casey, the mom friend of the glam fam, immediately engages him in conversation about the nuances of Armenian cuisine.

"So it's paklava, spelled with a *P*?" she asks. "How's it different from baklava? It looks identical."

Vahe chuckles. "That's because it's essentially the same pastry. The spelling can change by language and dialect, but typically Armenian paklava uses chopped walnuts and a spice-infused syrup, rather than pistachios and honey used in other Mediterranean and Middle Eastern cuisines. No matter how you make it, though, it's delicious."

The same can be said of all of Vahe's dishes. Everyone digs into the sarma and cheese boregs, and Vahe brushes off their effusive compliments, giving undue credit to me. But his kind words go in one ear and out the other because I'm too busy freaking out. If I keep seeing Vahe, keep sleeping with him, then I'm at risk of developing real feelings for him. And then what? There can be no future for us if we live hundreds of miles away from each other and have no intentions of moving.

Hooking up didn't take the edge off—it's put me more on edge than ever before. It has added fuel to the fire, one that's destined to blow up in our faces.

"You okay, Tori?" Vahe whispers, refilling our glasses of

champagne. With everyone else preoccupied in their own conversations, they don't notice his look of concern.

I flash him my most convincing smile. There's no need to pass along my anxieties to him—not when we should be patting ourselves on the back for a meal well cooked.

"Just plotting how I'm going to beat you when you come up to San Francisco," I quip. "And when I win, remember to make the check out to Tania and Nolan Beecher-Wells since they're both hyphenating their names."

I keep stone-faced so Vahe doesn't notice that I'm a bundle of nerves. I'm not sure if it works, but he remains unfazed. "We'll see about that," he says. "We still have tomorrow to go, and I've got a Sunday Funday for the record books. May the best city win."

He clinks my glass, content to spend the evening answering the glam fam's questions about enhancing their own recipes at home. But as rewarding as this meal tasting is after an entire day of cooking—among other things—nothing comforts me more than retreating into the confines of our little contest. When we're focused on the next round, I don't have to stress about Vahe fitting into my life, or me into his.

Because just like food always has an expiration date, eventually our game will end.

~

***TORI TOWNSEND's** search history on Saturday, November 25, at 11:34 p.m.*

WHAT's it like to live in Fresno

    How to survive 110-degree summers

    Fog-related deaths in Central Valley winters

    What's a foggy day school schedule

Do they still make cars where you roll down the windows
Why do we turn off the car radio to concentrate better
Best neighborhoods in Fresno
Best neighborhoods shouldn't mean the whitest
Best food in Fresno
What is a chuck wagon
Famous celebrities from Fresno
How famous was Kevin Federline really
Fun things to do in Fresno
Fun things to do in Fresno—not a three-hour drive away
What is the exact center of California
Why can't the high-speed rail get its shit together
Odds of long-distance relationships actually working
How to know if you're catching feelings
Can you catch and release feelings like a fish

When Vahe told me we'd be spending Sunday morning exploring one of Fresno's most hidden gems, I didn't know how he'd top Bloom & Brew.

But apparently what's more hidden than a beer garden tucked behind a nursery is a garden buried twenty-five feet underground.

"I didn't expect you to take 'hidden gems' so literally," I tell Vahe as we crane our necks to admire the orange tree standing tall in front of us. As the center of an agricultural mecca, Fresno certainly doesn't lack produce. But it's not every day that you see citrus reaching toward the skies through holes in the earth's crust.

"Touring the Forestiere Underground Gardens is a rite of passage. If it were up to me, every school in California would be required to take a field trip here. No student in this state should grow up without learning the extraordinary efforts previous generations of farmers made to keep them fed."

As we stroll along the labyrinth of tunnels, designed to emulate ancient Roman atria, Vahe tells the story of Baldassare Forestiere, a Sicilian immigrant who came to Fresno at the turn of the twentieth century to pursue his dream of becoming a citrus farmer.

"With just a pick, a shovel, and a wheelbarrow, he dug through this hardpan rock to create a subterranean oasis." Vahe runs his hand across the chiseled garden walls. "It took him forty years to excavate ten acres, and most of the fruit that grows here is harvested to this day."

Now I understand why Vahe told the Forestiere staff that we'd be taking the self-guided tour. I'm sure Vahe has spent so much time studying these catacomb-like courtyards that he's memorized their spiel word for word.

"But why grow underground? Clearly, the Central Valley's agriculture is abundant. Forty years is a hell of a long time to be chipping away at bedrock."

A shiver runs down my spine from the winter chill, and I take a sip from the hot coffee Vahe handed me at the start of the tour. Mine is blacker than my wardrobe, while Vahe's is so sweet that it could give Sabrina Carpenter a run for her money.

Vahe comes up behind me and rubs my back through my coat to keep me warm. "There's a reason I told you to bundle up. It can get ten to twenty degrees cooler down here. When you're farming in Fresno's triple-digit summer heat, creating your own shade is a huge advantage."

That makes sense. People don't give farmworkers enough credit—the millions of people picking our produce with the unyielding sun beating down on them. I don't blame Baldassare for carving out this sanctuary.

Vahe has me ruminating about what we as people leave behind, even after we conclude the tour and make our way back to the surface. I spent most of my life simply trying to break the cycle of my family's neglect. It's only been in the past few years that I've given any thought of what I'm running toward rather than away from.

I may be seen as more successful than Vahe on paper, if you're keeping track of my mega-famous friends and my hundreds of thousands of social media followers. But Vahe has something even more coveted: roots that go deeper than these underground gardens.

With the midday sun overhead and the winter fog dissipated, Fresno's moderate weather feels similar to San Francisco's this time of year. As if exploring a historic landmark wasn't enough, we drive over to the next spot on our itinerary: Dog House Grill, a popular sports bar and restaurant across from Fresno State.

From the way everyone in this joint breaks eye contact from the giant televisions streaming Sunday football to wave hello or walk over to give Vahe a fist bump, I expect us to settle in and stay awhile. But when the cashier at the counter asks him if we'll be dining in, he shakes his head. "Nah, man. I've got a hot date today, and she deserves the grand tour." He turns to wink at me. The butterflies in my stomach are so busy fluttering that I don't bother correcting him. As insistent as I was that these rounds weren't real dates, there's nothing fake about Vahe's arm around my waist.

I let him take the lead in ordering. I let him pay for the tri-tip sandwiches. And with every hour we spend together this weekend, I let him inch closer into my heart.

"Where are we headed?" I ask as we jump in the truck, trying to sound easy-breezy so Vahe doesn't catch the existential anxiety in my question. On the surface, I'm referring to our lunch plans, but between the lines it's a concern I've been grappling with. I blew my only bargaining chip when we hooked up yesterday. A true fuckboy would have gloated over me giving in and bounced, never to see me again. And here's Vahe Derderian, on cloud nine just to be in my company.

"You'll see." Vahe smiles, giving my hand a squeeze before

starting the ignition. "I can't have you head back home without taking you to my favorite hangout spot."

A few blocks later, we park near Fresno State's student union. If this were anyone else, alarm bells would be going off, wondering why the hell a man in his mid-thirties likes visiting a college campus.

But this is Vahe we're talking about. Whatever he's planned, it won't include leering at the barely legal.

We approach a stone structure positioned in the center of a square. It looks like a small-scale Stonehenge with pillars of rock connected by a circular metal beam.

"This is Fresno State's Armenian Genocide Memorial," he explains, pointing to the nearby sign that includes the years 1915–2015. "The university had it built with soil from the homeland, to commemorate the centennial. Since then, I like to come here and clear my head."

"It's beautiful," I say as we grab an empty bench and admire the view. Between the street art in the Mural District and the greenery in the underground gardens, I can't get enough of seeing life through Vahe's eyes. The pride he feels for his hometown is palpable. How could San Francisco ever win him over?

"I bet it's difficult for you to visit places that don't have large Armenian American populations," I suggest. "SF is one of the densest cities, with people from all around the world, and I've still met folks who couldn't locate the country on a map."

Vahe takes a moment to consider his response. "There is a comfort in not having to constantly educate people about your ancestral history. Fresno is so suburban that I didn't think of it having a distinct culture, but its Armenian community is unlike any other. That means a lot to me." He gets lost staring at the monument before bringing himself back to the present. "It's hard to quantify how many Hyes are out there. The latest census reported about a half million in the US, but Armenians are considered Caucasian, which is an obsolete racial classification for a host of complicated reasons. So I think the actual demographics are much higher, probably two to three times that. About the same number that were killed in the genocide."

We sit in the silence, the weight of that immeasurable loss as heavy as the stone monument itself.

I wrap my fingers around his abnormally large hand. "It must drive you up the wall to deal with people who don't know it even happened."

Vahe sighs. "They can't help it. They don't know what they don't know. The Armenian Genocide is one atrocity out of countless others, and if you don't live in Fresno, or LA, or some pockets of other major cities, you could go your whole life not knowing. Now what does drive me up a wall," he says with a smile, "is when the only Armenians someone knows are the Kardashians. You're telling me you don't know about Andy Serkis, Andre Agassi, Dita Von Teese, or the goddess herself, Cher? That's what's inexcusable, in my opinion."

I let out a hearty laugh. Vahe always manages to bring the light into even the darkest of circumstances. "You know, you'd make a great ambassador for Armenian relations. I could see you traveling around the world, sharing your Hye pride with everyone you meet."

Vahe beams. "That's kind of how I view myself. The easiest way for people to connect with a culture is through its food. The Armenian experience is marred by grief, but there's also so much joy, and that deserves to be celebrated. If we want to take 'Never Again' seriously, then we need to make sure our people are not forgotten. I may not be interested in having kids and furthering a bloodline, but I can still leave a legacy."

Amen to that. On that inspiring note, we unwrap our tri-tip sandwiches and dig in. The moment the juicy meat hits my tongue, I groan. It feels obscene to be eating something this orgasmic while the sun's still out.

When I look up from my meal and notice the blush on Vahe's cheeks, I break out into a doofy grin. I'm not sure what I adore more: being introduced to the most delicious food by Vahe or watching him get hot and bothered while I eat it.

If we were having a leisurely lunch somewhere more private, we could indulge in more than just food. But even though it's the Sunday after Thanksgiving and few people are milling about, Vahe doesn't take the bait. For now, good weather and better company are enough.

"I'm jealous of how much you love your hometown," I admit, washing down my last bites with the fountain soda we took to-go. "I don't know many people who would call the town where they grew up their real home."

"Is that what keeps you in San Francisco rather than returning to New York City?"

I give his question some thought. If I'm such a fan of big cities, why didn't I stay in the biggest one in the country? "I love being from Queens. It's a massively underrated borough, and I try to go back as often as I can. I'll always have a soft spot for where I was born and raised. I just wish I was fonder of who did the birthing and the raising. Putting a country's worth of distance between me and those memories has done wonders for my mental health."

Vahe waits for me to say more. I appreciate his efforts to get to know me better, but nothing will turn my scrumptious sandwich into lead in my belly like talking about my fucked-up family.

"I don't wanna get into it," I say, wiping my hands clean with a wad of napkins. "The only home that matters is the one I've made with the people I care about most. I followed Alex and the glam fam to San Francisco, and now it's the only place where I feel like I truly belong. Every single time I see the skyline, I want to pinch myself. I can't believe I got so lucky. People relocate to the Big Apple all the time to chase their dreams, but it wasn't until I moved out West that I felt like I made it."

Vahe wraps his arm around me, pulling me into his warm embrace. "You feel like you've made it because you literally made it. I merely inherited Fresno, but you left behind everything you knew and created a new home, a new family, an entirely new life for yourself. I've always felt like I've belonged here, but that's because I've never left. I respect the hell out of people who pick up everything and start over. What you did was brave, Tori."

I never thought of it like that. I met Alex not long after my mom died, and with my dad in prison, I had no one else keeping me in New York. Because I spent most of my time working, I didn't have any close friends, so when the glam fam fox-trotted into my life, moving seemed like a no-brainer. I would be gaining both a dream job and a built-in group of besties. It wasn't a difficult choice at the time, but maybe that's the plus-side of not having a hundred years of tradition holding you back.

We sit there cuddling on the bench, observing the birds perched on the monument and reflecting on what bravery means. Moving across the country of my own accord will never compare to the harrowing journey that thousands of Armenian Genocide refugees made in order to survive. But neither would have happened without taking one step forward.

I'm grateful that Vahe's ancestors found community here. But in the final few hours of our weekend together, I'm selfishly curious as to whether Vahe could find community elsewhere . . . with me.

But I can't get ahead of myself. The next round in our competition isn't for another three weeks. I need to make the most of our time now before we reunite in San Francisco.

I stand up to toss our trash in a nearby can when something white and bright catches my eye off in the distance.

"Is that . . . a giant letter *S* painted on the side of that hill?" I ask, squinting for a better view.

"Yeah!" Vahe exclaims. "That's the Sanger *S*, named after the town where Tania and I went to school. Sanger High has a fierce rivalry with neighboring Reedley High, so every year the student governments make the trek to Mt. Campbell and mark their territories. An *S* on the Sanger side, and an *R* on the Reedley side." He laughs. "We called ourselves the Sanger Bangers because it rhymed, but the city-sanctioned graffiti was an added bonus."

Sanger Bangers, eh? Now we're talking. "Say, how long does it take to drive to that mountain?"

Vahe scratches his head. "From here? Not very long. Thirty minutes, forty-five max. Why?"

I give him my most mischievous, seductive look, pulling him in close and giving his ass a quick squeeze. "Why don't you send me off to SF with a Sanger Bang? You can give me a knee-shaking *O* under that *S*."

He hesitates, until I rub his hard-on through his jeans when no one's looking. The *S* doesn't stand for soft, I'll tell you that.

Vahe seizes my lips in a kiss, holding my face between his palms while plundering my needy mouth. Forget the coffee earlier—making out with this man is the fastest way for my body to heat up.

When we come up for air, gasping, my lips feel bruised in the best way. Vahe steers me toward the truck, ready to get this show on the literal road. "You're making my teenage dreams come true," he rasps, "so it's only fair I repay the favor." He smacks my ass, sending a jolt of electricity straight my clit. If he keeps turning me on like that, I'm going to lose this bet. Because I won't be able to properly show him around San Francisco if he fucks the energy right out of me.

$\sim$

UPDATED *voicemail for Dikran's Deli on Friday, December 15, at 6:45 a.m.*

HI, you've reached Dikran's Deli. This is Queenie. For the most part, everything's business as usual over here. My son and daughter-in-law continue putting the bare minimum into this place, preferring to enjoy their retirement like suckers instead of working until they're dead. Look at me—I'm eighty-five years old, and I'm still kicking. It's not over until it's over.

They say greatness skips a generation, which makes a lot of sense. No offense to the big man Dikran, but you ask anyone around town, and they'll say the deli only stayed open for as long as it has because of me. One hundred years, can you believe it?

What I'm trying to say is you probably called to speak to one of my talented grandchildren. My oldest Mari is unavailable because quarterly taxes are due next month, and she's having a conniption with all the bookkeeping. Anush is unavailable because who else is going to ring up people at the cashier while I'm making my rounds and checking on everybody?

And my grandbaby boy Vahe is unavailable because he's in San Francisco this weekend. Mari's having a conniption about that too as we're not a family with much time for vacations. But his is for a noble cause. I've been pushing him to find the right woman for years—years!—and I've got a good feeling about this one. I'll even forgive her for pushing me off that ladder if she's my little esh's soulmate.

Needless to say, without Vahe baking up a storm, our pastry selection will be limited. Come get your paklava before it sells out! And be a dear and leave Vahe some marriage advice after the beep. [*beep*]

chapter
fourteen

After having such an amazing time with Vahe a couple weeks ago, I should be overjoyed to be showing him around my city tonight. So why am I wearing a circle into the carpet of my bedroom with my incessant nervous pacing?

The obvious answer is that I'm concerned about how the hell I'll ever be able to beat Vahe at his own game. I fully expected to face-plant on the cuisine factor. San Francisco's got more Michelin-star restaurants than most countries, but I can't compete with a fourth-generation chef and baker who has one hundred years of collective culinary expertise behind him.

And then Vahe made a strong case for Fresno's culture. The neighborhoods we explored were diverse and the right amount of rough-around-the-edges for a city girl like me. Before I hit the highway to return home, he stocked me up with apples and winter citrus from a roadside fruit stand. I can't even say I was craving SF's craft cocktails after Vahe bought me a bottle of a red blend from Fresno State's winery. A university that grows and sells its own award-winning wine! How the fuck am I supposed to top that?

So of the three criteria, I'm pinning *a lot* on San Francisco's cool factor. I should have this in the bag. While not as large as NYC, it's just as memorable. Fresno looks like a suburban wasteland on the surface with hidden gems you have to hunt for, but wherever you turn in SF you see views meant for the big screen. The Transamerica Pyramid, the Painted Ladies, and objectively the most iconic bridge in the world. Cap that off with gorgeous weather that hovers between sixty and seventy degrees year-round, and what could be cooler than that?

Yet, everything changes when you're seeing your city through the eyes of someone you desperately want to impress. I can't lead Vahe Derderian around Fisherman's Wharf like some knuckle-headed tourist. Sure, he hasn't traveled to every continent as part of Princess Alex's entourage—don't get me started about keeping skin moisturized in Antarctica—but he's still a man of taste. Where do you take someone who set such a sky-high standard?

While the competition has been the obvious concern that's kept me up at night, it pales in comparison to the tossing and turning I've been doing when I ruminate about what comes after our wager is over.

Man-hating me would thank Vahe for the multiple orgasms before kicking him to the curb. After all, I have zero interest in long-distance dating, especially long-term. I refuse to even travel across the Bay Bridge for a dude unless he's driving. Fresno, on the other hand, is two hundred miles away. I don't care how delicious his food is, or how thick his dick is. I'm uprooting my life for no man.

If that's the case, then why am I bothering with the battle royale? If I truly didn't give a shit about our potential future, I'd sabotage this weekend on purpose. Sort restaurants by least number of stars and devise an urban hike with the steepest hills. Make every moment miserable so neither of us could walk away thinking we're compatible.

No. Just like I did my best to keep my grades up and become a talented musician in the hopes of convincing my parents to give a shit about me, I want to plan the perfect weekend, so Vahe falls in love with San Francisco so hard that he makes me his highest priority. Which is understandably ludicrous when I'm not willing to do the same. And so I waffle between being singularly focused on winning and wanting to burn it all down to save myself the heartache.

Fuck it. Nobody ever moved forward in life by pacing in circles. The plans have been laid; the reservations have been made. Now I have to trust my instincts and let the chips fall where they may.

At around seven at night, Vahe texts me that he's left his downtown hotel, so I grab my things and head to the BART station to meet him at Ms. Maven's. I appreciate him respecting my boundaries and booking his own lodging like I did in Fresno. Although we've quickly moved into more-than-friendly territory, he didn't assume that meant he could crash at my place.

Thankfully, even if he did, I have two roommates I can blame. Som, Glen, and I don't have a rule against sleepovers, but Vahe doesn't know that.

What he also doesn't know is that I've never had a morning-after with a man. I consider myself more sexually adventurous than average, having fucked around in practically every nook and cranny in this city. I wouldn't bat an eye attending a play party or a tantric workshop.

But waking up together with morning breath and making pancakes? I'd rather strip naked and throw myself in the frigid bay.

As I exit the Civic Center train station and walk to the jazz club, I try to reassure myself that intimacy is a skill. I just need more practice than most people. It took me years to get good enough at piano that venues would pay me, and now I regularly perform in front of hundreds of strangers.

And tonight, one damn good-looking man who gets my heart pounding as hard as the pounding he gives when the clothes come off.

I thought there was no way I could find Vahe Derderian more attractive until I see him at the entrance of Ms. Maven's, laughing it up with Jerome like they're old pals.

"Is this dude harassing you?" I tease the security guard as I let Vahe capture me in a bear hug, breathing in his cologne. It's only been three weeks since we've seen each other, and I'm taken aback by how much I missed his scent.

Jerome grins at our goofy PDA. "On the contrary, Miss Tori. I had to make sure Vahe here wasn't lying about being your plus-one. I told him the last time a guy claimed to be your biggest fan, he was discovered in the ladies' room with his pants around his ankles."

I squeal with embarrassment, lightly smacking Jerome on the arm. I forgot about Mr. Manhattan the second I met Vahe, but that doesn't mean my penchant for fuckboys needs to be public knowledge.

"It's okay," Vahe reassures me, brushing his thumb against my cheek that must be beet-red. "I bet those yahoos did not come bearing gifts."

He reaches behind Jerome to pick up two items placed on the bouncer's stool: a bouquet of black roses and a box of choreg and paklava. The gesture stuns me. Vahe's presence is gift enough—I don't expect him to treat my regular gig with the same reverence as opening night on Broadway.

Jerome chuckles, nudging the baker with his elbow. "It's a good thing Tori doesn't sing because you just stole her voice, young man."

"Thank you," I whisper to Vahe, planting a tender kiss on his lips.

"It's not too basic?" he murmurs, and I shake my head emphatically, tears of joy threatening to escape my eye ducts and betray my badass exterior.

"They're perfect." *Just like you*, I want to blurt out, but I bite my tongue. Bringing me flowers to celebrate a performance is the most boyfriend-like gesture anybody's made for me, but that doesn't mean I'm girlfriend material. I can graciously accept his gifts, but it's best if we don't get ahead of ourselves.

I leave the bouquet and box of baked goods with the coat check attendant, giving him a stern warning that if one petal or pastry is damaged, I'll never let him hear the end of it.

Then I escort Vahe to his reserved VIP seat, right in the front row. Once he's settled in, I catch the eye of the bartender on duty tonight and give her a wave.

"Order whatever you want, and Barb will take care of you. I've never invited a special guest before, so I bet she'll hand deliver your drinks just to get a good look at you."

With another kiss, Vahe tells me to break a leg, and I take my seat at the piano, this time on stage with some traveling musicians I don't regularly play with. I knew Vahe would distract me like nobody else has, so I took twice as much time practicing this set. I don't want to make a fool of myself in front of him.

Usually, I overcome the jitters after a quick sound check, but it takes a couple of songs before I get into a groove. At first, I try not to fixate on Vahe's presence, but every time I steal a glance and see his gleaming smile, I experience a giddy surge of confidence.

Jazz clubs aren't for everybody, and each venue has its own etiquette. They're certainly more casual than a classical concert hall. But they're also not a free-for-all where guests can get away with rude behavior. A little chit-chat at a low volume while a band is playing is acceptable, but the worst thing someone can do is treat us like we're not there. I'm not an inanimate boombox, and I will not be drowned out by rowdy assholes.

But Vahe was raised right. He tips Barb in cash after each drink she makes him, he claps appropriately after each killer solo, and his phone stays out of sight. I know how hard it must be for him to be away from the family business for the weekend, and I don't take his full attention for granted. These days I'm lucky if I can keep an audience entertained and prevent them from doomscrolling every five minutes. And here's Vahe, not taking his eyes off me.

I never wanted to be worshipped by a man. But after watching Vahe's unconditional adoration, I'm starting to wish I was a woman worth worshipping. If I could be the person Vahe thinks I am, maybe we'd have a chance of being more than casual.

I feel like a fickle cat, treating my heart like a sliding glass door. I'm afraid the moment I let someone amazing like Vahe in, I'll sabotage things and push him out again.

You won't know until you try, that small, hopeful part of my psyche reminds me.

Two hours later, I finish out the show to thunderous applause, only because I swear Vahe's clapping can be heard on the Richter scale. The second I take a bow and exit the stage, he grabs me in his arms and spins me around like I've won a Grammy award.

"Tori, that was phenomenal! I don't think I've ever seen fingers fly like that. You blew everyone away!"

We head over to pick up my paycheck before grabbing his gifts on the way out, and Vahe's words of affirmation keep coming. He gushes about his favorite parts I played, how impressed the crowd was, how I knocked everyone's socks off. If he were any other man, I would think he was laying it on awfully thick, but with Vahe, the praise isn't over the top. He means every word.

I walk with Vahe to the parking garage where he's left his pickup truck. He insists on carrying my gifts, even though I have no problem holding things with my claws on.

"You just gave those hands a major workout," he says with a smile. "It's the least I can do."

We must be a scene of domestic bliss. There aren't any other folks around us in the garage, but if there were, I'm sure they'd see us googly-eyed and swoon. They'd think how sweet that this freak show managed to find herself a good man. Every pot has a lid, after all.

"Would you like to raid my mini fridge?" Vahe asks, as he opens the passenger door for me, and we get comfy in the cab. "I could drop you off at your place afterward . . . or not."

His words are hesitant but hopeful. If I let him take care of me, I'm sure he'd lean into the role effortlessly. He would have the front desk at the hotel send up a vase so my roses wouldn't wilt. He'd run me a hot bath and order everything off the late-night room service menu. He'd give me orgasm after orgasm, and that would be a fraction of the pleasure he'd experience turning his hotel room into our home away from home.

And that thought has me seized with terror. Because the moment I let down my guard, that's when tragedy strikes.

I know it's an irrational fear. I know the chaos of my childhood instilled an unhealthy hypervigilance and distrust in others, especially in the people I'm at greatest risk of falling for. You can't lose someone if you never loved them in the first place.

"What's the rush?" I say, as if I didn't just spend too many minutes being caught up in my own head. "We're all alone and we haven't christened this beater yet."

I may not be able to accept Vahe taking care of me, but I

can try to take care of him. And orgasms are the best way I know how.

"You were so sweet bringing me gifts," I say, biting my lip. "Now it's your turn to be treated."

I lock the truck from the inside—not because I'm concerned about break-ins or interruptions, but rather I want Vahe to know I mean business. After three excruciatingly long weeks, he's all mine now, and I'm going to make the most of it.

Sliding into his lap, I capture Vahe's mouth in a searing kiss. The cab of his pickup doesn't have the glamour of a four-star hotel, but what it lacks in ambiance it makes up in seedy sexiness. As Vahe intertwines his tongue with mine and grips my ass hard, I understand the appeal of hooking up with someone like me, somewhere like this. Similar to his truck in this concrete garage, I may be dirty and unpolished, but I can guarantee a good fucking time.

I grind against his hard-on until I have him moaning underneath me and at risk of ripping through his jeans. His hands are everywhere, pulling my hair, squeezing the side of my neck, and pushing my hips where he needs more pressure. It's my favorite part about fuckboys—unraveling them with lust, until they're just a boy who has to fuck as if his life depends on it.

But Vahe is so much more than your average fuckboy, a fact made apparent when he trails tender kisses down my neck and attempts to lavish my breasts. I'm used to men undressing me for their own benefit, but Vahe is itching to get my bra off so he can focus on pleasing me. A gentleman through and through. Well, not tonight, Baker Bro.

"Ah, ah, ah," I admonish, swatting his hands away. "You're not the one calling the shots. If you want to give your hands a job, you can pull down your pants, because your dick is the only thing I want right now."

To his credit, Vahe's a good listener. I relish the snick of his belt and the sound of his zipper moving at lightning speed. And I know it sounds cliché as hell, but the second his cock comes into view, I lick my lips. I can't help it. I don't eat much when I'm playing gigs, but now I'm starving for a different reason.

Vahe scoots toward the middle of the seat, so I can kneel down without hitting my head against the steering wheel. And then I settle in for a second, even better performance. I gently drag my nails across his length, before wrapping him in a firm grip. The finger rings don't affect my dexterity, and the little danger they bring only adds to their appeal.

"Oh, fuck—" Vahe groans when I take him into my mouth, savoring the way he tastes. I'm not one to romanticize bodily fluids—if anything, I appreciate that sex isn't sparkling clean and sanitary. I prefer it gritty and grungy, coated in sweat and musk.

But whether it's all the sugar he consumes or his adorable, breathy rasps, Vahe tastes sweeter than any other man I've had at my mercy. At the first drop, I need more.

"I'm not stopping until you fill my mouth," I tell him. "I want you dripping down my chin."

I swallow him down to the base like a threat, cupping his balls while working the shaft like I'm getting paid triple-overtime. Between the suction and sheer enthusiasm, I've never had a man last longer than a few minutes. When Vahe's hips thrust into my mouth with more vigor than most, I'm silently impressed by his stamina. But when his labored pants start being laced with painful frustration, I know I need to shift gears.

"Does somebody need a little backdoor action to get them there?" I say, pressing on his perineum. I'm happy to keep going and massage his prostrate, but he reaches down to stop me.

"I need you . . . to touch yourself." He shudders. "I won't be able to come if you don't."

I'm stunned. I mean, I always get what I want from hookups—life is too short to not get laid properly—but I typically have to take it without remorse. When you're hunting for bottom feeders, you have to accept a certain level of selfishness. I still have a great time because I'm not afraid to demand pleasure from men.

But for Vahe to be so preoccupied with giving pleasure that his climax is contingent on mine? That's a new phenomenon.

As part of the good, giving, and game philosophy, I'm down for whatever. And when that something is creaming my own pants, I'm not going to argue. That's the definition of a win-win.

I resume giving both wrists a workout this time, one working Vahe's cock while I slide the other beneath my black jeans. It helps that I'm already sopping wet—it won't take long to push Vahe over the edge when I'm already there.

Relishing the cool steel of my claws against my slickness, I rub my clit faster and faster, moaning around his dick as I keep pace. Now that I'm getting as much as I'm giving, Vahe doesn't hold back. He gets rougher, more urgent, fucking my mouth in a frenzy.

"Oh god, yes," he breathes. "You suck my cock so well. That's it, don't stop playing with that pussy."

Funny how I have no problem getting filthy with strangers, but Vahe's floodgates open when a woman is truly enjoying herself.

Eventually, I get so caught up in chasing my climax that my hand slips off Vahe, and if anything that drives him wilder. As I focus on the feeling building in my nerve endings, ready to snap, he holds my face in his palms, thrusting down my throat with conviction. We're playing alone, together.

Until I look up and meet his gaze. It's the easiest move to get a man to bust, but the intensity in Vahe's eyes takes me off guard. It's not the anger-laden greed that I'm used to, the male entitlement when they're stuffing a mouth to get it to shut up.

Vahe's staring at me with pure reverence. He's not just happy to be here, getting a blow job from any broad off the street. He's truly grateful to be here with *me*. In this moment when we're the only two people on earth.

His devotion would have knocked me over if I wasn't already on my knees. It crashes into me like a wave, and before I know it, I'm coming, sucking hard. Vahe follows quickly, and I don't break eye contact, smiling with my eyes as I swallow every last drop.

It doesn't matter whether or not Vahe is rock-hard. At heart, he's always a big softie.

"Wow," he says with a gulp, as if he's just completed a run. "I have no idea what I did to deserve that. Get over here." He shoves himself back in his pants, so he can pull me off the cab floor and kiss me. I've been with dudes who have refused to swap spit after oral until my teeth are brushed. Because god forbid I gargle their dick without gargling mouthwash afterward.

Maybe one day I'll stop comparing Vahe Derderian to every subpar lover I've had. But that would imply we have something more solid than an uncertain future ahead of us.

Vahe must sense me pulling away as I pull back from our kiss. "You wanna jump in my shower before we break into that box?" he asks, pointing to the choreg and paklava sitting beside me. His question comes out as a weak suggestion. It's easier to turn him down when he already expects to hear no.

"How about we save these for tomorrow?" I reply, trying to sound more upbeat so I don't ruin the mood. "I've got special plans for us, and these will make them even better."

His face falls, but he doesn't push it. I know he wants

more, but how disappointed can he be after that mind-blowing blow job?

"Of course they'll make them better," he replies. "I can't have you losing this bet by such a wide margin."

I chuckle, shoving him back to the driver's seat. It's safer when we retreat to being rivals. Eye contact during a simultaneous orgasm is one thing, but intimacy for any longer than that isn't going to come naturally to me.

Vahe drops me off at my apartment, and I give him the coordinates of tomorrow's secret destination.

"I know it's tempting, but do not look up this address in advance," I insist. "Just wear the swimsuit I told you to pack and meet me there at 9:15 a.m. It's a nonrefundable appointment, so don't be late."

He raises his thick eyebrow, like he doesn't wake up at the crack of dawn for a living. "Should I be excited or concerned?"

I give him a goodbye-for-now kiss, flashing him a devilish grin. "Anytime you're with me, you should definitely be both."

~

***TORI TOWNSEND'S** top ten worst dates in San Francisco (in no particular order)*

1. The first time, after moving from NYC, a guy invited me to a "rooftop" bar on top of a building, which I discovered was only five stories tall
2. Playing putt-putt at that mini-golf place in the Mission, which is so cramped that its tabletops fit three people's beers at any given time
3. When my date got so high at a music festival that he invented the concept of picnics while we were

having a picnic: "But what if they, like, brought a restaurant *outside*, man?"

4. The live action role-player who came dressed like a pirate because he believed there was actual treasure on Treasure Island

5. When I put extra effort into my appearance because my date offered to introduce me to "his best bros," and he ended up taking me to see a Giants game

6. The hipster who asked me if I wanted to go to Pier 69, which I realized didn't exist when he answered the door with his dick out

7. Staving off a panic attack when that car guy raced up and down hills like he was a Formula 1 driver

8. The "financial advisor" who promised to buy me dinner after a networking event, which was actually recruiting for a whole life insurance MLM scheme

9. Every time I didn't pay attention walking around and stepped into human shit

10. Being dragged to watch Shen Yun—no contest

chapter
fifteen

After being dressed to impress for last night's performance, I'm not proud to say my feminist brain fretted at the thought of being all natural this morning: hair pulled back into a low bun, dressed in a black, fleece-lined wrap dress, and without a hint of makeup on. But it's not until I make my way to Hunters Point and park along the curb of the Aphrodite Day Spa that I see I'm not the one who made a fashion faux pas.

"Are you modeling for Armenian *Sports Illustrated*?" I shout against the wind, exiting my car and waving to Vahe. He's standing outside the entrance of the nondescript midsize building in just a pair of flip-flops and short swim trunks in red, blue, and orange stripes to resemble his ancestral flag.

He instinctively covers the front of his shorts, as if that makes him any more modest when his chiseled body is on full display. "You told me to wear a swimsuit!"

"Yes, but under clothes like a rational human being." I pull down the V-neck of my dress to show a matching black one-piece underneath. "It's December, and the sun is nowhere to be found today. It's cold as fuck out here."

"Really? I couldn't tell." He rubs his arms energetically up and down to expel his goosebumps. "I would have gone inside to escape the elements, but you kept today's schedule a secret, so I have no idea which floor is supposed to buzz me in. And flagging down passersby doesn't help when I look like a patriotic perv in this."

Guilt washes over me like the waves of the Pacific Ocean off in the distance. If I wasn't so weird about intimacy, Vahe would have come with me because he'd be staying at my place. But instead he's booked a room in the cultural wasteland that is SOMA, aka South of Market Street. Downtown is the one area I tell tourists to actively avoid, but it's the only place that's zoned for commercial buildings higher than five stories, so naturally most hotel chains are clustered there.

"Okay, my bad. We're off to a rough start, but I know how to turn things around." I untie my dress and wrap us both inside the fleece lining. Vahe pounces, pulling me tight, both for warmth and to pick me up by my ass. His tongue slips past mine as I snake my legs around his waist, grinding against his rock-hard length. We tuck ourselves in the entryway to hide from the winter chill, but when Vahe pushes me up against the wall, something juts into my back with a loud dial tone.

"Ma'am," a perturbed man's voice rings from the intercom I slammed into, "we're not sure what you two are selling, but we don't allow solicitors of any kind on the premises."

Yikes. So much for an unobservant security desk. "You've got the wrong idea. We're here for our appointment at the Aphrodite Day Spa. The reservation's under Tori Townsend."

The man grunts before the tone goes dead. A minute goes by, and just when I'm about to beg to be let in, a buzzer chimes and the front door unlocks with a click.

We make our way through an empty, sparsely decorated lobby and up a rickety elevator to the top floor. With each step, I'm freaking out that the spa I selected might be a total dump instead of the award-winning establishment it claimed to be.

Relief hits me, however, when the number five flashes on the display and the elevator doors ding open to an immaculate, marble salon.

Vahe swears under his breath, unnerved by the sight of the spa instead of reassured. "Tori, I can't walk in a fancy-ass place like this with my junk in people's faces."

"Anybody with that opportunity should feel so lucky," I say, ogling the outline of his swim trunks. An impulsive thought strikes me, and I strip off my dress. "We just have to own it. If I'm paying to visit a fancy-ass place, then I'm showing off my fancy ass."

I hike up my swimsuit so even more cheek peeks out and strut to the front desk like I'm modeling Manolos instead of flapping my sandals annoyingly across the tile floor.

"Welcome," a blonde receptionist with flawless skin says with raised and meticulously manicured eyebrows. "Ms. Townsend, I presume?"

I nod demurely, as if I'm dressed in a politician's pantsuit and not exposing my tatted backside. "We booked the premium hammam package with the couple's massage."

She taps her keyboard to complete the check-in process. "Wonderful. After we drop off your belongings in our secure lockers . . ." She pauses briefly, scanning us from head to toe. "And give you some robes to wear, you'll have the best room in the house. Once your services are complete, you have until closing to enjoy the room's amenities—a sauna, cold plunge, and jetted tub—all to yourselves. Now, if you'll follow me this way."

She's about to direct us to separate men's and women's facilities to store our stuff when Vahe pulls me aside. "This seems amazing, Tori," he whispers, "but something about it makes me uncomfortable."

My heart catches in my throat. Did I make some kind of egregious mistake? I ask the receptionist for five minutes, and she leaves to give us a moment of privacy. "What's wrong?"

He fidgets with the drawstrings of his swimsuit. "I've never been to a hammam before, and . . . well, isn't it a Turkish bath? I'm not sure if me being here is the best idea. For god's sake, I'm wearing a Hye pride flag on my trunks like I intended to make a controversial statement. I might as well have 'Never Again' emblazoned on my ass!"

Whoa, whoa, whoa. This is escalating quickly if Vahe's mind is jumping to post-genocide politics. "I get that. I do. I'm a white woman who got her start working in Vietnamese nail salons. If anyone was conscious of cultural appropriation, it would be me." I take his hands in mine. "But public bathing has a long history dating back to ancient times, across so many civilizations. You wouldn't feel weird if I took you to a Korean spa, would you?"

He considers the question carefully. "I guess not. But this hits different. It's hard to explain."

"If it won't be a relaxing experience for you, then we can leave. For what it's worth, though, the people who work here are so bougie they should be ordering bottomless brunch in the Marina. The first time I did hammam I was with the glam fam in Vegas, and let me tell you, there was nothing sacred about that trip of debauchery. I'd hate for you to overthink this when people practice hammam around the world—even in Yerevan. I checked. Self-care is highly personal, but it's also for everybody."

Vahe smiles. "So you're saying spas have watered down Mediterranean and Middle Eastern bathing rituals like fusion restaurants have done with our food? Isn't that the definition of cultural appropriation?"

I swat him on the stomach and nearly break my fingers on his washboard abs. "Alright, smartass. Stage a protest if you want—that's your prerogative. But I'll have you know hammam is typically conducted in the nude, and I paid extra to get the staff to scram after our massages. You wouldn't want to let my money go to waste, would you?"

To make my offer irresistible, I leave hot kisses across his pecs and down his happy trail. Right as I flick my tongue along the waistband of his swimsuit, he pulls me up with a smoldering gaze.

"I don't need my raging hard-on to get us kicked out," he growls. "But the second we're left alone, I'm getting you dirty all over again."

Imagining my punishment for making Vahe wait has me shimmying with anticipation. We resume our pre-hammam prep, but I'm not paying much attention. When two more modelesque women escort us to the couple's suite, I don't even catch their names.

"Holy—" Vahe has to stop himself from swearing. I don't blame him. You'd have no inkling from the outside that the epitome of luxury would be behind these doors. The suite is gargantuan, with massage tables on the left next to a sauna and steam room. On the right sit two pools, one cold plunge and the other heated with jets. But the pièce de résistance is the massive circular stone in the center. Two stations have been set on top, with rolled-up towels for our heads and ankles.

"Have either of you experienced hammam here before?" asks the attendant standing next to Vahe. When we shake our heads, she proceeds with a brief rundown. First, we'll be cleansed with sudsy bubbles infused with mint tea, followed by a dual exfoliation with body buffing and a Himalayan salt scrub. Then we'll end with a mud mask and a honey-enhanced hydrating moisturizer. Between each step we'll be rinsed from basins of water that are collected and recycled through a filtration system underneath the stone.

Hearing her describe this process is enough to erase years

of stress off my life, and yet when the two women give us a minute to disrobe, I'm itching from the adrenaline running through my veins. Normally, these two hours would fly by, but I'm not with friends enjoying a laid-back getaway. Being a few feet from Vahe wearing nothing but two small towels over our nether regions is making me count down the minutes until our grand finale.

As the heated stone radiates warmth across my chest and an attendant uses traditional exfoliating gloves, known as kese, to scrub off dead skin, I can't concentrate on getting grounded in my body. I'm too preoccupied with what Vahe's going to do to said body when this is over. Every splash of water over my upper back is a stark reminder that my lower half is plenty wet already.

By the time we transition from the hammam stone to the massage tables, my limbs ache more than they did when we entered the suite. And from the glances Vahe and I steal lying next to each other, I can tell he's suffering from stiffness of his own.

A lifetime later, our attendants inform us that our time is up. When they suggest sitting in the sauna or steam room to keep our body temperature up and increase our circulation, I almost laugh in their faces. Given how hard my blood is pumping, the last thing I need is to feel even hotter.

Our services may be complete, but the real bodywork is about to begin. When the door clicks shut to leave us alone, it's like a gunshot has set us off to the races.

"Don't get me wrong," Vahe says, closing the space between us. "That was the best spa experience of my life, but it should be classified as cruel and unusual punishment."

I swallow. "I'll alert the UN for this blatant act of torture."

He smirks. "You don't know the half of it. Now, drop the towel, Townsend."

Gleefully, I obey his order. Vahe's mouth falls open, and at first I don't understand what the big deal is until I realize this is the first time he's seen me fully naked. Whether bent over the kitchen counter or underneath the brambles of the Sanger *S*, our previous hookups have been quickies with our pants around our ankles. I'm not one to dress modestly, but I forget how much skin he hasn't seen.

He reaches out to trace my underbust tattoo. It's a section of the sheet music to "Hurt," my favorite song. As iconic as the Johnny Cash cover is, nothing can beat the original by Nine Inch Nails, especially its haunting, monotonous repetition of A and E notes played together.

"I thought this was just a dotted line to accessorize your crop tops," he muses, enjoying the way my skin shivers under his touch.

My lips uplift into the tiniest of smiles. "That was the intent." I start singing the song softly, as fingers dance under the notes. "I had it placed this way so no one could decipher its meaning until I deemed them worthy."

He wraps his hands around my waist, despite my mental urging to drift toward my nipples. "How come I get the sense that very few of your bedfellows have laid eyes on it?"

"It's easy for it to remain a mystery when I rarely fuck in a bed in the first place."

Vahe bites his lip, his hands gripping tighter, as if weighing his next move. And then he does the last thing I expect: he grabs my robe off the hook on the wall and hands it to me.

"Wait—what's going on?" I take the robe between my fingers, dumbfounded. "I thought we were going to fuck all over the spa and risk a lifetime ban."

Vahe runs his fingers through his hair, which has gone curlier in the suite's natural humidity. "I may come to regret this decision, given how every fiber of my being resists the idea of turning down your exquisite body, but I have to pump the brakes."

"You were game until you saw my tattoo. You've never had any problems with the rest of my ink—you said you preferred it even." I angrily punch my arms through the sleeves of my robe. "Why the hell would you pull a one-eighty now?"

I can't recall ever getting rejected sexually in my life. The sting to my ego makes me feel more naked than I ever did without clothes on.

Vahe dons his robe as well, covering up the swim trunks I never got the chance to remove. "You said it yourself, Tori. You've been to bed metaphorically with plenty of guys—something I applaud, by the way—but a four-poster seems like a four-letter word to you."

His look of sympathy is so enraging I want to smack it off his face. "What's it to you where I like to fuck? Not once has a man ever complained about my sense of sexual adventure."

I make a motion toward the door, and Vahe reaches out to stop me. "Because I don't just want to have sex with you. Please, don't take this the wrong way. The sex we have is absolute fire, but I want real intimacy. If we keep sneaking around, then you'll never see me as anything more than the fuckboy from Fresno."

"What are you talking about? You had dinner with my best friends! That's more than I've done with anyone else before."

"First off," he retorts, "I didn't have dinner with them. I *made* dinner for them. And secondly, I'm a person with a lot to offer, and I don't think it's too much to want the chance to prove that to you."

I'm not about to argue whether Vahe has a lot to offer, but it's difficult to take him seriously when what I'm primarily interested in is packed inside a patriotic swimsuit.

"My eyes are up here, Victoria."

My gaze snaps back to his, and I can't tell who's more frustrated. I sigh. Even though we can use the suite's amenities until closing, the mood has been effectively killed. The idea of sitting together in the hot tub is more awkward than arousing. "What do you want from me? I spent the last three weeks planning the perfect weekend, and it doesn't feel close to perfect."

Vahe pulls me into a big bear hug. "Screw the competition. I appreciate your effort, and I'm sure whatever is on your schedule is going to knock my socks off. But what I really want —all I've ever wanted since you entered the deli—is to get to know you. The real you, deep down, beneath the ink."

I crane my neck up to pout at him. "I'm not sure what you're expecting. What you see is what you get. And you could have had me on that hammam stone if you weren't so hung up on a few bars of permanently drawn sheet music."

He kisses my forehead. "I may not have any tattoos, but I'd guess that nobody gets 'Hurt' below their heart unless they've had theirs broken before."

So he knew what song I was singing while he was admiring my tits. "Well said, for someone who's avoided needles jabbing into his skin."

He picks me up off my feet with ease and squeezes me tighter. "Hey, now. Having tattoos doesn't mean you're fucked up, and not having them isn't a sign you're not. But loving that song enough to get a permanent reminder of it does indicate there's a story there. I'd appreciate you sharing it. We could forgo all your plans and get food delivered to your apartment instead if it means I get to hear about everything that happened in your life before it brought you to me."

I resist the urge to make retching noises after witnessing that level of cheesiness—even if some small part of me likes the sound of it. Talking about my dead mom and my deadbeat dad doesn't get my engine revving, but it wouldn't kill me to open up for once.

"Okay, fine. You've made your point. I was going to take

you to this old-school Mexican restaurant for real Mission burritos, but we can grab them to-go and head back to my place. I'll unleash my trauma on you, and we'll *make love*"—I stretch out the vomit-inducing phrase with heavy sarcasm— "in my bed like a couple of normies. Will that make you happy?"

"As a matter of fact, yes." Vahe gives me a tender kiss before opening the door. "But more importantly, I think it will make you happy too, if you let it."

ROOMMATE GROUP CHAT ON SATURDAY, December 16, at 11:53 a.m.

TORI

Change of plans. We're coming back to the apartment, so I need you both to scram.

GLEN

Hooking up so soon? It's barely noon. Som is still asleep.

SOM

I'm awake. Barely. Note to self: never end a Friday night with a round of Fireball shots.

TORI

What year is it? Did we time travel back to Alex's twenty-first birthday party?

SOM

They're festive! I got caught up in all the holiday cheer, and cinnamon whisky sounded better when I was already drunk.

TORI

You know what sounds even better? You two vacating the premises.

GLEN

Nothing's stopping you from fornicating while we're here. It's not like you haven't done it before.

TORI

That's not what I'm concerned bout. Vahe wants to get to know me better and talk about our feelings.

GLEN

Oooh kinky. Can we watch?

TORI

No! My stomach's in knots, and I do not need more humiliation. I'll give you free facials if you make yourself scarce for the day.

SOM

Throw in some gua sha, betch, and you got yourself a deal!

chapter
sixteen

We wrap up our reservation at the Aphrodite Day Spa, stopping briefly at Vahe's hotel so he can change into normal clothes, then heading back to my neighborhood and taking two Mission burritos to-go. And no, I'm not going to reveal the restaurant because the last thing I want is for it to have even longer lines. Sue me for gatekeeping, but if your favorite joints kept getting overrun by yuppies every time SF Eater ran a review, you'd be territorial too.

"That's the opposite of my thinking," Vahe says as I explain this while we're seated at my dining table. "The more successful a restaurant becomes, the better a chance they have to expand and grow. Not to mention, more locations should mean fewer lines."

"But then it's not . . ." I trail off, grasping for why the idea rubs me the wrong way.

"Special?" Vahe suggests with a wry smile. "You're one of those people who doesn't like when something goes mainstream. How very San Francisco hipster of you."

I flick a pinto bean at his face with my claw, but his reflexes are too good, and it lands in his mouth. He chews it, victorious, and I laugh.

He makes a good point though. I never considered how my aversion for anything basic might be holding businesses back. Because if we're talking about Vahe's business, I would want his wildest dreams to come true.

Before I can ask what those dreams might be, Vahe gets up and starts walking the perimeter of the apartment, commenting about the various glam fam photos on the walls. I know this man has a hearty appetite, but I swear he inhaled his burrito just so he could wander around my apartment. As hungry as he may be, he's thirstier to learn more about me.

I don't mind indulging him when he's asking about my best friends. I regale him with stories of our travels—the fashion shows we've attended, the celebrities we've met, the hijinks we've gotten ourselves into. It's an outrageous life we get to live, I'll admit, and I never take it for granted.

"How did you get started?" Vahe asks as I re-wrap the remaining half of my hefty burrito so I can save it for later. "Were you always interested in beauty?"

I blink. It's such an innocuous question that I should be more prepared for it, but real answers are always more complicated than they seem.

"You know, I'm not used to being on the receiving end," I reveal. "My clients are the ones spilling their guts. I'm lucky to get a word in."

I see the lightbulb go off in Vahe's head. "How about you give me a manicure? Except this time, I'll be the one listening."

"You want a manicure?" I have a very progressive clientele, so I'm not surprised when men book appointments with me. I am surprised that Vahe wants to be one of them.

"Why not?" He sits back down at the dining table, assuming the position, hands splayed out. "I have to wear gloves while I cook anyway, so there's no risk of nail polish flaking off in the phyllo dough."

"Okay, then. Let's do it." I'm beaming, more excited than I expected to be. I grab my nail kit and prepare our station, running hot water into a bowl to soak Vahe's cuticles. Most men never push theirs back, so they need all the help they can get.

"What color would you like?" I ask, showing him my impressive collection of polishes. "I know a lot of guys go with black for their first time."

"Hey now, who said this was my first time?" Vahe exclaims, mock-offended. "You forget I grew up with two older sisters. When Mari wanted to play beauty school, I had no choice but to accept my fate." I chuckle, not surprised that Mari was cracking a whip from an early age.

"Plus, black is way too *basic*," he teases, scanning my monochromatic outfit. And I get it—a goth chick wearing all-black is about as groundbreaking as florals in spring. But if it's wrong, then I don't want to be right.

"Har har, what will it be then, smartass?"

Vahe gives it some thought before pulling a chain necklace from under his flannel. "How about matching this?"

I lean in, reaching for the small pendant to study it closer. "Is that an evil eye?"

"We call it an atchk, but its purpose is the same, to ward off evil spirits. I was taught that if your atchk breaks, you're not supposed to fix it because it's proof that it protected you. It's done its job."

I've screwed around with many a guy in a gold chain, but Vahe's the only one with a more admirable reason than his own vanity for wearing one.

"You're in luck," I say, selecting the perfect cobalt blue and giving the bottle a good shake. I'm almost jealous how fantastic it will look against his olive skin.

To his credit, Vahe doesn't dive straight into an interroga-tion. He waits for me to prep his nails—clipping, filing, and buffing at my own pace. It's not until I start applying the clear base coat that I decide to reward his patience.

"For a long time I thought I fell into the beauty business because I had no other choice," I say, returning to his question. "Teachers and guidance counselors drilled into me that I was supposed to attend college, and since my parents had talked about a college fund when I was young, I assumed that was the plan. I was naive about a lot of shit back then." The words come out with a dark edge, and I have to take a deep breath to reset. "My mom and dad both suffered from addiction, and it got worse the older I got. By the time I was filling out university applications, they claimed I never had a college fund, and why the hell did I think otherwise? That's when I knew the money was gone. I know they were in the throes of an insidious disease, but parents are supposed to sacrifice everything for their children, and mine spent my future on their next hit."

I can tell it's killing Vahe that he can't hold my hand because I'm busy painting his nails blue. "But what about scholarships? Or going to community college?"

It warms my broken heart that Vahe's instinct is to go into fix-it mode for a problem that's seventeen years old—mature enough to graduate if it were a person. "I was smart—don't get me wrong—but I was never going to get a full ride. It was like when I found out my family gave up, that's when I gave up too. I thought I didn't deserve to go to college, whether it was for four years or two. By then I had saved a small chunk from working in nail salons on nights and weekends, so I figured I might as well turn my after-school job into a real career. Took out cosmetology school loans, and that was that."

Vahe shifts uncomfortably in his seat, frowning. It must be difficult for him to reckon with how differently we got our starts in life. We both work in the service industry, but he inherited his business while I was ready to do anything to survive.

"It's okay," I reassure him. "There's a silver lining to this sob story. My point is, I originally thought I became a nail tech because I didn't have any other options, but that wasn't the case. I could have bailed and done something else, but I fell in love with making people feel beautiful. My instructors told me that I had a real knack for it."

Vahe's smile returns, lighting up the whole room. "I bet you were a nail-painting prodigy."

He's not being patronizing. He'd say that about anything I did. "Possibly. I took to everything naturally—facials, brows, waxing—but nails were a unique talent. They're what I love doing the most."

"More than playing piano?" he asks as I apply a second coat.

"I adore both, but yeah, I would say so. Jazz is a hobby of mine. It's nice to make some extra cash, but I wouldn't ever want it to be a full-time thing. I like blowing off some steam at the end of a long workday. Playing for an audience is great, but even if there's nobody around, I do it for me." I meticulously paint matching evil eyes on Vahe's ring fingers, appreciating their hypnotic stare. "Nails are something I do for others. Music and manicures are both art forms, but there's some-thing tangibly rewarding about making someone feel more put-together for a couple of weeks."

"I can see that," Vahe agrees. "Whenever my barber shapes my beard with a straight razor, I feel fresh as fuck." He can't stroke his chin, but he strikes a pose like he's shooting a commercial, which sends me into a fit of giggles. Thank good-ness the top coat I'm applying is clear.

"Precisely." I finish off with a few drops of quick-dry, so Vahe doesn't have to sit around forever. "Every woman I know feels like her life is on track after getting her nails done.

In fact, I looked forward to the times my mother would get a manicure—it meant she was sober enough to get her act together, at least for a day or two. Beauty was hope in my house."

"When you put it like that," Vahe says softly, "I think you ended up exactly where you're supposed to be."

I smile, grateful that he understands. I can't stand being pitied for where I've been because I want to celebrate where I am now—in a field I love, in a city where I belong. And maybe, just maybe, with someone I belong with.

It's customary for me to end a manicure with a hand massage, and I reach for the lotion without thinking. As I knead Vahe's fingers and forearms, it doesn't take long for the air to shift between us. I know I'm not the only one imagining our hands being put to better use when I see an intensity in Vahe's eyes that mirrors his atchk.

"I know we just had a full-body massage, but would you be opposed to two in one day?" Vahe's gaze flicks down the hall as if his proposition wasn't obvious.

"That's an offer I will never refuse," I say, taking his well-moisturized hand and leading him to my bedroom. I'm glad I removed my one-piece but kept my fleece wrap-dress on, so I have a second opportunity to let it fall to the floor. Whatever curiosity Vahe had to explore my belongings is squashed by a chance to explore my naked body instead.

I move in closer, tipping my head back to kiss him, and Vahe puts his hand up to stop me.

"Am I an evil spirit you're trying to ward off?" I tease, settling for kissing his fingertips.

Vahe jerks his wrist before I can suck on his index finger and show him what he's missing. "You changed your plans so I could get to know you better, and I appreciate that. It means a lot to me. Let me take my time with you."

I can't argue with that. I may be the queen of quickies, but if Vahe wants to reward me like this, I'll open up way more often.

Always happy for more pampering, I lay face-down on my bed while Vahe strips down to his red boxer briefs.

"I'm just getting comfortable," he warns as I ogle his chiseled body. "Being around you gets me hotter than a shift at the deli in 110-degree summers."

I can't even. In all my years of hitting it and quitting it, I've never met a man who gets overheated from looking at me in the nude.

Vahe waffles on how to maneuver himself, before settling in between my legs. The position is delicious and torturous for both of us, especially when he squirts lotion onto my back and his rigid cock makes contact with my ass cheeks every time he slides his hands forward. With every slow stroke, he thrusts against me, with only a thin layer of cotton keeping him from driving home inside me.

Even in my lust-addled state, I admire how good Vahe is with his hands, tracing my tattoos and kneading my muscle knots with careful attention. He's both gentle and firm, smoothly transitioning from delicate scratches to tugging on fistfuls of hair.

And true to form, he respects my request to not constantly reaffirm consent. He doesn't waste his precious time asking if he can touch me. He knows if I take issue with anything he's doing, I have a mouth and I'm not afraid to use it.

It's the assurance that I'm down for whatever, whenever, that gives him the confidence to move his fingers to more salacious destinations. First, he inches toward my breasts, running his thumbs along the sides. I lift my weight slightly off the bed and allow him to cup underneath, massaging my nipples until I'm arching my back and moaning for more.

Then he slides down my hips, and I widen my legs, giving him access to all of me.

He travels up my inner thighs, running his fingers along my folds. It's obvious he no longer needs the lotion as I'm soaking through the comforter.

"So wet for me," he murmurs as he resumes his massage, one hand reaching around to touch my clit while the other slides two fingers inside my aching pussy.

He's patient, content to stroke at a steady rhythm, feeding me praise with each pump. I can't get any leverage while on my stomach, and my legs are spread open as wide as they can go. I want to be filled up so badly, but Vahe does not share my sense of urgency.

"No need to rush this," he says, simultaneously circling my clit and thrusting in and out without speeding up. "Let it happen."

I whimper and babble my brains out, cycling between chanting his name and cursing his existence. But the pressure building finally breaks, and I fall apart around him. He coaxes my climax out of me while I groan, face planted into my pillow.

"See? That wasn't so bad." My limp body is exactly what he needs, so when he flips me over, I'm as compliant as a pool noodle.

Vahe takes off his underwear, freeing his hard dick from its prison. As excited as I am to move on to the main event, my body is restless for another reason. This time I'm not bent over the kitchen counter or on my knees in his pickup truck. I'm in a bed, about to engage in the most vulnerable sex act I can think of: the missionary position.

What's natural for most people has me breaking out into hives. But if I can endure the pain of needles for my body mods, I can overcome this fear.

"Open your eyes, Tori." I meet Vahe's gaze, unaware I had squeezed my eyelids shut. He sits back on his knees, dick good to go but face unsure. "I don't want to do anything you're uncomfortable with."

I beckon him closer. "I'm just inexperienced in this department. I've fucked so many guys I've lost count, but this whole 'making love' thing is new to me."

Vahe smiles from ear to ear. Making love is not the same as being *in* love—I think—but he takes great pride in it anyway. "Allow me to be your first."

He kisses me deeply, enveloping me in his arms, and we indulge in holding each other close. I can't remember the last time I made out with someone for the simple enjoyment of it —not since high school, at least.

When he's got me grinning and loosey-goosey, I feel relaxed enough to take things further. I reach down and stroke him, appreciating the weight of him in my hand. I grab a condom from my nightstand and unroll it around him, squeezing at the base. He moans into my mouth as I guide him to my entrance, ready and waiting.

"Mmmm, fuck, you feel amazing," Vahe groans, sliding inside, going deeper as I acclimate to his size. "You won't be in this position for long because I won't be able to last."

That may be true for him, but he's got me in missionary on hard mode. Every time my eyelids flutter closed, Vahe brings me back to the present with a teasing "eyes on me." He leans back and lifts my legs, keeping my gaze locked on his cock thrusting in and out of my folds.

For how flustered our intense eye contact makes me, it is hot as hell. It's like Vahe is urging me to come without words, daring me to lie back and take it. To take him into my body and let him into my heart.

"You can do it, Tori. I know you can." His encouragements send me in a tailspin. When he throws my legs over his shoulders and pinches my clit as he pounds into me, I come unraveled all over again.

Vahe settles his chest on top of me without crushing the air out of my lungs. Skin to skin, he continues pumping, chasing his own release. His body is like the perfect weighted blanket. My fingers are digging into his shoulders, but my claws are off. Literally and figuratively.

With my defenses breached, I give Vahe a kiss that tells him everything I can't yet. How much I care about him, how much better my life is with him in it. I kiss him—not just to bring him home, but to show him he *is* home.

That's what tips him over the edge, and I squeeze my inner walls to drain him to the last drop. If I'm going to be overrun and ragged, so will he.

When we're utterly spent, we catch our breath in each other's arms. I feel rubbed raw and exhausted. When I wipe my damp face, I assume I must have broken a major sweat. It takes me a minute to realize that the moisture is from my tears. The first time I open myself up completely with a man, I end up crying.

It's a mortifying blend of happy and sad. In a couple of weekends, I find myself falling hard for Vahe, and there's nothing I can do about our circumstances. How far we live apart, how dedicated we are to our loved ones and our careers. Making love is one thing, but shaking up your entire world for love feels insurmountable.

Vahe runs his thumb along my damp cheek. "Would you like me to go?" he says, unable to hide his sadness.

I hiccup, shaking my head with force. "Stay." Stay the night, stay forever, I want to tell him. Just stay. Don't be like everyone else in my life. *Don't leave.*

When a new river runs down my face, it dawns on me that Vahe's tears have joined mine.

～

TORI TOWNSEND RUINS popular San Francisco destinations

1. **Fisherman's Wharf**. Known to locals as Pier 39, this place is like if Times Square was oceanfront property. With shitty chain restaurants, overpriced gift shops, and a questionably small aquarium for one of California's largest bays, it never met a tourist trap it didn't like. Sea lions are cool, but if I wanted to watch grunting, territorial animals, I'd go to Equinox gym.

2. **Lombard Street**. Ah, yes. The perfect activity for out-of-towners. Make them drive down the windiest street in the world when they can't even handle parking on the city's steep hills. They should have to experience a smash-and-grab when they reach the end because if they're gullible enough to fall for this attraction, they deserve to get scammed.

3. **Alcatraz**. If you asked native San Franciscans if they've been to Alcatraz—by themselves and not with their visiting families on vacation—I bet most of them would say no way. If you want to waste several hours learning about San Francisco's criminal history, just stroll down Billionaire Row.

4. **The Painted Ladies**. I mean, if you love a nearly forty-year-old show so much that you're willing to take a photo to immortalize it, you do you. But I don't need to make a special trip to gawk at houses I can't afford. That's called living in San Francisco.

chapter
seventeen

It's no surprise to anyone who knows me that I pride myself on going off the beaten path. If it were up to me, Vahe and I would stick to my original plan of showing off San Francisco's seedy underbelly—or at least its kookiest quirks. We'd uphold the time-honored tradition of taking edibles and navigating Magowan's Infinite Mirror Maze, followed by downing overpriced boozy punch at the iconic tiki bar Anthony Bourdain himself adored, and then perhaps ending with a historic sex dungeon tour if Vahe was up for that kind of thing.

But after he convinced me yesterday to share stories from my painful past and give myself to him, body and soul, I did the one thing every tech startup in this city has done a million times.

I pivoted. Which is how I find myself on a Sunday morning riding a motherfucking cable car.

"Tell me again," Vahe ponders, holding my hand as we make our way down California Street, "why didn't we catch a car where all those people were standing near the mall?"

I scoff. "Classic amateur move to wait forever for the Powell line. I mean, both routes are out of our way, but if you want to play tourist, we're doing it like locals. Plus, this has the better view, by far."

We take in the sights, from the Wells Fargo Museum to Grace Cathedral, until we reach the end of the line at Van Ness and transfer to Muni to complete the rest of the trip by bus. It crushes my city girl spirit to be so inefficient with planning public transportation, but after I already vetoed Vahe's other San Francisco date suggestions, a cable car ride was the least offensive alternative. Because you sure as hell aren't going to see me at Alcatraz again unless they've reopened the prison specifically to punish me for the homicidal rage I'll inflict after wasting another day on stolen Indigenous land.

"So where are we headed?"

Vahe's innocuous question distracts me from getting irrationally angry about a destination we're not even visiting. After arriving at our bus stop, we walk around the corner to the edge of the vast Golden Gate Park. My blood pressure is already falling to a more peaceful level. "To my favorite moment of zen," I say with a relieved sigh.

Vahe crosses his arms. "I thought you said you wanted to avoid places overrun by tourists and transplants. Isn't this the same as a New Yorker making an exception for Central Park?"

"It's not making an exception if it's a legitimate part of the city. I didn't drag you on a day trip to Napa or Santa Cruz and pretend it counts as being in San Francisco proper. And as a New Yorker, born and raised, I'll always be the first to promote green urban spaces. Golden Gate Park is actually twenty percent bigger than Central Park, which means you'll never run out of things to do, and you have plenty of room to avoid other people. Hence why my city beats yours any day of the week."

"Got it. So it's a sanctuary from all the signposts of an urban environment—the skyscrapers, the dense concrete jungle, and a metric shit-ton of strangers living on top of each other. Doesn't sound like it beats anything if you spend most of your time trying to escape it." He smirks. "But what do I know? I'm just a country bumpkin."

He strides off and I have to walk twice as fast to keep up. That is, until he abruptly stops short, and I collide with his toned traps. "Where the hell are you going—oh *no*."

Stepping aside, he brings a fleet of Segways for rent into view. "Oh *yes*."

I'm convinced Vahe is trolling me now, committed to making me do the cringiest activities. But from the way he's egging me on like a boy on the playground, I find myself relenting without too much resistance. My friends can attest that I've dumped dudes for meaningless infractions, like the time I ditched that biotech guy at a Mexican restaurant after he ordered a quesa-dilla, pronouncing the *l*'s as a joke. How have I let someone I used to call Baker Bro jeopardize my too-cool reputation?

After we both cried our eyes out during the most emotionally exposed hookup of my life, the Baker Bro nickname is like a jacket that no longer fits him. He's got the physique of a douchey prick, but he's not obsessed with his own body. I get aggressively bored with gym talk and not once has he mentioned how much he can lift. I've never even seen him gulp down a protein shake, so if he's your typical bro, he's doing a great job of hiding it.

As for being a baker, that may be technically true, but I've learned Vahe is so much more. Which is how he successfully convinces me to get off my high horse and onto a Segway for the first time.

I anticipate face-planting within seconds, but the discomfort is only mental, and it doesn't take long for me to get used to powering this ridiculous looking scooter. As we veer further into the park, appreciating the lush landscape, the ride is more enjoyable than I expected. And when Vahe leans forward to accelerate and challenges me to a race, I'm actually, dare I say it, having *fun*.

We zoom around the park until we arrive at Stow Lake, and Vahe jolts upright to stop, in awe of the idyllic scene. Although the lake is man-made, it's still a sight to behold. A tranquil moat surrounds a small island, which hosts a gorgeous green and red Chinese pagoda.

Watching Vahe take in one of my favorite places has me imagining what it might be like to spend time here with him regularly—if he, by chance, lived in San Francisco. That same curiosity from yesterday gets the better of me before I can squash it. "Have you thought about maybe expanding Dikran's?" I ask, as we park our Segways.

He gives me an amused look. "Oooh . . . a contentious conversation about entrepreneurial ambition? Sign me up."

My eyes widen. "Who said anything about making it contentious?" I backtrack so he doesn't take my conversation starter the wrong way. "I just think it's a shame that more people don't know the healing power of your Armenian pastries."

"I know," he says with a smug grin. "And I have no problem answering, but you should know I'm gonna immediately throw it back and ask why the most talented pianist I know doesn't have a single album available for purchase."

I bristle at the assumption. "You tried to find my music?"

"We've been over this before, Tori, when I followed you on social. You forget I'm the youngest raised alongside two nosy sisters. When it comes to cyber snooping, I learned from the best. Now, come here. I found the perfect way to hash this out."

He points to the boathouse in front of us where a large sign advertises pedal boats by the hour. They bob at the dock, in shades of yellow and turquoise and hot pink. Even though they aren't shaped like giant rubber ducks, with their carnival vibes they might as well be.

I scoff. "Why do you insist on being so—"

"Charming? Adorable? Delightfully entertaining?" He steps up to the ticket counter and pays for a two-seater. "Despite your mission to rip apart every shred of joy on earth, Tori, I am immune to your efforts. Plus, I read somewhere that it's easier to be vulnerable with someone when you're sitting next to them instead of across. I got my dad to finally agree to draft a will on a long car ride to visit family in Glendale, so I figured you'll open up while paddling around in circles on this beautiful winter day."

"Not if I don't push you into the lake first." It's an empty threat, of course. When he selects a boat as green as a scoop of mint-chip ice cream and extends his hand, I take it to step inside. Not that I didn't consider sending Vahe into the depths below, but honestly at his size I'd be less successful than if I tried to beat the Hulk at arm-wrestling.

"See?" he enthuses as we get settled into our seats. "We're taking part in a mass-produced, pleasurable activity like millions of couples before us, and you didn't spontaneously combust into flames. We should have brought a bottle of Fresno State wine and a charcuterie board to have ourselves a little picnic out here."

I channel my disapproval into my paddling until we pass a family of ducks. All of a sudden, having some berries on hand doesn't sound like a terrible idea. "Back to my original question: why not build an Armenian bakery empire?"

We stare at the water, content to take the conversation at our own pace, and I have to admit Vahe's right. I spend so much of my time facing people directly in my manicurist's chair, listening to clients use the salon like a confessional, that I never considered how refreshing it would feel to talk to someone on equal footing with all the time in the world.

Vahe resumes paddling, steering us around the bend of an artificial waterfall. "The same reason you were shut out from attending a university and still living in a tiny apartment with two roommates who never learned how to knock."

I chuckle, thinking back to Som and Glen barging in during our second, less sentimental hookup last night because they thought I was in pain. I agreed to have sex on a bed, but I never said it wouldn't be rough. "Hey, we could've fucked in the spa, so that's the risk you took. But I hear what you're saying. All of us in Alex's glam fam make enough now to live on our own if we wanted, but when I was starting out, roommates were a must-have, not a nice-to-have. Money gives you options."

"Exactly. I'm damn successful by most standards—I co-manage a family business, and I own my home. I can not only invest in my future, but also in our employees by paying them a living wage and offering them full benefits with profit sharing. But restaurants have notoriously thin margins, and the capital I'd need to open a location in San Francisco is outrageously high. Care to guess how much?"

Oh god. Breaking though SF's red tape to get a restaurant off the ground must be as challenging as climbing Everest. "I'd say six figures, minimum, right?"

"The barest of minimums." Vahe laughs darkly. "Between rent and utilities, construction and permitting, design and decor, kitchen appliances and equipment, not to mention advertising and consulting fees, I'm looking at least a half-million in startup costs."

Oof. I know firsthand how hella expensive it is to live here, but being a brick-and-mortar entrepreneur is on another level. "Sounds like you've done the math." I nudge him with my elbow. "Did I hear you correctly that you crunched the numbers for SF specifically?"

Vahe smiles grimly, pausing his paddling as if lost in

thought. "You did. It'll sabotage my chances of winning our wager, but I went pretty far down that rabbit hole in my planning a few years back. Talked to banks, consulted my accountant, the whole nine yards. I've had this nagging feeling that however well Dikran's Deli does, that success isn't really mine because I inherited the business. So I thought if I opened a second location in San Francisco, that win would be mine and no one else's. But I could never get the numbers to add up."

My heart can't help but flutter at the idea of us sharing a zip code. Maybe if I knew more about what led him down that path, I can keep that door open a little longer. "But why San Francisco? Why not LA or another city with a larger Armenian population?"

"I think the fact that the diaspora isn't as strong here is a pro rather than a con. As you've noticed, there are tons of restaurants in the city that offer a fusion of Mediterranean and Middle Eastern flavors. But I can't recall one still open that was advertised as being distinctly Armenian. The last great establishment I've been to closed down years ago. It was located all the way down in Sunnyvale, and the owner was also from Fresno. Go figure. Anyway, I like the idea of catering to a community that deserves so much more love and attention. Plus, I can introduce Hye culture to the rest of you odars who don't know what you're missing."

Vahe playfully shoves my shoulder, and I laugh in agreement. "Yes, SF is overrun with clueless tech bros, but some of us still have great taste. And as someone who now gets chauffeured around to some highfalutin eateries, I know you could go toe-to-toe with any of them. It would be a grave injustice to keep your talent from reaching more people. They would absolutely love you. I know it."

We've completed the two-and-a-half-mile loop, and the boathouse is within sight. But Vahe isn't in a rush to cross the finish line because he's too busy staring deep into my eyes. "I only care about convincing one person to love me," he whispers.

At the dropping of the L-bomb, my back stiffens, and my feet slip off the pedals. Vahe doesn't wait for my objections. All the words I wear like armor—we live hundreds of miles apart, we've only known each other for two months, neither of us has had any success with serious relationships—die in my throat the moment Vahe's tongue slips past mine. I can feel his yearning, the desperation to evolve our kiss into something more—not physically, but emotionally. Like if he places his lips on my metaphorical walls in just the right way, they'll finally come crashing down. He pulls me into his seat, crushing my body against his, and I want to give him everything he's asking for without using words.

"Come celebrate Christmas with me," he exhales into my ear, kissing that spot behind it that drives me wild. I'm taken aback by how simple his request is. I had been bracing for him to coerce a love confession out of me, which would be nothing short of miraculous. But moving around my schedule to spend more time together? Now that I can do.

I grab my phone from my jacket to check my calendar. "The glam fam throws a party to decorate sugar cookies and dress up like baddie Santas à la *Mean Girls*, but they'll forgive me if I bail one time."

Vahe reaches out to stop me from saving the date. "Sorry, not the twenty-fifth. I should've clarified. I mean Armenian Christmas on January sixth. You wouldn't have to join any church services, but my family caters Christmas dinner at the Old Armenian Home, where Queenie lives. We share the typical holiday traditions odars are used to—a giant tree, gift exchanging, and someone dressed as Gaghant Baba, which is what we call Santa Claus—but our version has the added benefits of watching the community elders get drunk and sing Armenian carols. And, obviously, the holiday would not be complete without all your new favorite foods."

It's so cute how animated he gets sharing about his culture, but it's difficult to pay attention when my brain is hung up on a single word. "Your family? You want to introduce me to your *whole* family, on Christmas?"

I start paddling anxiously, as if to escape this conversation, and Vahe helps out to keep me from spinning in literal circles. The second the boat makes contact with the dock, I jump off, and Vahe has to scramble to catch up without tipping over into the lake. "Tori, wait!"

I'm tempted to grab a Segway and scoot off into the sunset, never to return. The charges I'd pay for stealing one would be astronomical, but at least I wouldn't have to face the Derderians' disappointment when they find out I'm Vahe's new girlfriend.

"Tori, do not make me chase you all over the park. It's not a good look when a big, hairy man stalks a distraught woman, and I'd rather not get arrested if I can help it. Will you please step away from the Segway?"

He makes a good point. I have plenty more of the city to show Vahe, and my plans will be for naught if the only tour he's allowed to take is through the county jail.

The second I let go of the handles, Vahe wraps himself around me—a gesture of comfort and support, I'm sure, but also to ensure I don't escape again. "Now, what has got you so scared? You've already met Queenie and my sisters, and they're exponentially harder to impress than my parents or extended relatives."

My eyes bulge, flashing back to my first encounter with the women of Dikran's Deli. "Mari and Anush mistook me for a vagrant breaking into the bakery, and I scuffled with your grandmother so badly my car became collateral damage."

Vahe shrugs. "Hey, at least they'll remember you. Consider that a good thing."

"I'm not so sure about that. I'm not someone who impresses the kind of tight-knit families who take their kids to the zoo and spend holidays at senior living communities." Vahe stares blankly as if he can't understand my logic, forcing me to state the painfully obvious. "Have you forgotten what I look like? The only untattooed skin I have left is on my face, and my earlobes are so large you can stick your fingers in them." I put my index finger through my tunnel to illustrate my point, wagging the claw ring in defiance. "Does this scream classy and wholesome to you?"

The hopeful part of me expects Vahe to laugh off my concerns, but when his arms fall and his lips recede into a fine line, I know I'm right to be paranoid. I'm not ashamed of my alternative appearance—every needle I endured is proof I turned my pain into pride—but I'm not naive. There's a reason I paint nails instead of collate paperwork. It doesn't matter that I'm a successful business owner in my own right, not when all people can see is a bad role model who performs satanic rituals and drinks the blood of puppies.

I've never had any trouble getting laid, because most men are hypocrites with Madonna-whore complexes. They'd take me home, but they all stopped short at introducing me to their moms. So I decided to throw my hands up in the air and say fuck it. Shaved half my head, spent every paycheck on new ink, and never looked back. I avoided every clean-cut dude with a nine-to-five. If I wasn't a good girl, then I sure as hell wouldn't waste my time pining after good guys.

Until I met Vahe. And now our already precarious relationship is going to come crashing down because the sweetest man who's ever crossed my path is now blinking at me like he didn't think his Christmas plan all the way through.

"Everybody's going to love you," he says, more to reassure

himself than me. "My family did not escape a genocide to discriminate against people for the size of their earlobes. After I spent so many years fucking around, they'll be so excited for me to settle down that they won't care what you look like."

Not the ringing endorsement I was hoping for. But Vahe mentioning his past momentarily distracts me, sparking my curiosity. "Not that I'm advocating against fucking around, but why haven't you settled down by now, if your family has been dying for you to?"

He runs a hand through my hair. "I'm honestly as surprised by my change of heart as you are. I mean, you get it —fucking around is fun. And I was working all the time, so I had no qualms about keeping things casual. Until I met you." He tips my chin up to meet his gaze. "All of a sudden, casual wasn't good enough. I realized that laying down roots could be about a person even more than a place."

I want to believe him, to trust that his opinion is the only one that matters. But that doesn't mean his family won't convince him we're not a good match. I know how the world treats you when you come from less than desirable circumstances. I can't tell you how many people have assumed I'm broken just because I'm from a broken home. It's taken me my entire life to undo that internalization myself. If it weren't for the glam fam, I'd still believe I'm a worthless shelter mutt barred from receiving the kind of love that's reserved for people with better pedigrees.

Vahe must see the skepticism all over my face because he doubles down on his conviction. "Please, Tori," he insists, taking my hands in his. "I want you with me. Holidays are infinitely better when you have someone to share them with. I know Christmas can come with a certain gravitas, but it's really an excuse for my family to drink brandy and sing our favorite songs. January sixth is on a Saturday, so consider this just another weekend date."

I try laughing, but the sound comes out hollow. Look where our competition has gotten us—betting with our wallets and risking our hearts instead. "And what about our other dates? Is our wager all for nothing?"

It seems ridiculous now, caring about this silly little contest, but Vahe doesn't take offense. In fact, he squeezes my hands like he's experienced an epiphany.

"I'm ready to admit defeat if you'll agree to this. Let's not kid ourselves anymore, and call it what it is. You won, Tori."

All our camaraderie rushes out of the conversation, like a balloon losing its air. Without our friendly rivalry, I feel deflated. In fact, I'm seething at how easily Vahe tosses aside the very thing that brought us together.

"Are you bribing me?" I clench my fists. "The weekend isn't over yet, and I made plans to beat you fair and square. And now you're telling me none of it matters. Are you seriously going to guilt-trip me with thousands of dollars in free catering, so I'll spend Christmas with you and your family?"

Vahe looks toward the crystal-blue sky, and it's the first time I wish the weather wasn't always so perfect in San Francisco. I'd rather fight through a torrent of wind and rain, if only so the outside can match how turbulent I feel on the inside.

"You were always going to be the winner, Tori. And not because I intended to throw the game. As soon as we agreed to the criteria, I knew I was a goner."

My brow scrunches at such a nonsensical statement. "What are you talking about? Honestly, the way things were going, I figured you would take the tahini cake—literally. When it comes to the three C's of the Michelin guide, you already had cuisine in the bag. And while San Francisco is a juggernaut of culture, I can't say it's mine. I don't have one hundred years of tradition with this city like you do with yours. Even if SF were to win the cool factor, that means

Fresno wins two out of three. Why the hell would you willingly walk away from a victory?"

He shakes his head, slowly and deliberately. "You don't get it. It was never about our cities, not really. San Francisco could have been as dull as waiting for bread to rise, and I would still have conceded to you, because *you* are the cool factor. You are, by far, the coolest person I've ever met, Tori Townsend. I can't go back to my old life, pretending any date I go on could hold a candle to the time I've spent with you. I would give you and everyone you know free food for life if I can be on your arm and in your heart. If you say I'm yours."

How the tables have turned. I thought we'd spend today gallivanting around Golden Gate Park, gorging ourselves at the best eateries, and perhaps, if we got drunk enough, we'd take the party to Japantown and belt our lungs out at karaoke. I expected to celebrate my win with a smug victory lap around the city, not a confusing conversation that's left me wondering how I went from planning a dear friend's wedding to getting on the fast track to coupledom myself.

I should be jubilant. Not only did I become the best bridesmaid of all time by getting Tania and Nolan's catering comped, but also a man fell for me so hard he invented a ridiculous ruse to be by my side. The first man to rebuff my sexual advances so I'd take him seriously. I may have won this contest by default, but did I conquer the fuckboy, or did he conquer me?

"Just one more weekend, Tori. That's all I'm asking. One more pedal boat around the moat, and we'll cross the drawbridge when we get to it."

I smile weakly. What a silly analogy to make. Is the drawbridge supposed to be our uncertain future or my ironclad heart? Am I the princess in the castle to save or the final boss to destroy? We may have ended one game, but another more treacherous one is about to begin.

With only two months until the wedding, it would be hella lame to back out now. Life's thrown a lot worse my way, and I manage to keep going. I may regret everything in the end, but I won't know until I give it my best shot.

So let's play.

~

GLAM FAM GROUP chat on Monday, December 18, at 3:05 p.m.

TORI

Hey, I know everybody is hella busy in the run-up to the holidays, but can we schedule an emergency makeunder?

CASEY

Was that a typo? You mean a makeover, right?

GLEN

If you're ready to shave the other half of your head, I think you'd look killer bald.

ALEX

Oooh—or I've got a new pink wig that would be perfect for you!

TORI

No, no cueball or wild colors. I said a makeunder. Vahe's invited me to join his family for Armenian Christmas, and I need to tone my look down several notches.

SOM

. . . why, exactly?

TORI

I've never met a guy's family before, and I just want to make a good impression. Som, can you bring your heavy-duty makeup to cover my tattoos?

SOM

I can, but I can't hide the fact that your ears have giant holes in them.

TORI

I can dig through Alex's wig collection to disguise the gauges. Tasteful, natural colors only. Same with the outfits—I need to look like I'm in a family-friendly holiday rom-com.

CASEY

As a preppy Southerner, I know what you're going for, but I have to say the thought of putting you in clothes like that makes me sad.

TORI

Me too, but we gotta suck it up, buttercups. My game with Vahe is still on, and I came to win.

eighteen

I'm not one to ask for help, but when the glam fam realized how serious I was about this makeunder, they rose to the occasion. Thankfully, Tania and Nolan are hunkering down at home during the holidays, so we're off the wedding planning clock. Alex is preoccupied, per usual, with maintaining her social media empire, but the rest of us were able to grab some of the dead time between everyone's Christmas obligations and whatever New Year's Eve party that our princess is being paid to attend.

That doesn't mean they're happy about helping.

As the sun sets on San Francisco, Casey sighs for the millionth time, flicking through the racks of clothes that she schlepped to the apartment. "So, you're telling us that this man is head over heels in love with you, exactly as you are, and you still want a squeaky-clean wardrobe?"

"It's one party," I hedge, trying not to grimace at the available options. I enlisted the right stylist, since Casey was raised by a Southern sorority sister, but I didn't anticipate the cardigans. So many cardigans. "It's not like this is a permanent about-face."

"Until his family insists on spending more time with you

—holidays and vacays, brunches and baptisms. What happens then?" She hands me a long-sleeved dress with a houndstooth pattern, and I want to hurl. This is something worn by an Upper East Sider named Poppy. Not *me*.

Not with that attitude, at least. "They're just clothes," I say with resignation. "I'm sure I'll get used to them."

She stares back as if in physical pain, and I turn around to try on the dress, so I don't have to wither under her wounded expression. Clothes are Casey Holbright's calling. Her life's purpose. And I'm stomping all over it in patent kitten heels I don't even like.

Glen pipes up from the loveseat, a glass of red wine in his hand. "Sounds like a lot of effort for a man who never asked you to make it." Awfully rich coming from him. Other than recommending me wigs from Alex's collection and teaching me how to wear them, this makeunder has required zero effort on his part.

Sitting next to him, Som clinks her glass against his. "Yeah, whatever happened to the Tori who would say men ain't shit?"

She's right. That was my motto, until I walked into Dikran's Deli and was thrown off my axis. "Vahe's different. He wouldn't change a single hair on my shaven head." I gesture at the glam fam. "But you know what it's like when we're around people who aren't in the beauty business. How they look down on us."

Glen nods. "Like every prick who's asked where I went to university and told me cosmetology school doesn't count as 'real' college."

"The tech bros are the worst," Som chimes in. "Asking if I'm doing makeup as a side hustle while I'm completing a coding bootcamp or something."

"Yes!" I say, swapping the dress for a sweater and maxi skirt that are more appropriate for a kindergarten teacher than a gothic nail tech. "Normies never understand how we make a living outside of a cubicle. Or, worse, they believe you're selling an overpriced luxury and don't deserve to get paid for your work. Like everyone who thinks an at-home manicure will ever compare to going to a licensed professional."

"Omigod, betch, preach." Glen snaps his fingers. "People out there would never DIY a tattoo, but they think it's totally chill to bleach their own hair."

Looking over to Casey, I wait for her to add her own pet peeves. She raises her hands in defense. "Hey, I completely agree. I've had more than my fair share of mouth-breathers who think dressing up rich people is a useless job, but they shut their trap when I tell them the rich person I'm working with is Alex."

I get where Casey's coming from, but name-dropping has always been a double-edged sword. Sure, whenever I reveal I'm the personal aesthetician of the most followed social media celebrity on the planet, people take me more seriously. But then I have to deal with their reinvigorated excitement that I'm someone worth talking to.

People always fall into one of two camps: either they're diehard fans of Alex and desperate for details from someone who knows her or they're a hater with an axe to grind, intrigued to discover whether my best friend is a secret bitch when the paparazzi aren't looking. Regardless, I become tabloid fodder for a never-ending line of social climbers and clout chasers. I'd rather be written off as worthless than suffer through Christmas dinner playing six degrees of Princess Alex.

Once Casey and I have narrowed down all the outfits to the best selections—or at least the ones I can stomach—it's Som's turn at bat. We migrate to the kitchen, so she can set up a makeup station at the dining table while Glen and Casey shift their responsibilities to cooking a light dinner. Usually, Alex is footing the takeout bill, but when she's not around, we've gotten good at whipping up dishes that are easy to eat when you've got a full face on: chopped salads, fruit medleys, and bite-size pastas like cavatelli that won't screw up your lipstick.

While our stylist and hairdresser take care of food, Som shows me how to tone down my face. I don't usually need assistance in the makeup department, but nothing about my appearance could be described as subtle. Kids these days are obsessed with the clean beauty aesthetic, whereas I perfected the 2016 cut crease and never looked back.

"So, you think I'm ridiculous for going through with all this?" I ask, gesturing to the pile of piercings as I pull them out from my nose, eyebrows, lips, and ears. I keep missing some like I'm in an action flick, handing over all my concealed weapons.

She chuckles. "Ridiculous would have been if you split your tongue—I'm so glad we were able to talk you out of that." No kidding. I've made plenty of body modifications over the years, but at least I steered away from the inside of my mouth.

Som starts priming and color correcting, so she can hide my neck tattoos underneath a heavy layer of stage makeup. "You forget who you're talking to sometimes, Tori. If anyone could understand a desire to look a certain way to gain societal approval, it would be me."

Fuck, she's right. I'm freaking out over some ink, and Som's here, navigating life as a trans woman, someone who immigrated from Thailand to a country arguably more hostile to gender fluidity. As in awe as I am of Som's makeup artistry, I have to remind myself that her ability to transform is a survival skill.

"I'm being strategic," I explain as Som paints on heavy-duty foundation. "We're the glam fam. We know how important first impressions are."

She gives me a mischievous smile. "Do you know what my first impression of you was?"

Jeez. I flash back to what must have been a decade ago. Alex and Casey grew up together as childhood friends, and they picked up Som and Glen along the way, jet-setting around the world in their raucous early years of adulthood. When we crossed paths in the ladies' room of a New York jazz club I was playing at, I was five years older and about fifty years more jaded, barely scraping by.

"I remember meeting Alex first. She was crying over some loser who was treating her like dirt, and you and Casey were trying to cheer her up. I must have come in hot with my man-hating that night."

"White-hot. Guns blazing." She takes a pause from applying concealer, so she doesn't stab my eye while in a fit of laughter. "But that's not what stood out to me. I can't recall what you were wearing, but what was clear as day was our immediate connection. Underneath your 'men ain't shit' fury was someone who told us we were the sweetest, most gorgeous women she'd ever seen."

I brush off her compliment about my compliment. "I was drunk as fuck. It was one of those cliché Roaring '20s themed parties, which annoy me to no end. But when I saw you crowded around the sink, you all had matching flapper dresses that sparkled on the bathroom tile. My bad mood vanished in an instant. You literally lit up the place. It was the truth, and anyone else would have said the same."

Som points her makeup brush at me. "I never expected a compliment like that from someone with that much stainless steel in her face. You might have thought the party was lame, but you never thought less of us for being there. Despite your alternative appearance, Tori, you are very much like other girls."

I reflect on Som's words, grateful the glam fam wasn't

scared of me or turned off by my prickly exterior. At my worst, I make snap judgments, writing off strangers without a second thought. It's happened so often to me that it's a reflex, pushing people away before they have a chance to do the same to me. But I could never be a pick-me around the glam fam. We picked each other, and I would defend them to the death.

"So you're saying I should get Vahe's family drunk and show them the healing magic of the women's restroom?"

She bops me on the nose with her brush. "I'm saying you're hardworking, talented, and fiercely loyal. Vahe knows that about you, and once his family does too, it won't matter what you look like. Give them time, and let them learn how to love you."

My cheeks burn, and I want to tell Som to go easy on the blush, since I must be plenty red already. "You know, love is a strong word. I was thinking of playing it by ear and seeing how it goes—"

Another bop on the nose, and highlighter goes flying into the air like fairy dust. "Tori Townsend, I swear to god. You better give yourself even more time, so you can learn how to love that poor man back."

Som finishes up my face, before setting the table for Glen, so he can teach me the finer points of wig installation. I run my hands through the natural, chestnut-colored hair, placing it in front of my ears to hide my gauges. I get a jump-scare when he turns Som's vanity mirror so I can sneak a peek, wondering who let the trad wife in.

To their credit, the glam fam takes my makeunder in stride, complimenting me on how well I dress the part, even if this one seems better suited for a little house on a prairie. I like this look as much as I like admitting my own feelings, but I can sit in the discomfort of both.

Because the first step to loving Vahe is giving myself the permission to do so.

***Tori Townsend's** search history on December 29 at 10:54 p.m.*

WHAT HAPPENED on January sixth
    Not that January sixth, the first Armenian Christmas
    How Armenians celebrate Christmas
    Names for Santa Claus around the world
    Why are the Dutch so weird about blackface
    Why do we shorten Christmas to Xmas
    Xtina music videos
    Armenian alphabet
    How to learn a new language in one week
    Duolingo on fast mode
    What to wear to Armenian Christmas party
    Festive gloves to hide finger tattoos
    Has anyone ever been smited before
    Past tense of smite
    Sneaking in a Christmas quickie without getting caught
    Is there a hell and what to do if you're going to it

chapter
nineteen

"You don't have to go through all this effort, Tori. If you make a complete one-eighty from when they first met you, they'll think I brought over a different girlfriend."

I huff, turning away from the mirror in Vahe's room. "If I don't make at least some effort, they'll wish you did." I fidget with the waistband of the burgundy silk skirt, debating whether I should do a French tuck with my cream cashmere turtleneck sweater. The pieces go together perfectly—everything Casey picked out for me is elegance incarnate, even if I'm not. The longer I stare, the less confident I feel.

Vahe comes up behind me, kissing my neck and wrapping his arms around the very waistband I'm grumpily glaring at. "You've already covered most of your tattoos and removed every facial piercing. At least throw on some jeans so you're comfortable. Tonight is supposed to be fun!"

I bite back a hollow laugh. Fun is the exact opposite of how I'd describe the level of intense preparation I've undergone. But no matter how many times I repeat Casey's sage words of wisdom—shoulders back, head high, only imposters don't get imposter syndrome—it won't erase the fact that my earlobes are the size of quarters or that I have STAY SHARP inked across my knuckles. The tattoo is a nice reminder to keep both my nails and wits about me, but it won't prevent the judgment I'm sure to receive from Vahe's extended family.

I take his advice and swap the skirt for jeans—not the faded, distressed pair I typically wear, but they're black so I already feel a sense of relief. I leave my combat boots in the closet, selecting tasteful ankle booties instead. If you saw me passing by on the street, you'd assume I'm on speaking terms with my parents and have a tried-and-true bundt cake recipe to impress at dinner parties.

But I'm not about to make the amateur mistake of gifting baked goods to a family of bakers. Instead, I reach for the only thing I can offer as holiday spirit: my portable keyboard.

"Are you sure I won't come off pretentious if I bring this?" I ask as we lock up the house.

Vahe packs the case into the bed of his truck, wrapping it in a moving blanket and securing it with bungee cords. "Absolutely. Live entertainment is a rarity at senior homes, especially at the low, low cost of zero dollars. They're going to be delighted you went to such lengths to learn their favorite Armenian Christmas carols."

I sure hope so. The music was easy to memorize, but the lyrics were on a whole other level. Why didn't anyone tell me the Armenian alphabet has thirty-eight letters? As long as the residents don't expect me to join in the singing, I should be safe from embarrassing myself.

After a short drive, we arrive at the Grapevines community. I assumed a place colloquially known as the 'Old Armenian Home' would have Armenian architecture, but the mid-sized buildings look more like historical Californian missions with their stark-white walls, rounded arches, and terracotta roofs.

While most the buildings are dedicated to independent

and assisted senior living, Vahe steers us toward a social hall on the lefthand side where the residents congregate for events.

"It looks a million times better after the recent renovation," he explains as we approach the entrance. "When I heard that they're planning on offering it as a wedding venue, I thought they were nuts, but it's not half bad if you're looking to get hitched on a budget."

I'd be worried that Vahe has thought about how to make a wedding wallet-friendly if I weren't distracted by the spectacle in front of us. Because when we walk into the hall, I realize he's undersold it. Not half bad is how I'd describe the latest *Fast and Furious* movie, not a lavish ballroom decked out in holiday cheer. I'm a heathen whose only reason for the season is hot cocoa and stocking stuffers, but even I can't deny the impressiveness of the ornate orthodox crosses adorning the warm beige walls and the massive Christmas trees in each corner of the hall. With so many lights and tinsel and ornaments, you can barely see any branches underneath.

The staff from Dikran's Deli is busy setting up the buffet line, and the aromas from the trays of shish kebab and pilaf have got everybody's mouths watering. Residents wearing Santa and elf hats occupy themselves by mingling and helping themselves to drinks, but every so often their eyes dart to see whether dinner is ready to be served yet.

I consider sneaking a sarma the moment the staff's not looking, until I remember that team includes his siblings, both of whom are making a beeline toward us.

"Tori, good to see you again!" Anush waves and goes in for a hug. Her warm intro, however, gets cut short when a pre-K-aged boy in a reindeer sweater pulls a glass orb off the nearest tree. "Armen, no! What did we say about not throwing the ornaments?"

She dashes off, berating her husband for being glued to his

phone. Mari approaches with her husband and their gaggle of three kids, all of whom tackle Vahe on sight.

"Speak of the devil," Mari says, presumably to me, with a smirk. "I was just telling our parents how busy we were while Vahe was on his little weekend getaway."

Vahe gives Mari a 'watch it' glare but doesn't push it, instead steering me toward the large table where his parents are sitting with a handful of friends and extended family. They're cordial, but nobody jumps out of their seat or acknowledges me with more than brief smiles. When Vahe introduces me with a quick "This is Tori," I wonder if he already gave everyone a heads up in the family group chat. Did he refer to me as his girlfriend? Or is Mari so annoyed about picking up her brother's slack that she's poisoned them against me? I expected dirty looks, but this apathy feels even worse.

While Vahe goes around the table to extend his well-wishes, I try to reassure myself that everything's fine. So much is going on as people arrive, and maybe it's been a long time since the whole family got together. It's only been a few minutes, and there is plenty of time to get to know everyone. It's too early to throw myself a pity party.

As if on cue, Queenie bursts into the ballroom to get the actual party started. "Alright, the queen is here!"

She's carrying a cane, but from the way she raps it on the tile floor, it's clear she doesn't need it to walk. I got to hand it to a woman so secure in herself that she uses a dedicated accessory to demand attention. And it works. The crowd disperses like she's Moses parting the Red Sea, and a staff member hands her a flute of champagne—no tray, and no drinks for anyone else—waiting for her to drain it before taking the empty glass and resuming his buffet duties.

Fucking hell, this woman's got swag.

"My little eshes!" Queenie claps her hands, shuffling in our direction. At barely five feet tall, she squeezes Vahe around the waist and makes him bend down so she can pinch his cheeks. "About time you brought Miss Tori around. You know, my nails have been absolutely dreadful, and now no one in this town can come close to her shaping skills."

She shoves her cane into his hands and turns to grasp mine, commiserating over her most recent manicure. She's being melodramatic, of course. A woman of her status would never show up to an event with subpar nails. But I agree the rounded look isn't the best for her regal fingers.

"I'll come around tomorrow and square off those edges. Promise."

She pats my hands with a warm smile until she looks up, concerned. "Where are your rings, dear?"

Self-conscious, I pull back, knowing full well my favorite sets are back at Vahe's house. They're as much a part of my identity as a cat's claws, but under no circumstances did I think full-knuckled talons were an appropriate accessory for a Christmas party at a senior home. "I don't have any worthy of this festive occasion."

Queenie frowns, taking in my outfit as if she knows I've never worn anything cream-colored in my life. "Hmm, well, next time you should come prepared. You wouldn't be able to tell from looking at them, but some of these old rascals can get real feisty after a game of dominos and one too many drinks. I'd stay sharp if I were you."

She touches her nose in reference to my hand tattoo before waltzing off to the buffet. Like magic, as soon as she picks up a plate, the room simultaneously rises out of their seats and forms a line behind her.

"How did she become such an institution?" I ask Vahe in awe, watching her greet each server by name as they pile food high on her plate.

Vahe beams with pride. "That's exactly what she is. Every time someone praises Dikran's Deli for its long history, I say it's because of her. Dikran may have built the four walls, but Queenie is the reason why we're still standing a hundred years later."

He gestures toward my clothes. "And as you can tell from the way she stared straight through your borrowed outfit, Queenie has a knack for seeing into your soul. She can strong-arm you into becoming the person you were meant to be."

Vahe can say that again. Starting with nearly falling off that ladder and cracking my head on the pavement, nothing about my interactions with Queenie have been delicate. I'm not surprised to hear she spent her entire existence securing her family's legacy through brute force and zero tolerance for bullshit.

I'd take her critique of my cream sweater over fake niceties with the rest of the Derderians. At least I know Queenie's judgement comes from a good place. She only wants me to achieve my true potential. It's not unlike my relationship with the glam fam. As someone who calls her best friends betches, I'd rather spend my evening with an imposing biddie who calls her grandson a jackass.

Unfortunately, I can't stick by Queenie's side all night. As soon as she's filled her plate, she flits from table to table, eating upright while she catches up with every single resident. The misanthropic introvert in me is horrified, but I admire her ability to gain more sustenance from good conversation than cheese boregs.

I decide to take the opposite approach to surviving this Christmas party. Instead of cheerfully yapping away with everyone in the room like Queenie, I pack as much food as I can fit on my plate. Now I can keep my mouth stuffed, using each course as armor against awkward conversation. Sorry, did you ask what I do for a living? I can't hear you while I'm chomping this marinated meat on a skewer.

My plan unravels, however, when Mari pushes into our

already cramped table, right next to me, and goes on a warpath.

"So, little bro, how was 'Frisco? Hopefully, you didn't step in too much human excrement on your mini holiday."

I'm not sure what I'm more disgusted by: Mari's literal shit talk or her notoriously gross nickname for the place I call home. It's either called SF or the city, and nothing else.

"We had an amazing time," Vahe says, squeezing my hand under the table. "Everything Tori planned was wonderful, but I got to hand it to Golden Gate Park. Did you know it has bison? I never thought in a million years I'd see a whole herd in the big city—"

"Sounds like fun," Mari interrupts, poking irritatingly at her food with her fork. "It doesn't matter if Dikran's is disposable to you as long as you're having a good time."

Our table goes quiet, but a quick swivel confirms everyone else is oblivious to the tension. Queenie's across the ballroom, cheers-ing a group of ladies with yet another glass of champagne. Anush and both sisters' husbands are preoccupied at the kids' table, making sure grains of bulgur and pilaf don't end up all over the floor.

"I don't know why this is an issue," Vahe says, his tone as sharp as the knife he uses to slice his shish kebab. "I gave you plenty of heads-up that I was taking the weekend off."

The cutlery can't compete with the daggers Mari's throwing in my direction. She's obviously upset about more than a few extra hours of overtime. I'm not going to say I won't start a fight—because let's face it, I've gotten into my fair share of trouble—but I'm too protective of Vahe to let his sister stomp all over him.

"Mari, what is your deal?" I butt in. "I doubt I've said more than ten sentences to you, but you've had a problem with my existence from the moment we met."

She tosses her fork with an angry clang. "You mean when I

thought you broke into our business? Or when you almost cracked my grandmother's skull on the sidewalk? Or when I found the invoice for the Beecher and Wells wedding adjusted from five thousand dollars to zero? So before you start on my so-called deal, Victoria, why don't you enlighten us on the deal you made with my brother."

My stomach drops. I've only had a few bites, but I couldn't fit in more food if I tried. "What are you talking about?"

Mari looks triumphant, like she's been searching for a justification to hate my guts and is thrilled to land on something with this much meat on the bone. Like the mascot of Fresno State, she's a vengeful bulldog prepared to strip the flesh from my limbs.

"I always found it odd that a bride wouldn't coordinate her own catering. Why wouldn't she be more hands-on? The meal is the one thing guests are going to remember long after the flowers have died. But if her plan was to scam a small business by getting my sucker of a brother to agree to charity work, it makes sense the honeypot she'd send would be you."

"What the hell is that supposed to mean?" I spit out. I mean, I know Tania and Nolan have been stressed about their ballooning guest list, but fucking honeypotting? How paranoid do you have to be to think I'm only dating Vahe for free food?

"I've seen your social media," Mari continues, sneering like she's unearthed a military-grade secret and not a public profile. "Gallivanting around to all those trendy restaurants and five-star hotels. Of course when your best friends are celebrities you expect to get everything comped, but we can't afford to live on exposure. Five thousand dollars may be a drop in the bucket to you, but it's our livelihood. How long were you planning on stringing my brother along before you cut him loose—for a few more months or right after the reception to save yourself a trip?"

Mari could have slapped me across the face, and it wouldn't have hurt as badly as thinking I'm nothing more than a spoiled moocher.

Alex receives this kind of vitriol all day every day, but she's a billionaire who can withstand criticism. I wasn't born to astronomically wealthy parents, and I refuse to be painted with the same brush. Alex could have replaced her ragtag glam fam with the most renowned beauty experts, but she chose us —me, Casey, Som, and Glen—despite our lack of pedigree. She believed in us when no one else did. Not once have I taken that for granted. For every private jet ride I've hitched, there are a thousand other handouts I've turned down out of pride.

I sleep in a shoebox apartment with Glen and Som, and I've never name-dropped Alex to skip a line or receive a discount. But if Mari is going to treat me like an entitled diva, then I'm going to act like one.

To his credit, Vahe starts to defend me, but I'm already locked and loaded. "Do you hear yourself?" I push my chair back. "If I live such a lavish lifestyle, then why am I here? San Francisco has over thirty Michelin-star restaurants. If I'm so well-connected, why would I bother scamming for free food from a hole in the wall in the middle of nowhere?"

Someone one table over gasps, and that's when I realize my indoor voice is anything but. And it's not just my volume that has amplified to an unacceptable level. I couldn't care less about Mari seeing red, but Vahe looks so wounded I might as well have pistol-whipped him.

I reach for Vahe's arm, half-formed apologies bubbling up my throat, but he pulls away and tosses his napkin onto his plate. "I may have been born the youngest," he says, jabbing a finger at his sister, "but the only baby I see here is you, Mari. If you had pulled me aside to discuss the contract like adults, I would have told you it was just a joke. Right, Tori?"

He turns in my direction but doesn't wait for me to chime in. "Tori and I made this stupid bet with each other about whether San Francisco or Fresno was the superior city. If she won, I would comp the catering for Tania's wedding. But it was a flimsy excuse to get into each other's pants and now that's taken care of, we don't have to keep up with the charade anymore. I'm sorry if I made it sound more serious than that."

Vahe storms off, leaving me stunned and surrounded by hundreds of side-eyes. I catch Queenie's glance from across the room. Her lips have receded into a grim line, but the slightest trace of sympathy gives me hope. She jerks her head toward the door as if to kick my ass into gear, and it's the wakeup call I need. The competition may have started as a joke, but our chance at a relationship wasn't. That was real, even if my callous remarks have made Vahe wish that wasn't the case.

I grab my travel keyboard case and sprint for the entrance. I feel bad that I'm ditching this party so dramatically and leaving the Grapevines residents without live music for their Armenian Christmas carols. I feel worse that I may have sabotaged Tania and Nolan's special day and left them without a caterer six weeks before their wedding. But as awful as their contract being null and void may be, I realize my entire world will crumble if my life with Vahe is too.

～

UPDATED *voicemail message for Dikran's Deli on Saturday, January 6, at 8:45 p.m.*

Hi THERE, you've reached Dikran's Deli. This is the owner and chief whip-cracker Queenie. If you're calling on

Armenian Christmas and wondering why we're not open, then I'm afraid common sense isn't as common as it should be.

I'm updating this voicemail to let you know that due to an unforeseen family matter, we will also be closed tomorrow on Sunday, January 7th. It's not something I'm thrilled about, especially when our weekend brunches are out of this world, but sometimes we have to do things we don't want to. My father escaped a genocide, and I grew up in a time when it wasn't socially acceptable for women to wear pants. I'm not saying those two things are weighted equally, but this world isn't fair in so many ways.

We'll re-open on Monday, January 8th, during normal business hours, which is whenever I decide them to be. In the meantime, I will be busy preventing my grandchildren from murdering each other. You think I'm being dramatic, but you don't know my eldest Mari. After tonight's little fiasco, I'm starting to think she's capable of making the Ottoman Turks look like Care Bears.

Pray for me, and leave your message after the beep. [*beep*]

chapter
twenty

I explode out the entrance of the Grapevines community ballroom into the parking lot. Expecting to see Vahe peeling onto the street, I'm prepared to dump my keyboard, never to be seen again, if it means I can catch up to his pickup truck. But when I hear his voice behind me, it hits me that he never left.

"Tori, what are you doing?"

Vahe pokes his head out of the truck, which is parked in the front row. "I thought you drove off without me."

"And left you in an unfamiliar city, at night, on Christmas? I'm pissed, but I'm not heartless. Now get in."

I open the door and tentatively slide into the passenger seat, leaving the middle seat open between us. Given his permafrown, it's best if I give him a buffer of personal space.

A long beat passes until I recognize he's waiting for me to explain myself, at which point I fall over my words. "I'm sorry. I shouldn't have said those things about the deli, especially not when your food is the best I've eaten in my life. Truly. I mean that." Vahe doesn't accept the compliment, so I continue. "I just couldn't believe your sister was accusing me of scamming you for free catering, and I lost it."

He gives me an annoyed look, like, *No shit, Sherlock*. But this time I wait him out, desperate to hear how he's feeling.

Vahe sighs. "Look, I get it. You're always beating yourself up for being raised in a rough environment, as if you had any control over who brought you into this world. But just because I run a business with my family doesn't mean I don't want to wring their necks sometimes." He twists the steering wheel with both hands to make his point. "For better or worse, Mari's got eldest sister syndrome. At her best, her attention to detail is impeccable, and she steers this ship with the leadership of a naval admiral. But as you witnessed, that also means she's fiercely protective. I'm sorry you bore the brunt of it. I should have given her a heads up about the contract before she had a chance to go ballistic on you."

There's so much he could be saying but isn't. He's not promising to smooth things over with his sister. He's not reassuring me that he won't send Tania an itemized bill for catering that was supposed to be comped. The last thing she needs six weeks before her wedding is me dropping the bomb that she's on the hook for thousands of dollars. If I can't come up with the funds fast enough with a marathon of manicures, I'd sooner sell my dirty underwear and feet pics than make my fuck-up Tania's problem.

Still, even though I'm a contender for World's Worst Bridesmaid, I don't have it in me to push Vahe to honor our bet—not when there's so much more at stake.

No, what I'm more hung up on is that Vahe hasn't said anything about repairing our relationship. Because what's obvious between the lines is that we won't have one.

"We're not sitting here because I talked back to your sister," I say, ripping off the emotional bandage.

Vahe shakes his head in agreement. "If that's all it was, I'd be making you two hug it out so we could spend the rest of the party barreling into tomorrow's hangover—"

"Then what is it?" I interrupt, my voice reaching a frantic pitch. "Because I said I'm sorry about insulting the deli. I didn't mean it—"

"But you *did*," Vahe asserts. "This is way bigger than the deli, Tori. I can excuse you calling Dikran's a hole in the wall. I'll be the first to admit that we're not in the best neighborhood. And I'm damn proud of how many folks flock to us despite being in the center of an industrial wasteland. No, this is about Fresno."

My eyes bulge in bewilderment. "What about it?"

"Exactly. You've already forgotten, but I can't. You said Dikran's was in the middle of nowhere, and that frankly isn't true."

Refusing to be caught in a trap of semantics, I backtrack. "No, no, no. That's not what I meant. I was referring to the block it's on in that dreary downtown, I swear."

"And what about now? Are we in the middle of nowhere?" He gestures across the street where a warehouse supermarket and a sad strip mall sits off in the distance. Row after row of SUVs in various shades of gray and silver, as far as the eye can see.

I understand the point Vahe's making. After so many years of following Alex around the globe, I have yet to experience a culture shock like the one I have every time I enter suburbia. The obsession with space only to fill every spare square inch with concrete. The ironclad resistance to build denser housing and better public transportation and flourishing downtowns that people of all ages actually enjoy. Not that San Francisco doesn't have its fair share of NIMBYs, but urban priorities are different when there's no room for McMansions with four-car garages.

"It all clicked when you used that phrase," Vahe says with an eerie sense of calm. "You're helping to plan a wedding for a couple who lives on the edge of a national park, and yet it's

Fresno that doesn't count as real civilization to you. Despite being home to over half a million people. It's the fifth-largest city in this state, and you act like I live in the sticks. You know what city is number four on that list, by the way?" He doesn't pause for me to state the obvious. "Sure, Tania may have colored your opinion of what to expect from Fresno, but my family's business has been at its heart for a hundred years. This whole time you've treated this contest like it's the big city versus the small town, and that couldn't be further from the truth."

I can't resist letting out a little scoff. "Okay, let's not get carried away. I apologize if I insinuated that Fresno is a ghost town, but come on—we both have eyes. Population by itself doesn't say much when those people live radically different lives. San Francisco has like three hundred thousand more residents, and they're sharing less than fifty square miles of space. Fresno, on the other hand, is nearly three times larger in pure land mass. The one city that's denser than SF is NYC, and guess what? I've lived in both places. So sue me if every other town pales in comparison."

Vahe grips the steering wheel in frustration. "Strong words for someone who's only been here a few times."

Alright, now his stubborn hometown pride is getting on my last nerve. "What do you want me to say, Vahe? A few trips is frankly more than I expected to make, but that's what I get for running bridesmaid errands." I brace myself for the fallout from what I'm about to say next, but we might as well get it over with now that our relationship is on life support. "And as long as we're being honest with each other, it wouldn't take many more trips before I'm bored out of my mind. I'm grateful you showed me some of Fresno's underrated spots, but the true hidden gem was you."

My lip wobbles, and I soldier through as fast as I can before the tears pooling behind my eyes flood the pickup. "I lashed out back there because I'm fucking angry at myself for doing the one thing I promised I wouldn't do. I fell in love with a man in a city I don't. I don't love Fresno, and I have no intention of living here."

Silence fills the cab. As we stare out the windshield, I'm reminded of our pedal boat excursion in Golden Gate Park. Vahe was right about having difficult conversations sitting side by side. If I had to look directly into his eyes, I'd jump out of this truck and run straight into oncoming traffic.

He sighs, hunching over the steering wheel until his forehead kisses the top, and it takes everything in me not to place my lips there instead. I hate that the first time I use the L-word with a man, it's during a fight. But as much as I want to let our bodies do the talking, these words need to be said.

"When we first made our wager," he says, lifting up his head, "it felt ridiculous because who concedes to a stranger that their city is better than where you've lived your whole life? But you were confident and smart as hell. The most stunning woman I'd ever met. The second you took off your claws and I saw your finger tattoos, it made complete sense because sharp was exactly how I'd describe someone with that much attitude. I couldn't let you walk out of the deli and never see you again."

I want to tell him I don't deserve compliments and force him to take them all back. It would be so much easier if he screamed and spat that I was a worthless bitch. He'd just be at the back of a long line of men who treated me terribly, starting with my sperm donor.

His gaze drifts off, as if recalling memories from another lifetime and not three months ago. "I'm not sure the exact moment I fell in love with you, but that's when our game wasn't so fun anymore. I knew Fresno would never be able to win you over, but I held out hope that maybe *I* could, if I showed that you had a welcome place in my family. That you had another home where you could belong." His eyes return to mine, pained. "I'm sorry Mari soured tonight because I was foolish enough to think she wouldn't discover Tania and Nolan's catering contract at some point. But it sounds like it wouldn't have mattered if everyone was on their best behavior. I was open to the idea of relocating to San Francisco, but you never considered compromising for one millisecond. Am I supposed to pine for someone so opposed to making room in her life for me?"

I can't help it—even through the pangs of guilt that I'm not considering a potential move for Vahe, my heart still lifts at his admission that he would move for me. But I can't get attached to that idea because that's all it is. A possibility, a passing fancy. Eventually, Vahe would come to his senses and leave me behind, like everyone else in my life.

"That was your first mistake," I tell him. "Thinking any family can remain picture-perfect long enough to convince me that people aren't bound to disappoint you. Everybody I know always goes away in the end, remember?" I point to where my Hurt tattoo sits underneath this sweater that's starting to itch real bad. "It's not Mari's fault. Even if she didn't verbally tear me to shreds, I wouldn't have changed my mind. If anything, I should be thanking her for jolting me out of this Hallmark fantasy. Contrary to what small-town romances try to sell us, love isn't enough to upend your entire life—"

Vahe slams the steering wheel. "But I would!"

"Oh, sure," I sneer. "Let's play this out to its inevitable conclusion. You'd abandon one hundred years of tradition and the only city you've ever known to . . . do what? Work food service in one of the most expensive places in the country? Do the napkin math—three thousand a month for rent, plus another four hundred if you want to park your truck—and tell me how you'd get it to add up. I live in a tiny apartment with two roommates and one bathroom because I can't afford to buy a home that's not a complete dump. And I work for a billionaire! I'm guessing, like me, you're too proud to take handouts, so let's face the hard truth. If you had a legit chance of relocating to SF and opening your own restaurant, you would have done it already. I don't have anything to do with the fact that you're priced out."

The moment I spit out the words, I'm overcome with regret. I've heard the saying "Hurt people hurt people" so many times it had lost all of its meaning—until now. My claws may not be on my fingers, but Vahe looks as shocked as if I took 'stay sharp' too literally and stabbed him in the gut.

To be honest, it's not the most heinous thing I've said to someone, but I already know it's what will haunt me. I've never loved anyone like I love Vahe, and whatever could have bloomed between us, I killed it with surgical precision.

"You know, Tori," he says softly, "we may have had our fun teasing each other over our cities' stereotypes, but had I known you were the living embodiment of a coastal elite, I would have told you to get your paklava somewhere else. Glad to know that someone who busted her ass to get to where she is kicks the ladder out from underneath her the second she reaches the top. God, you're so close to actually getting it, it's laughable."

"What do you mean?" I anticipated a host of angry, vengeful responses—not for him to throw my air of superiority back in my face.

"You say you despise suburbia for being basic. Boring families with cookie-cutter homes in cities where—how did you put it?—where dreams go to die?"

I blink, simultaneously impressed and unnerved by his uncanny ability to recall what I've said.

"What you can't seem to connect," he continues, "is how much you get off on feeling better than those so-called basic bitches. You told me that living in SF was proof that you made it. You broke out of generational poverty and built a one-in-a-million celebrity beauty career. You should be proud of all you've accomplished. But cities have become status symbols—not because they're the only places where smart, talented people live, but because of simple supply and demand. No one's inherently special for coming out the other side of a housing crisis and suppressed job market, not when luck has so much to do with success. Good for you for winning the geographic lottery and fuck right off for looking down your nose at those who didn't. For feeling smug at people who—like you said—couldn't get the numbers to add up right and were priced out. People like me. Hope you enjoy your empire of dirt, Victoria Townsend."

Vahe puts his key in the ignition and starts the truck, the finality of his words ringing in my ears. Sitting side by side serves as the smallest relief. Because after our gut-wrenching, relationship-ending conversation, we can avoid each other's eyes and pretend like there's nothing left to be said.

～

Tori Townsend's text history

SATURDAY, JANUARY 6, AT 11:38 P.M.

> Hey, Vahe, I just wanted to tell you I made it home safely. I know you wanted me to stay the night so I wouldn't have to drive back so late, but I figured it was best to give you space. Don't worry about giving me space, though. You can call or text whenever, and I'll answer. I promise.

Sunday, January 7, at 6:25 a.m.

> I don't know about you, but I barely slept. I kept tossing and turning over how sorry I am and how much of an apology I owe you. Would you be able to talk later today? I'm around anytime.

Monday, January 8, at 8:33 p.m.

> I'm trying to respect your boundaries, and I'm doing a terrible job at it. I'd even appreciate you calling to tell me to fuck off just so I can hear your voice. My life is better when you're in it, and I'm sorry I took you for granted. If there is the smallest chance that you still hold hope for us, give me a thumbs-up emoji or a "K." Anything. Please.

chapter
twenty-one

You would think I would be more experienced when it comes to grief, but when dysfunction is the air you breathe, pain that most people would consider insurmountable becomes ordinary. So much has been taken from you that when you experience actual tragedy—like my mother's liver finally failing—loss feels like relief.

Not this time though. This grief keeps coming in waves, each knocking me over with the force of a tsunami.

The first week back in San Francisco I am little more than a pulse. I cancel my client appointments and jazz gigs, claiming I've succumbed to a monstrous flu. I stay in bed all day, watch TV I can't retain, and only bother to eat when Glen and Som bring me meals during their wellness checks. They don't ask questions because they don't need to. They can tell Vahe and I are over from the way I stare at my phone for hours, waiting for it to ring.

The second week the pendulum swings in the opposite direction. Fueled by caffeine and self-loathing, I throw myself into my work, picking up extra nights at Ms. Maven's and discounting beauty services to make sure every day is fully booked. Meals are liquid so I don't have to take any breaks. If

I'm too busy to taste anything, then I definitely don't have time to cry the river of tears I'm holding back.

By the third week, my schedule reaches more of an equilibrium. If you're under the impression that I would use my free time to process my emotions in a healthy manner, you would be wrong.

Instead, I find myself racked with such all-consuming guilt about letting Tania's catering slip through the cracks that I'll do anything to make up for it.

Not that Tania has any idea though. I mean, she must have learned about my breakup from the glam fam because she hasn't asked me about Vahe since Armenian Christmas. There's no reason to make my problems her problems anyway. She has enough stress with chasing down RSVPs and finalizing the seating chart that the last thing I need to toss on her plate is the possibility that she won't have any food to offer her guests.

Vahe has yet to answer my calls, texts, or DMs about the contract—despite my repeated promises that I'll pay the full amount and whatever interest he wants to charge for emotional damages. But as much as he may hate me with the fire of a thousand suns, I refuse to believe he'd burn down Tania's special day because of how cruelly I acted.

I'm not ready to throw in the towel. If he really has gone full revenge, I'd rather beg every restaurant in the city to cater this wedding than come clean to Tania about my complete failure as a friend.

It's the first Saturday in February, which means it's the day of Tania's bachelorette party. I'll admit I haven't been in the best headspace, so I've been out of the loop. By the time my suffocating breakup-induced brain fog lifts, the glam fam has already taken care of the party planning. They're keeping tonight's destination a secret, but I know my best friends. We won't be spending a cozy sleepover in our pajamas. My agenda is clear: I'm going to look my fucking best. I'm going to dance until the sun comes up. And, most importantly, I'm going to get rip-roaring drunk.

But before I set myself up for the mother of all hangovers, I have a job to do. While the rest of my friends are putting the glam in glam fam and giving Tania the glow-up of a lifetime, I'm spending the day being the best bridesmaid I can be.

It's a chilly but bright morning as I make my way down Valencia Street in the Mission District. Tania hasn't had time to cross thank-you cards off her to-do list, and rather than order from some faceless conglomerate, I offered to drop by the cute little stationery store that's a short walk from my place.

"Welcome!" The door chimes as I enter and a bespectacled, middle-aged white woman greets me at the cashier, surrounded by shelves of San Francisco souvenirs, kitschy gag gifts, and cards of all kinds. As someone with not much room to spare, I'm not one to collect trinkets, but I can't help but smile at the stuffed sea lions and Karl the Fog stickers. It's been so long since my mouth has formed a grin that my cheeks hurt.

The staff member hands me a comically large catalog of custom cards that can be personalized with photos from Tania and Nolan's engagement shoot. My eyes go wide as I flip through the endless number of options. And these are just the thank-you cards. I can imagine how many decisions Tania has had to make while planning this wedding. I've only taken a few of them off her plate, and they're still overwhelming.

"It's a lot to go through," the woman says sympathetically. "Grab one of the chairs up front and take your time. I'll be here if you have any questions."

Grateful for her no-pressure approach, I take a seat next to an intoxicating tower of candles and start narrowing down my selections. I'm consumed by color palettes and typefaces until someone walks past with a side profile that's eerily familiar. A prominent nose and a luscious head of dark, wavy hair that I'd recognize anywhere. But by the time I jump up and peer out the glass storefront, the figure is gone, hidden among the stream of folks on the sidewalk, going about their weekend business.

It's a ridiculous notion. Vahe is hundreds of miles away, working hard and wanting nothing to do with me. I'd be an egomaniac if I think otherwise.

I wrap up my task the best I can, on edge, eyes flitting to the window hoping for another impossible glimpse. After placing a bulk order and scheduling a pickup time in a few days, I exit the store, itching to expel this restless feeling.

Dandelion Chocolate, the bean-to-bar chocolatier and café, calls my name down the block. I've been drowning in melancholy for weeks, and I could use the dopamine hit. Dandelion is a foodie's dream: small-batch, single-origin, and quintessentially San Franciscan. What's not to love?

Apparently, love itself. For a brief moment, I forgot that Valentine's Day was ten days away until I walk into the café and am bombarded by bon-bons and truffles, wrapped in red and pink packaging. Tania and Nolan are getting married on the holiday, so I shouldn't be surprised by the festivities. It's just a painful reminder that I'm out a plus-one, that no one will be asking to be my valentine.

I decide to swallow down that bitter pill with the most decadent hot chocolate on the menu. How ironic that when I first met Vahe, I teased him for drinking coffee as sweet as chocolate milk, and here I am, ordering exactly that to cheer myself up.

It is a fantastic idea, though. The barista calls my name, and I lurch toward the pickup counter, taking a big gulp of the rich concoction. I don't even bother blowing the steam off the top. My life feels like scorched earth, so who cares if my throat is burnt to match.

I'm too distracted by the deliciousness to take a seat. I stand off to the side, eyes closed, sipping pure bliss. I'm wearing a black hoodie over my head, warmed both inside and out. Feeling the stress and sadness escape my body, I take a deep breath, appreciating the comforting smells of cocoa, plus vanilla from the house-made marshmallow I added. Until notes of honey and amber musk infiltrate my nostrils, overwhelming my senses.

That smells *exactly* like Vahe's cologne.

The realization knocks me off-balance. I manage to avoid dropping my mug and shattering it into a million pieces, but the second my eyes snap open, I spit out hot chocolate all over the floor.

Fuck. As I grab handfuls of napkins to clean up the mess I've made, I try to get a good look at the owner of that signature scent, swiveling to locate that looming hulk of a man who should be impossible to miss. But just like at the stationery store, he's gone without a trace.

There is no trace, I tell myself, because he's not here. This is all in your head. You've spent the past three weeks so haunted by his absence that you're hallucinating his ghost.

At this point I can't stomach another possible sighting, so I decide to head home and resume my bridesmaid duties where I know Vahe can't torment me.

I spend the rest of the day creating props for the wedding's DIY photobooth and packing hundreds of mugs with Earl Grey tea bags and sugar cubes for Tania's Yosemi-tea party favors. If I keep my hands busy, I won't be as tempted to text Vahe and accuse him of stalking me.

Determined not to unravel, I don't pick my head up until the sun is setting and I hear the front door open. Of course, Tania's bachelorette. I need to get my ass in gear—starting with downing a drink to kick this party off right.

"You betches ready to pregame?" I call from the couch.

"I'd love to, darling," Glen answers, "What can I fix you—margarita or martini?"

"Martini, please." I turn around, wondering why Som isn't demanding hers be made extra dirty, but she's not with Glen.

"Where's your partner in crime? I thought you were beautifying the bachelorette."

From behind the kitchen counter, he stirs the liquor. "We were, but she had to hang back to help with some last-minute items." No word on what those might be. "Someone has to drag you away from your to-do list and remind you to wash your hair."

I raise an eyebrow as Glen passes me the martini and clinks my glass against his. "You know I take morning showers. But I wouldn't mind your styling if you're offering."

He matches my wry expression. He's not offering, but we never have to the way we swap services. It's an unspoken rule in the glam fam: as long as no one takes advantage, we've got each other's backs. Literally in my case, considering the monthly waxes I've given Glen since we started living together. "Get in the bog, betch," he says, pointing to our shared bathroom.

Although he normally upholds the stereotype of the gossip-obsessed gay man, I appreciate that Glen hasn't interrogated me about my newly single status. He doesn't need to use his words when his weapon of choice is a round brush. Because as he puts the finishing touches on my look, wafting hairspray over my side-swept grungy waves, I can tell the glam fam has a new mission: make Vahe Derderian rue the day he dumped me.

"Oh yes, gorgeous," he drawls in his British accent. "I swear, Tori, the moment you step into what Casey's picked out for you, you'll have me questioning my sexuality."

Glen's enthusiasm is infectious, even though I know for a

fact he hasn't so much as kissed another woman on the mouth since he outgrew his posh mother's coddling.

When I pad barefoot over to the towel rack where our garment bags are hanging and pull the zipper down for a peek, my giggle comes out like a garble. "Are you sure Tania's on board with this? I thought only the bride's allowed to party in white."

"You would think." Glen applies a drop of shine oil to his burly beard. "After she paid for that color consultant to label her a Cool Winter or whatever, she's avoiding any hue that makes her pale skin look washed out. She even had her wedding gown dipped with a pink ombre."

I'm taken aback. While I was falling in love for the first time, our bride-to-be was writing off white. But I'm counting my bachelorette blessings. "More for me, then, because this is fire."

I strip off my clothes and slip into the pair of bright white shorts. They gleam with a metallic sheen and have barely enough fabric to cover my butt cheeks. Then I toss on the black bandeau top. After dressing so modestly at the Armenian Christmas party, it feels euphoric to leave nothing to the imagination.

"Damn, talk about putting the hot in hot pants." He slides a hand in my back pocket.

"Wow, Glen. I'm flattered to be your first, but you gotta give a lady a heads up before going straight to butt stuff."

"Where's the fun in that, love?" He winks and pulls out what he was fishing for: a pair of white suspenders studded with sharp, steel tips. "Trust me, I saw the price tag on that suit." He gestures to the matching white blazer on the hanger. "You'll want to take that off before it gets drenched in sweat." He clips in the suspenders and pulls the straps up my shoulders, careful to avoid pricking his fingertips. "Now you can serve and stab your enemies at the same time."

No kidding. Casey has perfectly threaded the line between glamorous and dangerous. It feels like her way of apologizing for dulling my shine in those family-friendly clothes, even if it was my idea to wear them in the first place. As I lace up my steel-toed combat boots, I'm more comfortable than I've been since the unfortunate incident at the Grapevines.

What the hell was I thinking pursuing someone like Vahe? In no universe am I supposed to settle down with a sweet baker from suburbia. I'm a heartless bitch from a broken home. I've got terrible posture from being weighed down by the massive chip on my shoulder. I'm better off dumpster-diving for dirtbags like I've always done. It's what I'm good at.

I anoint my fingers with a shiny set of silver talons and swipe on a coat of wine-red lipstick, aptly named Poison. It's what I drink, it's who I date, and it's what I am, deep down inside.

"Let's go, Glen. Time to grab our coats and slit some throats," I say, reaching for the blazer. "I'm ready for my trampage tonight."

~

TORI TOWNSEND'S *rules for bachelorette parties in a perfect world*

1. **The first rule of bachelorette parties is you get one day.** Not a whole weekend. Not a three-day holiday extravaganza. Certainly not a weeklong horror show. You're only going to get married once, right? No pre-wedding party should take longer than your actual wedding.
2. **The second rule of bachelorette parties is you reread the first rule.** Seriously, my social meter is

like my phone battery. It craps out after four
hours. What makes you think you're more
entertaining than a half day of mindlessly scrolling
social media?

3. **Equally important as time is distance.** If time is
money, so are miles, because the farther you make
me travel to a party, the more moolah I could have
spent on a luxury vacation without a dozen rowdy
women using their outside voices wherever they
go. If I'm getting drunk, I prefer walking distance,
not a destination you read about in Bougie Bridal
magazine. And if it requires a passport? Piss off.

4. **Lose the mass-produced memorabilia.** And I'm
not talking about the penis straws (see next point).
I mean the shit you buy in bulk for your "bride
tribe"—by the way, gross. Nobody needs a
monogrammed tumbler or a cheap, ill-fitting shirt
just so we can remember the moment. That's what
photos are for, sweetheart. All this manufactured,
mostly plastic nonsense is going to end up in a
landfill, along with your sense of taste you threw
out the second he put a ring on it.

5. **And ditch the fake dicks while you're at it.**
Okay, back to penis straws—and cookies and
balloons and whatever else you can make phallic-
shaped these days. What are you, twelve? If a
plastic dick in your drink makes you giggle, you
clearly haven't had enough real ones in your
mouth.

6. **It's supposed to be a celebration, not a death
sentence.** I like things that rhyme as much as the
next person, but "final fling before the ring" has
got to *go*. If you're just alluding to having a trashy
girls' night with your closest friends, then you're

being dramatic, seeing how you can get shit-faced any night of the week. But if the reason you're throwing dollar bills at strippers is because you're lamenting you'll only have access to one penis for the rest of your life, maybe monogamous matrimony isn't for you. It's the twenty-first century, and at least in San Francisco, open relationships are all the rage. It's totally fine if two or more men aren't your style, but at your bachelorette, you can't have your cock and miss it too.

chapter
twenty-two

When our rideshare pulls up to the corner of Ninth and Howard, it's like we've arrived at a celebrity nightclub, instead of the low-key bars we usually frequent. As Glen and I approach the entrance, I can see a step-up where a professional photographer is snapping pics of guests before they gain admission.

"Where the hell is Som?" I project into Glen's ear as pop music booms from a speaker over the front door. "She's never one to turn down the paparazzi treatment."

"I told you already while we were primping. She had some pre-party planning to take care of first. She'll meet up with us later." Glen gives our names to a slender Asian man in an all-black suit. "We're with the Beecher party," he clarifies as the gatekeeper scrolls a tablet to check folks off the guest list. "The one surrounded by a SWAT team, I'd assume."

It's standard procedure for Alex's glam fam to require the strictest of security measures whenever she joins us at a public function. After all, she's more famous than most royals and state officials combined, so everywhere we go it's always the same. Secret aliases, disguises, a wall of bodyguards with a license to kill. The whole shebang.

I don't have time to wonder why Glen's being evasive about our roommate. We get passed off to more men in black suits, communicating to their higher-ups via headset. They escort us around to the back, where a nondescript door opens into a dark corridor. I don't even know the name of this joint, and I'm being told to follow complete strangers like they won't kidnap us for ransom.

Fortunately, my not-so-irrational fears of being abducted over Alex's billionaire fortune are alleviated when we see our princess and the bride with a handful of ladies I've never met. A mix of childhood friends and work colleagues if I had to guess. They're congregated in a VIP booth in the corner, all dressed in black and white like sexy salt and pepper shakers.

We cross the massive, dimly lit room. Dozens of tables are stationed around an abnormally long bar that spans the room from end to end, supported by thick columns that connect to the ceiling. This hub would have the vague appearance of a stage if it weren't for the squadron of bartenders around it, frantically fulfilling orders and stacking colorful cocktails on server trays.

"Betches, get your fine asses over here and come take some shots!" Alex screeches, giving away that this isn't her first round. "Casey, where are the limes?"

The stylist points to a bowl of citrus wedges at their table and finishes adjusting Tania's tiara, which knowing her and Alex's designer taste is adorned with Swarovski crystals. Usually, with their matching blonde curls, Alex and Casey could be mistaken for sisters. But tonight, discretion is a bigger priority than playing twinsies, so Alex's luscious locks are tucked under a mousy ginger bob. Not that she can ever truly fly under the radar when our booth is roped off and flanked by what must be the venue's entire security team.

I jerk my head toward the nearest bodyguard as Alex shoves a tequila shot and a lime wedge into my hands. "Did you get one of these beefcakes to taste the liquor first for poison?"

She winks. "Gotta enlist more than we need in case you want to take one of them for a spin. Donovan here let me know his shift's about to end, and he got us access to our own private dressing room if you two want to get more comfortable."

I catch his eye. After lewdly scanning me from tits to ass, he gives me that universal dude-nod that indicates he's down to fuck. On any other night, I'd say hell yeah without a second thought. But something seizes in my chest—an omen that I'd be making a terrible decision. And I'm too sober to do things I'll regret. At least for now.

I toast Terrible Decision Donovan with my shot glass. "Come back after I've had three or four of these, and maybe we'll talk."

Throwing back a shot, I brace myself, still expecting to taste the cheap jet fuel I subsisted on during my days of NYC club hopping. Instead, the smoothest tequila I've ever tasted hits my tongue. I should know by now that Alex never steps outside without having the best of everything at her fingertips. If a bar doesn't have a tippy-top shelf, her team will bring their own.

Tania's entourage, however, isn't as acclimated to the good life as we are in the glam fam. I squeeze past the huddle indulging in the bougiest bottle service of their lives to give the bachelorette a bear hug. I'm not one for displays of affection, public or otherwise, but whether it's the tequila or the incessant guilt I've been swallowing, I feel the urge to smother us both in my shame.

"You look stunning," I say into her ear, catching a whiff of peonies from her dark hair and admiring her naturally silver streaks. As an honorary member of the glam fam, having been adopted by Casey two years ago as one of the stylist's clients, she's the least interested in the world of beauty. I get restless when my hair is the same color for too long, but I've always appreciated how Tania can rock her never-been-dyed tresses. The mood lighting bounces off her white strands like the tinsel on the Christmas trees in the Grapevines ballroom. The image seeps into my brain before I can stop it. Tania's going on about how she and Casey found the pink flamingo–colored dress she's wearing, but I can't absorb any of the conversation because I keep replaying my last, spineless words to Vahe in his truck.

The memory is too much to bear, and I resist the urge to push Tania out of my way and bail on this bachelorette. I blurt out a quick congratulations before pouring us both another shot.

With my mind successfully dulled by tequila, it returns to the same pesky question I had when we arrived. "Where the fuck is Som?"

All of a sudden, the room darkens. Walk-on music starts blaring, and a spotlight illuminates the center of the bar, indeed turning it into a stage. A middle-aged Asian woman with a fire-engine red wig struts out and hits her mark, wearing a Jessica Rabbit–inspired crimson dress and elbow-length purple gloves. Her impressive stature is amplified by the fact that she's standing several feet above our heads, all of which are craned to find out what's about to happen.

"Hellooo, San Franciscoooo," she bellows, "and welcome to AuroraSF. I will be your most illustrious emcee this evening. You can call me Yassica, because if there's anything you should be screaming at the top of your lungs tonight, it is YASSSS."

Hoots, hollers, and thunderous applause breaks out, and Yassica eats it up. "Thank you, I agree. I am a motherfucking big deal. And in case you were wondering, I am one hundred percent Filipina—emphasis on the peen because that is what I am on the hunt for, honeys! Who else is with me?"

The room explodes again, and Tania's hometown friends get particularly rowdy. That's when it hits me. Is this a strip show of male entertainers? Am I going to spend the night gawking at bulges in banana hammocks? It's bad enough that Vahe already looks like he can star in the next Magic Mike movie. I don't need a bunch of strangers' dicks reminding me of how much of a dick I was to him and how I'll never see his again.

Thankfully, though, Yassica rids us of that notion real quick. "Yeah, well, calm your tits. The only thunder down under you're gonna see is from Aussie, our maven from Melbourne. That's because AuroraSF isn't a strip club or a drag show. As part of our mission of supporting the trans-gender community for over twenty-five years, all our performers are trans women of color."

Wait a minute. Don't tell me—

"As much as we love dudes in dresses, that's not what's on the menu here at AuroraSF. Trans women are women, and if we hear you're acting anything other than grateful for these gorgeous goddesses, we will not hesitate to kick your asses out. Now put your glasses down and get your hands up for tonight's special guest. She's best known for painting snatched faces on the hottest princesses, some of which are gracing us with their presence tonight."

Holy shit. I can't believe it. With Yassica blowing kisses in our direction, the message is clear. Everybody in the glam fam has been here the whole time.

"Let's get loud for Darla Dragonfruit!"

At the cue of her stage name, Som bursts onto the stage, lip-synching to J. Lo. I'm mesmerized by how jaw-droppingly beautiful she looks. Dressed in a black and gold brocade leotard and dangerously tall stilettos, she's made her legs look a mile long. And with extensions in her jet-black hair, pulled up into a sky-high ponytail, it's like there's a perpetual arrow pointing to her gloriously plump ass.

It takes all my strength to turn back from watching one of my roommates and best friends strut and shimmy around the columns like they're stripper poles. But when I see Tania and her friends lose their minds over such a perfect surprise, I just wish I could have played a part in it. The rest of the glam fam stands off to the side, dusting their shoulders off on a job well done.

"So why wasn't I in on Som's epic slay?" I ask pointedly at Alex, Casey, and Glen while pouring myself a third tequila shot. "Hella unfair considering I'm the one most likely to keep a secret."

The accusation comes out angrier than I anticipated, and as much as I would like to blame my confrontational attitude on the booze, I know this resentment has been simmering for months. It's how I felt when everybody participated in Tania and Nolan's engagement photoshoot without me. I have a high tolerance for being slighted—I've had a lifetime of it, after all—but eventually my pent-up rage will boil over and burn everyone I come into contact with.

The glam fam simultaneously winces, and I'm starting to think I can't do anything as well as cut the people I love most with my callous remarks. Casey is the first to speak up. "We didn't want to burden you with bach party planning. You already have so much on your plate with the wedding itself—"

"And it's not like we don't get enough of Som's lip-synching when she's prancing around the apartment," Glen adds.

I inhale a self-righteous breath, nostrils flaring. "With that logic, I don't need to be invited to happy hours because we have liquor at home. Don't take Tori to the mall because she's got an online order waiting for her in the mailroom. What else have you been excluding me from lately?"

Alex adjusts her ginger wig, even though it's not the synthetic hair making her uncomfortable. "Look, Tori, we love you. But every time we've suggested going out, you've turned us down, either to run an unnecessary errand or wallow in bed. Don't get us wrong—we understand breakups are a bitch. We've tried to get you to open up about what happened with Vahe in Fresno, but if you don't want to let us in, you can't expect us to wait forever."

Easy for Princess Alex Waterston-Gardner to say. What does she know about breakups? She's been with her douchebag boyfriend Dominic for years, even though he doesn't seem serious about her. Boy, I can't fucking wait when the two of them inevitably implode, sinking her into the worst pain of her life, so I can dish her the most deserved 'I told you so.'

Alex must sense from the daggers I'm shooting at her that I find her hypocrisy laughable. "But we're all here now!" she segues. "What do they say about moving on? The best way to get over somebody is to get underneath someone else, right? Sounds like we should throw another round back and get Donovan over here, stat!"

It takes me a beat to process her suggestion. I'm not sure if it's the tequila that's causing my stomach to lurch or the thought of following through on this rebound. When I put on this smoking hot outfit, I intended to leave a trail of men in my wake. And when I first locked eyes with Donovan, I was open to hooking up, whether or not the decision was terrible. He was clearly on board, so why can't I take Alex up on the offer?

"I don't know if I'm interested . . ." I hedge, biting into the lime chaser to mask my reluctance.

"Interested in what, betch?" Som says behind me. "Joining me for an encore?"

I whip around, taking in Som's flushed face. I must have been so preoccupied with my existential crisis that I didn't notice the room erupting in applause at the end of her performance.

Alex nudges my elbow like we're totally chill and weren't having a tiff about how our friendship's taken a back seat. "We're trying to convince her to go guard the body of that hot-as-hell bodyguard over there. He's been relieved of his duties, but I think his last job tonight should be working Tori out."

Someone on staff at AuroraSF hands Som a bouquet, gushing their congratulations, and the second the interaction's over, she drops the flowers on the arm of the booth to return to the more important matter at hand. "Girl, what the hell are you waiting for? I would climb that man like a tree. I would ride his face reverse-cowgirl and lick liquor off his abs like an ice luge. I would—"

"I get it," I try to interject, but Som's off to the races. She loops Casey and Glen in, and everyone is having a ball listing off all the ways they would do the dirty with Donovan. Any other time, I would join them, but something about their blatant objectification rubs me the wrong way. What if Donovan is secretly tired of sleeping around? What if he goes along with the casual hookups because they're fun in the moment, but what he desperately wants to find is love? He could be hoping to meet the person he'd throw his playboy lifestyle away for, but nobody believes him because he's always surrounded by horny drunks.

Okay. Wow. I truly am dense.

The reason I can't drag Donovan to our private dressing room and have my way with him isn't because he's not my type or my eyes are broken. Precisely the opposite, in fact. He reminds me so much of Vahe that I'm projecting my emotional baggage onto the bodyguard because I pity him.

I can't fuck another guy and toss him to the side like Som's bouquet—which is soaking up spilled tequila just to stay hydrated—because that's exactly how I treated Vahe. I had zero intention of dating long distance and couldn't see how we could be compatible, so I never took him seriously, until it was too late.

It took me my entire adulthood to unlearn my parents' toxic messages about my worth and rebuild my sense of self. And to protect that newly found confidence, I wore my upbringing like a shield of armor. People from the big city who were raised by wolves don't date those softened by suburban bubble wrap. People with dead moms and deadbeat dads don't end up with partners who love their family so much they work in close quarters with them daily. And people who have never experienced real love before don't accept it from those who were bathed in it from the beginning . . . lest they drown.

Speaking of drowning, if I don't stop drinking shots, I'm going to rip the figurative brakes on my brain and careen into the Bay. I wish I could say after suffering from the neglect of an alcoholic and drug-addled mother that I never touched a mind-altering substance, but it's harder to break old habits when they've been ingrained since birth. Because I would bet my life savings that Mama Townsend didn't put down the beer bottle when she was supposed to be shopping for baby bottles. Usually, I have no problem indulging in my vices in moderation, but I'm suffocating from so much self-loathing that if I don't sober up quick, I will be pulled into a pit of despair deeper than the Pacific Ocean.

"I can't do this. I'm sorry," I blurt out to no one in particular. Thirty minutes into the show, and I've already had four shots. I'm not in the headspace for drunken fun and frivolity. If I keep powering through, I'll black out—and not in the silly 'passed out with friends in the back of an Uber' kind of way, but in the self-destructive 'who cares if I wake up' kind of way.

I push past the wall of security around the booth, not bothering to say goodbye to the glam fam and delay my exit any further. They're too busy cheering as several performers approach with magnum bottles of champagne, each lit with VIP sparklers. I don't even need to extend my apologies to Donovan for insinuating he'd get a happy ending on his shift or for my friends treating him like man-meat. Women are tripping over themselves to hand him a glass, and he's thoroughly enjoying the attention.

That's where the comparison to Vahe ends. Even at our spa date where women were mingling in bathrobes and bikinis, he couldn't stop staring at me. And now I've ruined any chance I had with him, because I couldn't push past his baker playboy persona.

I wasted so much time thinking I couldn't picture a life with Vahe, and now I can't picture one without him.

~

***Tori Townsend**'s text history*

Saturday, February 3, at 7:45 p.m.

> Hey, Vahe, it's Tori—figured I should clarify in case you deleted my number. I know I shouldn't be reaching out since you haven't responded to any of my messages, but you also haven't told me to stop so . . .

Saturday, February 3, at 7:48 p.m.

Sorry, I'm a little drunk. I'm at Tania's bachelorette party, but I need to leave before I kill the mood and ruin it for everyone.

The glam fam kept encouraging me to hook up with one of Alex's bodyguards. I'm not going to lie and say I didn't think about it. I just couldn't go through with it—not when every man I see reminds me of how much I miss you.

I guess I should take a vow of celibacy and become a nun. I know that's a Catholic thing and not an Armenian Orthodox thing, but if Holy Cross Church is ever looking to recruit, you know where to find me.

Before I can exit AuroraSF and escape into the night, I hear someone behind me call my name. I pretend I don't hear, but as I reach for the doorknob, Tania's hand grips my shoulder.

"Tori, why are you leaving so soon? There's going to be cake later!"

I brushed off the glam fam's suggestion that I fuck my problems away, but Tania's wholesome enticement to stay is too much to bear. My mind is filled with flashbacks of tahini cake and paklava and these custard-filled donuts called ponchik, and I can't hold it in any longer. Much to my horror, what bubbles up my throat isn't regurgitated tequila, but rather a hearty sob.

"Hey, hey, what's wrong?" Tania exclaims, alarmed by the tears gushing down my face. She pulls me aside and through a narrow hallway on our right, where a private dressing room is marked with a chalkboard sign that reads BEECHER PARTY. Once inside and out of view from prying eyes, I unleash the full waterworks. Racks of performer costumes flank us on one side and several vanities are stationed on the other. Tania locates a tissue box on a table among piles of makeup and hands it to me so I can save my white blazer and shorts from catching my mascara.

"Let me guess," she says, "those bodyguards were so bodacious, they moved you to tears."

I chuckle, in spite of the snot dripping down my nostrils. After a loud, cathartic honk into the tissue, I sigh. "I don't want to ruin your bachelorette party with my bad vibes, Tania. I really don't. Honestly, I wasn't even dating Vahe that long, so I don't know why I'm taking the breakup so hard. Our relationship was over before it started. I'm not sure it even counted."

"If it made this much of an impact on you, it absolutely counted." She encloses me into a tight hug, and I bite back another rush of tears. I've never had a geyser burst from my eyeballs over a guy, but if this is a side effect of falling in love, I must say I'm not a fan.

Tania releases me from her grip. "And don't you dare worry about ruining my bachelorette. It's my party, and you can cry if you want to."

Okay, that gets me to laugh for real. Words are Tania's specialty as a top-tier marketer, but I take for granted how witty she can be when she's not stressed about seating arrangements.

Assured by my smile that I'm not going to have another emotional breakdown, Tania cuts to the chase. "Now tell me why our toughest chick is tied into knots."

I summarize the debacle that was the Armenian Christmas party, pouring salt on a wound that's still fresh and has no hope of scabbing over any time soon. Tania's bullshit meter is strong. I watched her carry Habituall through its biggest scandal and into a successful IPO, and I know she can instinctively tell what's genuine and what's good PR.

So I lay out all the facts, without sugarcoating anything: my classist insults about Dikran's Deli, unchecked bias against suburbia, and, most regrettably, distrust that Vahe could ever be a viable option as a life partner. I list off the very factors I'd hate to be judged for, like where I live, how many people I've fucked, and how I was raised. I purge my most revolting thoughts, until my voice goes hoarse. Neither Tania or I believe in an afterlife, but after airing the worst of myself as if I'm confessing my sins, I wouldn't be surprised if the earth were to open up and drag me to an eternity of damnation.

When I'm done spewing my word vomit, I brace myself for Tania to call me a toxic, self-serving bitch, or at the very least, berate me for hijacking who knows how many minutes from her bachelorette party. Only a truly heinous person would steal the center of attention from a bride-to-be.

What I don't expect is for Tania to chuckle. "Oh, honey, is that all?"

"What do you mean?" I hiccup, wiping my damp cheeks with one tissue and blowing my nose with another. "I just told you that not only are Vahe and I fundamentally incompatible, I also insulted him for it."

Tania waves off my concern. "Puh-lease. I'm marrying an elite rock-climber, remember? Me, someone who used to spend my corporate fitness stipend on massages and referred to camping as 'cosplaying a caveman's lifestyle.' When I first met Nolan—about a year ago, mind you—the man was living in his van and shitting in the woods. Incompatibility doesn't begin to cover it. If you asked me at that time to dream up my perfect partner, Nolan would have been the exact opposite of my answer."

She's not exaggerating, that's for sure. Tania's the most Type-A friend I have, and that's saying something, considering how Casey organizes her personal wardrobe by color, season, and designer. I always assumed Tania would end up with yet another tech bro with a trust fund, not an athlete who gave up his inheritance to scale mountains for a living.

"But how were you able to set aside your differences without sacrificing everything you stand for? You two had only been dating for a couple of months before you just up and quit your job, got engaged, and bought a home in—"

I bite off what I'm about to say, but Tania already senses where I'm going. "In the middle of nowhere?" she says with a knowing smile. It's not the first time I've used the phrase around her, and now I'm mentally kicking myself for being just as judgmental with my best friends as I was with Vahe. How has anyone managed to stick around in my life without throwing in the towel?

"In Oakhurst," I correct myself sheepishly. "You completely changed your life, and it happened so fast. How did you know Nolan was worth it?"

Tania finds a wastebasket and hands it to me so I can toss my used issues. "I didn't. Admittedly, our situation was different because of Nolan's mission to free solo the Dawn Wall. Would I have been as eager to lock things down if Nolan used ropes and safety equipment like a sane person and it wasn't a matter of life and death?"

She pauses to consider the question. "Maybe, maybe not. I can understand your hesitation to upend your life for a man you've only known for a few months. Goodness knows the thought of abandoning my dream job and dream city terrified me. But I have a diagnosed anxiety disorder, so everything terrifies me. If I was ever going to make room for new dreams, my life needed upending."

Tania gestures for me to sit at one of the vanities, so she can fix the makeup I've smeared in my hysterics. She's not a certified cosmetics expert—that title goes to Som, of course—but she manages to do a decent job cleaning up my eyeliner with a Q-tip. "You could take it slow with Vahe," she says, dotting concealer on my puffy undereye circles. "Do the long-distance thing for a while until you decide on a compromise that works for both of you. That's what Nolan and I intended to do, but it turns out I'm a bigger risk taker than I thought. And if a scaredy-cat like me can put it all on the line for love, I know you can too."

She taps the side of my nose with the concealer tube, where my amethyst stud sits. "With how many needles you've endured for your piercings and tattoos, telling Vahe how you feel should be a piece of cake, right?"

I laugh at the comparison. It may have taken until her mid-twenties for Tania to get her ears pierced, but I'd gladly split my tongue if it meant I could magically make up with Vahe without having a heart-to-heart conversation. But conversations are a two-way street, and our relationship has hit a dead end.

I tell Tania as much, about Vahe's radio silence and how he hasn't responded to any of my messages. As the words tumble out, it's impossible to avoid the implication of what the fallout means for the wedding catering, and I can tell by Tania's wide eyes that the hamster wheel in her mind is spinning. Calming a friend through her relationship drama is one thing, but I bet potentially losing one of her biggest and most crucial wedding vendors isn't how she wants to spend her bachelorette.

"I fucked up, didn't I?" I say hesitantly. "This is a crisis of epic proportions if he hates me so much that he's refusing to fulfill our order, whether or not we pay him."

Tania lifts her hand in protest, as if she won't consider the thought. "Let me handle damage control with the Derderians. The Armenian community is close-knit—we're not ones to leave each other hanging. Our ancestors survived a genocide, so it would be a dishonor to abandon a Hye in need. And I'm prepared to go full bridezilla if I have to. I'll go above Vahe's head and give his grandmother a piece of my mind."

With that cold edge in her voice, I don't doubt her for a

second. Fortunately, Tania's villain origin story is interrupted when my phone vibrates in my back pocket. An unknown 559 number pops up on the display, and I immediately answer, recognizing Fresno's area code.

~

A *list* of things Tori Townsend has learned from the elderly

1. **No one talks more than the Silent Generation.** Best believe Ethel is getting a pedicure every week —not because her cuticles are in dire straits, but so she can regale the salon with stories about her Yorkshire terrier, Yippie (my name for the dog, not hers).

2. **They make a good point.** Everybody likes to make fun of Karens, and rightfully so, but bossy Baby Boomers have nothing on Marys and Judys who are minorly inconvenienced. The difference is that their complaints are usually justified. You're right, Betty—the yams do suck, and the AC is too cold!

3. **Their fashion is fire.** People assume you become more conservative as you age, like harrumphing over property taxes is a degenerative disease, but they clearly haven't played the game "Drag Queen or Dolores?" Nobody does maximalist beauty like an eighty-five-year-old woman with permanent eyebrows, jet-black hair, and enough chunky costume jewelry to fill a thrift shop in the Castro.

4. **They throw the middle finger at longevity.** Notice how almond moms exist, but not almond

grandmas? These biddies and baddies were born during the Second World War, so they inherently understand we're here for a good time, not a long time. Every article about a centenarian asks their secrets to remaining on this earth past your expiration date, and the answers are always eating whatever the hell you want and drinking a pitcher of red wine with dinner. So go ahead and count every calorie, but Barbara's on her third pack of cigs for the day, and she's damn near indestructible.

5. **The best don't care about your labels and quirks.** There's something about careening toward your own funeral that makes you give zero fucks about how others live their oppressively short lives. If they're grateful for how they're going out, they won't care how you turned out. Gay or straight, hustler or hippie, settled down or sowing your wild oats, nothing fazes those in their final stage of existence. Your grandma remembers not being allowed to have a credit card, so trust her when she says she just wants you to be happy.

chapter
twenty-four

It's the Saturday before the wedding when I walk into the
Golden Poppy. It's a casual Chinese restaurant in downtown Fresno, a few blocks away from Dikran's Deli. Immediately, I lock eyes with my lunch date—not the Derderian I
want but the one I need.

"Fancy seeing you here, Queenie," I say as I slide into the
red booth across from the matriarch, as if I didn't agree to
meet her here after that fateful call at Tania's bachelorette
party a week ago.

She scoffs. "Nothing fancy to see here, but that's why I like
this place." There are no menus on the table, but it's clear
Queenie doesn't need any when she cranes her head toward
the back where two middle-aged Chinese women are talking
animatedly. One rings up orders while the other washes a stack
of Coca-Cola tumblers, red and plastic like the seat that
squeaks every time I fidget. "Sunny! The usual," Queenie calls,
startling the few other lunchers. "Then come here and meet
my grandson's girlfriend."

I sink into the booth with a high-pitched *eeeek* (the uphol-
stery, not me), too mortified by Queenie interrupting
someone on the job to correct her with a quick "ex-girlfriend."

But instead of accosting her presumptuous customer, Sunny drops everything she's doing, sends her coworker to the kitchen, and shuffles over to our table as if she expects to see an Oscar-winning actress, which is what I feel like considering the smile that's plastered on my face.

"Aiya, so beautiful," she gushes. "So this is his type, eh?"

There's an unspoken undercurrent to Sunny's gawking, like out of all the women she expected Vahe to date, a tatted, pierced punk in black would be her absolute last guess. But her fussing is good-spirited, so I feel less like a circus freak and more like a celeb worthy of running around with my more famous friends. As she fawns over me, I'm thankful I took Queenie's advice and refused to cover up like I did at Christmas. My hair's been lightened to a glossy lavender, and my tattoo sleeves flash through a fishnet mesh top. Ears, eyebrows, nose, lips, bellybutton—none of my body mods got left at home this time.

And, of course, my trusty amethyst claws tap on the table. Sure, it's a tad embarrassing to field compliments from total strangers, but anyone with my kind of look is comfortable being the center of attention. If anything, I'd rather be in public getting triple takes than spend my life getting effectively ignored like I did as a kid. I may not have known my grandparents, but this wholesome moment is like a balm to my bruised inner child.

Eventually, Sunny's coworker comes by to drop off plates of food that make me salivate: succulent beef and broccoli, pork with crispy pan-fried noodles, dry-fried string beans, and piles of fried shrimp with a variety of dipping sauces. It's more than we could ever possibly eat, but my growling stomach is determined to make a dent.

I've seen Queenie in her element at the deli, so I know she's more than comfortable making small talk, but she's clearly not in the mood today. After the women return to their stations, Queenie lets me get three bites in before she jumps straight to business. "Alright, Miss Tori, what's it going to take for you and my grandson to get back on speaking terms?"

I can't swallow my pride down with my lunch, so I nearly choke on a twirled forkful of noodles. "You tell me! He's the one who won't answer my calls and texts."

She brushes off that fact as if it's an irrelevant nuisance. "I know my grandbaby, and Vahe is torn up inside. He hasn't been the same since you left the Christmas party. Moping about, being moody with customers. More than once I've heard him letting it out, yelling in the parking lot like he showed you the day you met. At first, I had sympathy because I've never seen him this brokenhearted, and I assumed he'd come to his senses. But it's been over a month, and it's bad for business, honestly."

A pang of guilt shoots through me as I imagine Vahe shouting until his voice goes hoarse. I've got too many neighbors in my apartment complex to risk disturbing them, but my pillow's been pulling double-duty these days, muffling my screams. "I don't know how else I can apologize," I say, tossing up my hands, "if he has zero interest in hearing it."

Queenie bites off a massive fried shrimp down to the tail, all in one chomp, and it feels like there's a metaphor in there somewhere. "I didn't ask you here to demand that you beg for him back. On the contrary. I have half a mind to smack some sense into him, but I figured I should run it by you first before I take such drastic measures."

We share a knowing smile about the men in our lives— how we can't live with or without them—but I don't let it go to my head because she would just as quickly smack me around if it meant she could rein in the chaos. She's not Team Tori or Team Vahe. When it comes to Dikran's Deli, Queenie is royalty, and we exist to serve.

"Even if your punishment is cruel and unusual, I'm not

convinced it will change Vahe's mind." I move food around my plate glumly. "And I don't blame him. After how I acted, I can't see him ever going out on a limb for me."

Queenie finishes off the fried shrimp and sits back in thought. "What do you know about the genocide, Miss Tori?"

Woof. Talk about a hairpin turn.

"I did a b-bit more research after meeting Vahe," I stammer, unsure why she's made such an abrupt shift in subject matter. "From what I understand, over a million and a half Armenians were killed by the Ottoman Turkish regime during World War I. It emboldened Hitler to proceed with the Holocaust, as he was quoted, 'Who, after all, speaks today of the annihilation of the Armenians?'" I gulp down water to lubricate my dry throat before powering through. "Horrifically, over one hundred years later, there's been no equivalent of the Nuremberg Trials. To this day, Turkey denies committing the Armenian Genocide, despite mountains of evidence, and it wasn't until Biden took office that the US officially recognized it because apparently our military alliance was more important than the healing of an entire civilization."

I pause, waiting for her validation like she's my history teacher giving me a pop quiz. When she finally nods, a sigh of relief escapes me.

She does a quick scan around the room as if she's being mindful of whether there are any children in the vicinity. "Here's the thing about mass genocide. Ignoring the utter immorality for just a moment, do you know how difficult it is to round up nearly two million people—logistically speaking? That's more than both our cities' populations combined. You don't go from zero to death march overnight, is what I'm saying."

I gulp, shell-shocked by the thought.

"In the years before the genocide," she plows ahead, "my father was an intellectual and an entrepreneur, but more importantly, he was *observant*. And the only reason he wasn't forced to dig the ditch he would have been shot into was because he got the hell out of Dodge, years before the deportations started. Was he ready to leave his entire way of life behind? Of course not, nobody ever is. But if you don't proactively embrace change for the better, I fundamentally believe it will be inflicted upon you for the worst. Call it a survival instinct, but if there's anything I've been bred to be, it's decisive. You dawdle, you die."

My mind flashes back to our battle over the signage, and a missing piece of Queenie's psyche clicks into place. Here's a woman who will never wait for anyone to get shit done, whether she's twenty-five or eighty-five. I have to admit—her mindset on embracing change has me rethinking what I'm capable of.

"Now I'm not comparing Fresno to a war-torn country, of course," Queenie continues, "But I can tell when someone's spirit is dying. My grandson will live a much more rewarding life if he takes it by the reins when he's given the chance."

I understand her point of view. Never in a million years did I think I'd be reconsidering my ironclad stance on leaving my favorite city in the world, but when the person who makes your heart sing isn't by your side, it defeats the purpose of staying.

"But Queenie—aren't you concerned you'll be losing your precious grandbaby to a badmouthed heathen who sharpens talons for a living? Not once have I ever been seen as a positive influence on anyone."

"Ha! And you think I must be some hoity-toity gal just because I collect Social Security, don't you? Oooh, you should have seen the headaches I used to give my father every time he caught me with a boy in the back of the deli's supply closet. But you don't build a booming business without flirting with the regulars. These days everyone calls me Queenie because

I'm the boss, but back then it was because of all the men I had wrapped around my finger. And to be frank, given all my gentlemen callers at the Old Armenian Home, times haven't changed." She smiles, a devilish twinkle in her eye.

"My point is, I recognize a firecracker when I see one. You may be explosive and a danger to people who get too close, but damn are you a delight to be around. And from the way Vahe's been auditioning as Eeyore for a live-action adaptation of *Winnie the Pooh*, he believes that too."

I snort with laughter, in awe of this feisty woman and her unapologetic ability to tell it like it is. "Okay, let's say you're right, and Vahe is as torn up about our breakup as I am. Then why the fuck doesn't he answer my messages? It's not like I'm the one who's been ghosting for weeks."

Queenie lets out a huff. "You kids and your newfangled devices. You spend so much time attached to your so-called smartphones, you'd think they would make you less dumb. Ghosts aren't brought back to life by texting, Miss Tori. So get off your ass and have a real, face-to-face conversation. Like the one we're having right now. I'll have you know I smoothed things over with your friend Tania, so Vahe will be at the wedding. Perfect chance for a second chance, no? I'll give him the push he needs if you promise to catch him. After all, no one falls harder in love than a man who never saw it coming."

She calls over Sunny for the bill, and I have to wrestle her for the check holder, sliding in my credit card before she can beat me to it. What is with this woman and her iron grip?

As a peace offering, I pass her both fortune cookies that come with the receipt, and she opens one with a resigned huff.

She breaks off a piece, tossing it back, and pulls out the strip of paper with a raised eyebrow. "Hmm, this one must be yours," she says, mouth full, handing the fortune to me. It reads, *Say yes—then figure it out later*. Not the home run I was hoping for—it doesn't matter how many times you say yes if the other person doesn't hear it.

"Now that's what I'm talking about!" Queenie barks, munching the second cookie. She holds out her fortune for me to read: *A romantic rendezvous is in your future*. She pauses, tilting her head to the side as if trying to recall something. "You're a full-service aesthetician, yes? After hashing out the catering kerfuffle, Tania mentioned something about you being the bridal party's beauty expert."

"You could say that . . ." I hedge, hesitant to ask what she's getting at. It's true my hotel bathroom is stacked to the brim with nail equipment, skincare products, self-tanner, and a million other bits and bobs in case a beauty emergency strikes in the final days before the wedding. But if giving Queenie a free rejuvenating facial is what it will take for her to convince Vahe to come around, that's a bribe I'm willing to accept.

"Great!" She claps her hands and ushers me out the restaurant door toward my car. "I've got a few plus-ones in mind, so if I want one of them to water my garden this weekend, I'm going to need a landscaper. Do you do Brazilians?"

Oh god. I thought the figurative Band-Aid on my bruised ego was the only thing I'd be ripping off during this wedding, but I was very, *very* wrong.

~

Email from Tania Beecher on Tuesday, February 13, at 7:30 a.m.

To: The Glam Fam
 From: Tania Beecher
 Subject: Wedding day timeline (important, please read!)

. . .

I CAN'T BELIEVE the big day is tomorrow! Thank you, everyone, for all your help in making this wedding a reality. I've attached the bridal party spreadsheet with the full details, but as a reminder, here is our agenda:

- 8:00 a.m. – Wake up (I will be up at the crack of dawn due to my crippling anxiety, but this is our start time in case you need to set an alarm)
- 9:00 a.m. – Breakfast in the bridal suite (and yes, there will be mimosas!)
- 10:00 a.m. – Hair and makeup (aka Glen and Som's time to shine)
- 12:00 p.m. – Lunch break (a light array of salads, sandwiches, and protein smoothies I can drink through a straw without screwing up my lipstick)
- 1:00 p.m. – Getting ready shots (photographs, not tequila, but I'm not opposed to that either)
- 2:00 p.m. – First look (if Nolan bursts into tears when he sees me, I'll call it a win)
- 2:30 p.m. – Portraits (because people who schedule photos during happy hour are monsters)
- 3:30 p.m. – Last-minute prep (don't forget to grab your bouquets!)
- 4:00 p.m. – Ceremony starts (and, as they say, I can finally let out the breath I've been holding)

chapter
twenty-five

After spending the last few days completing my bridesmaid to-do list—spray-tanning skin, grooming brows, painting nails, you name it—the big day is finally here. It's brisk in Yosemite outside the Granite Grove Lodge, and while there's snow on the ground, we lucked out with plenty of sun shining during this picturesque ceremony.

I'm standing stoically with the glam fam, listening to Tania and Nolan read off their promises to each other, when it dawns on me. Some people make public declarations of love by vowing to stick by one another's sides for better or worse, in sickness and in health. And others—namely, me—prove their love by giving their boyfriend's grandmother a bikini wax. I'm praying we can reconcile because those are thirty harrowing minutes I'll never be able to get back.

For all the effort I put into this wedding, I should be paying more attention, but my eyes keep getting pulled away, scanning both sides of the aisle for a glimpse of Vahe. I thought by getting the vendor contract back on track, crisis had been averted, but I didn't anticipate the worst outcome could be him not even showing. Regardless of where we stand, Vahe's known Tania forever, so the least he can do is attend her wedding and support her like any childhood friend would.

Didn't Queenie say he'd be here? The reason she called me was to demand we put our egos aside and have a real conversation. It's Valentine's Day, but the way Vahe continues to ghost me, you'd think it's Halloween.

It doesn't help that the guest list ran away from Tania, so of all the men dressed in impeccable suits, the majority are Nolan's famous rock-climbing friends and other elite athletes. That fact would be comforting—knowing I could end the night against a stranger's chiseled body instead of being alone—but now the thought of hooking up with a man in peak physical condition means nothing if he's not Vahe.

Cue the early aughts R&B because I got it bad.

Cheers erupt, breaking me out of my spiral. Tania and Nolan sealing their vows with a kiss is my cue that the ceremony has ended. I hold my bridesmaid bouquet with one hand while locking arms with one of Nolan's groomsmen. I'm glad I splurged on a new set of finger claws for the wedding: a gleaming gold filigree studded with flowers made of rubies. Because if I were ever going to believe that love conquers all, this jewelry is the inspiration I need.

We follow the bride and groom down the aisle, with the rest of the glam fam trailing behind. I'm used to bringing up the rear, but Alex insisted she take the position furthest away from the happy couple so as not to overshadow them with her immense celebrity. It sounds narcissistic when you say that out loud, but she's not wrong. I mean, would WeWork have been such a corporate disaster if it wasn't co-run by Gwyneth Paltrow's cousin? Bad things happen when someone gets jealous of their more famous loved ones.

Thankfully, everyone's focused on Tania, until we reach the end of the aisle, and I see Vahe's gaze locked on . . . me. I brace myself for a dirty look—or worse, stone-faced disregard

—but in those few milliseconds, his lips turn up. Tangible proof that he's happy to see me. Instantly, I'm flooded with relief. It's not his usual ear-to-ear grin I've come to miss, but it's a start. We may not be out of the woods yet, but this single exchange fills me with hope, nonetheless.

An immaculate planner, Tania runs a tight ship with everything she does, which means I'm now relieved of bridesmaid duties. Instead of being dragged to take a million bridal party portraits, I can make a beeline to the bartender in the hotel ballroom for a shot of liquid courage. But as I'm throwing back my favorite bourbon, I never let Vahe out of my sight. I've come this far to make amends, and now it's game time.

While everyone else is preoccupied with mingling during the happy hour, I catch him hovering near the back of the crowd. I pay for two beers and make my move.

"One olive branch for Vahe Derderian," I declare sheepishly, presenting the beer to him.

He takes me in while twisting off the top—I'm not sure if it's actually a twist top or if his grip is just that impressive. "Not as inventive as a carnivorous plant, but I guess two man-eaters would be more than I can handle." He smiles to reassure me he's not being passive-aggressive, handing me the beer back so he can uncap the other. "Cheers. You look phenomenal, as always."

I fidget with the half of my lavender hair that's braided, uncomfortable receiving a compliment when I don't deserve one. But part of me feels lucky that I'm seeing Vahe on a day when I've never looked better. Casey did a bang-up job custom-fitting us into our emerald velvet gowns, and Tania encouraged me to go with a deep-V neckline so I could show off the tattoos on my décolletage. The look is more traditionally feminine than I typically tolerate, but I feel like a regal badass who could—maybe, possibly—win back her boyfriend.

I gesture to his crisp, black suit, hugging his muscles in all the best places. "Right back at ya, little esh. I'm guessing Queenie doesn't have you on catering duty if you're dressed like that."

Vahe opens his mouth as if he's about to say something before changing his mind. "You know, Tania's a damn good negotiator. When we discussed the terms of the contract, I fully intended to honor our arrangement and comp everything, but that wasn't good enough for her."

My eyes bulge, heart racing at the thought of Tania shaking him down over my mistakes. That doesn't sound like her at all. "What do you mean? Where is she?"

He pulls me back by the shoulder, breaking me out of my unhinged impulse to interrogate a bride on her wedding day. "Chill out, Townsend. It all worked out, actually. She ended up paying me the full amount—and fundraising another twenty-five-thousand dollars—as long as I promised to use the funds for one thing."

I'm stumped. "Getting Mari off my back?"

Vahe guffaws. "Now that you mention it, it would get her off both our backs." He takes a big breath. "The money is to help open my own restaurant."

His words echo in my ears, and before I know it, I'm squeezing him in a celebratory hug. "Wow, Vahe, that's amazing!"

He's said nothing about next steps or whether he'll be taking Tania up on her offer. We both know that amount of money is a generous start, even if it's not enough to cover all the startup costs required for a brick-and-mortar business.

For once, none of that matters because I'm so, so happy for him. If we never speak to each other after tonight—as much as that would crush every fiber of my being—at least I know that Vahe is one step closer to living his dream, whether I get to be part of it or not.

Beats pass, and I'm still pressed against his chest, clinging to his suit jacket. And yet, Vahe doesn't push me away. If anything, his hands grip my waist like he's been lost at sea and finally found a buoy.

I want to ask a million questions about his plans for his restaurant, but it's intoxicating to be back in his arms, and I don't want to ruin this moment. It's not reconciliation, but it feels like it, and that's good enough for now. "I've been hallucinating while we've been apart," I admit, mumbling into his lapel. "Wherever I went, I kept seeing glimpses of you. I was so frustrated you were ghosting me, and there I was, wishing you would haunt me. Like I deserved to suffer a break with my reality if you weren't going to be a part of it anymore."

Vahe strokes my hair, careful not to unravel the braid, before meeting my gaze. "I'll admit I was angry. We both said things we're not proud of, but you kept trying to make it up to me and I didn't give you the time of day. That was a juvenile overreaction, and I'm sorry. Even after I realized I fucked up, my twisted logic told me it made more sense to leave you on read. That way I could surprise you."

He pulls out his phone and shows me a series of selfies he took: posing in front of street art in the Mission, drinking a hot chocolate from Dandelion. But then he swipes through snapshots of locations I'm not familiar with, this time of empty commercial spaces and glossy office interiors with venture capital–sounding names on the marquees. And that's when I understand what he's been planning.

"I wasn't an apparition driving you mad," he explains. "You probably did see me around San Francisco. As much as I wanted to loop you in, I needed to decide if I wanted to relocate whether or not we got back together. I had to explore SF on my terms, to see if it could feel like my city and not just your city. So between meetings with potential investors and landlords, I walked around a variety of neighborhoods and had conversations with locals. I did the most touristy, basic things I could think of and also took recommendations off the beaten path."

He tilts my chin up, his remorse apparent. "It killed me to ignore your texts and send your calls straight to voicemail, but I needed time to myself. To figure out if I could love the Bay as much as I love you."

My heart tumbles, and I have to remind myself to breathe. "And do you?"

"Not a chance."

I jolt as if electro-shocked, and Vahe laughs at his own joke. "I'm kidding. I mean, I'm always going to have pet peeves with ultra-urban living—like the fact that sometimes BART trains screech like dying walruses or when I step in shit, I can't always tell if it's from a dog or human. But you were also right about many things. The weather is an eleven out of ten, every meal made me jealous for not being the genius behind it, and even though it would be less expensive to live on the moon, the costs are worth it if I can be part of a thriving community that wants what I have to offer."

He tucks a loose strand of hair behind my ear. "But no matter how much I grow to love San Francisco, it can't compare to how fast I fell in love with you, Tori. You're not the only reason I'm moving, but you are the most important. You're my home now, and I will follow you around the world if you'll have me."

Fighting back tears, I don't wait. I don't deliberate. Instead, I grab his face and pull it toward me, planting the biggest, most enthusiastic kiss I can muster. "That's all I've ever wanted," I say breathlessly. "To be loved so deeply by someone that they'd never let me go. I never understood the idea that home could be a person and not a place, but you taught me that, Vahe. You're my person, and I love you. So goddamn much."

Relief pours out of me. I was so desperate to hold on to Vahe that I was considering a move of my own, but I'm grateful that he beat me to the punch and was brave enough for the both of us.

I mean, I've never dated anyone significant enough to be called a significant other, let alone lived with one. There are still so many questions on my mind: Where exactly are we going to live? What are Glen and Som going to do without me as a roommate? And how are we going to juggle cohabitation and getting a new business off the ground without wanting to murder each other?

But I'd rather be relegated to the Outer Sunset or risk double homicide if it means Vahe and I have a second chance of being each other's first priority. A particular fortune cookie calls to me: *Say yes—then figure it out later.*

"So what now?" I muse, feeling like anything is possible on this magical night. "Should we grab Queenie and the glam fam for a little cha-cha slide?"

Vahe's eyes darken, and his hands glide down the soft velvet dress, settling on the small of my back. "I was thinking we could sneak away and throw ourselves a more *intimate* party."

He presses me against the stiffness in his suit pants, as if I didn't already catch his drift, and I'm immediately ready to ditch this popsicle stand without an ounce of guilt. In fact, if Tania was here, she'd bless this reunion herself.

"Your room or mine?" he says, lust dropping his husky voice an octave lower.

I tug on his tie and lead the way. "I've got a better idea."

∼

Glam fam group* chat on *Wednesday, February 14,* at *7:25 p.m.

ALEX

Where's Tori? Tania wants to get everyone together on the dance floor.

GLEN

She's not here at the bar—anybody want me to bring them a nightcap?

SOM

She's not at the dessert station sneaking a second helping of paklava . . . which means she's probably sneaking around with her baker boyfriend.

ALEX

Omg they're back together?

CASEY

Well, I don't see either of them in the ballroom, so let's make some bets on where they're currently canoodling.

GLEN

I call dibs on the coat closet.

ALEX

Oooh, maybe they're in the bridal suite?

SOM

My guess is the women's restroom—they've got a couch in there!

CASEY

Vahe drove his truck, and my Southerner spidey sense says even Tori can't resist a rendezvous in a beat-up pickup. Let's break —whoever finds them first gets all their treatments paid for by the losers during our next spa day.

SOM

Oh, it's on.

chapter
twenty-six

Now that Vahe and I are officially back together and planning on cohabitating, we have all the time in the world to *make love* in our future home.

But that doesn't mean I'm ready to settle down completely and swear off more unconventional hookup spots. I haven't fucked in a public bathroom in forever, and that changes tonight.

"In here," I command, but Vahe stares at the women's sign, unconvinced.

"Here? Right now? Someone could walk in on us!" he hisses.

It's almost like that's the point, my guy. I'm too horny to launch into an explainer on exhibitionism, so instead, I push him through the door and jump into problem-solving mode.

After kicking open every stall door to ensure no one else is inside, I notice our solution in the back corner. "There! A janitor must have left behind an out-of-order sign. Go place it outside the door."

Vahe follows my instructions, still on edge. "And what if the cleaning crew is called to take care of things?"

"Jeez, how long are you planning on lasting?" I say, more exasperated than impressed. "I've been aching to get you inside me for weeks, so I anticipate coming in like five minutes, max."

His face softens with sympathy. "Moving forward, I promise to never let you go without again." Pain flashes across his face as he shifts his erection. "And trust me, I'm about to explode too, which is why I want to guarantee we won't get interrupted until we do."

"Fair enough." I scan the space, all gleaming tile and mirrors. I can tell why they're called restrooms. This one feels as relaxing as the Aphrodite Day Spa. If adrenaline wasn't coursing through my veins, I'd enjoy sinking into the tufted sofa next to the vanity.

A sofa. Of course. Cheers to outdated gender norms that expect women to suffer fainting spells at the slightest distress.

"Help me push this against the door," I say, pointing to the high-end furniture. I've never needed to move heaven and earth to get laid, but in dire circumstances, I will move a couch.

Vahe completes the task without much effort, his biceps bulging as he slides the sofa to block the entrance. I wrench my glance away from his muscles and meet his gaze. The only reason he's breathing heavily is because he can't take his eyes off me.

"What are you waiting for, Tori?" His dilated pupils have a predatory glint. "We don't have much time before someone discovers our shenanigans, so you better hike up that dress and assume the position."

About fucking time. "Yes, chef."

With the couch out of commission, I enter the first stall, not wanting to waste another second. It's not exactly roomy, but compared to most public restrooms I've debauched, it's positively pristine.

Vahe, however, isn't as forgiving. "You couldn't pick the handicapped stall?" he says with a huff, struggling to close the door around his massive body without crunching me against the side.

"Quit your moaning. I thought you liked a tight fit."

He spins me around to face the wall and bends me over the toilet. "Ha. If anyone's going to be moaning, it will be you, sweetheart."

I hear him unbuckle his belt and unzip his pants. Those sounds alone have me arching my back before he even puts his hands on me.

"So needy." He chuckles. "Have you been dying to get my dick inside you?"

My ass grinds against his crotch in response. "What do you think?"

Vahe growls at the contact, gliding his hands underneath my gown to remove my underwear, hesitating when he realizes I'm not wearing any. "I think you wanted easy access because you knew I'd have you ass-up tonight."

"I had hope." An unexpected pang hits my heart. "Same reason why I went on birth control and got tested when I returned to San Francisco. I never needed to before because I wasn't interested in serious relationships, but I didn't want to give up on us."

"Fuck, Tori, come here—" Vahe's hands slip, and he tries to turn me around to face him, but I dig in my heels. Literally, so hard I'm afraid they'll crack the tile.

"No way. Not because I'm allergic to you getting all soft and mushy on me, but because any minute now someone is going to barge in and put the kibosh on our sexy times. We can get sentimental later, but right now—" I gather my dress to my waist and pull Vahe's hand back to my aching, wet pussy. "I need you to fuck me."

He sharply inhales, relishing the slickness, and slides one

finger inside, then another. True to his promise, I let out a low moan, but it's not enough fullness to satiate me. "More, Vahe. I need your cock. Now."

He doesn't wait or crack a silly quip this time, just shoves downs his tented boxer briefs and buries himself in my pussy. We're well past the warmup stage now. Every inch of me is on fire, and I need release.

"I've never been harder in my life," he says, emphasizing his words with each thrust. I spread my legs wider to accommodate his sizable length and take every inch. "You're telling me I'm the first man to fuck you raw like this? Claim you fully inside and out?"

"And the last," I whisper without thinking. It's the most serious, permanent thing I've ever told somebody, but it's true. I don't want any dick if I can't have Vahe Derderian's, and he deserves to know that.

"Fuck, Tori. Now you've done it." I thought my admission would slow him down, melt him into a puddle of lovesick goop. But he pistons harder, holding me in place with one hand firmly around my neck and the other circling my clit. "I'm gonna come so fucking hard, I'll be dripping down your legs the rest of the night. Reminding you that you're mine."

"Yes, *yes*, I'm yours." He's got me at his mercy, whimpering and panting and chanting his name like a woman in heat. It's primal, this urge to bare everything open for him. Sex has always been a roaring good time, but this? This is transcendent.

I can't tell if we're getting progressively louder or if our moans are simply echoing off the bathroom tile, but we lose ourselves in the moment. I'm so relieved and grateful to be reunited with Vahe that I don't care who hears.

Between the rhythmic pounding of my pussy and Vahe's fingers stroking my clit, again and again, the pressure inside me mounts, and I can feel it—I'm *so* close.

"Faster," I gasp. "Fill me up. I can't hold out much longer."

Vahe obeys my desperate pleas, ramming so hard I revel how his balls slap against me. I'm a woman on a mission, and he's here to serve.

"You better come for me," he says, kissing the back of my neck. "I want this pussy clenching around my cock." To drive his point home, he wraps his hand around the base of my braid and pulls with one swift, sudden tug.

The delicious sting sends me over the edge, and I let out a groan that's been trapped inside me for a hundred years. Vahe holds my body as my climax comes crashing in waves, squeezing tighter when his follows suit. His cock pulses, and my pussy's walls clamp down, draining him to the very last drop.

"God, I needed that," I exhale, wincing slightly as Vahe pulls out and tucks himself back into his pants.

"You and me both. I got to guzzle down some water to rehydrate because I don't think I have any bodily fluids left."

He quickly re-braids my hair, turning it from a well-fucked, tousled mess back into being bridesmaid-worthy.

"Who knew dating a man raised with two sisters would come in handy like this?" I tease, turning around to face him.

Vahe gives me a tender kiss. "I was taught to take care of family. And that includes you, Tori. You're family."

Before I can move past my kneejerk cringe reaction and let his words sink in, my own found family calls my name.

"Tori Baker-Fucking Townsend!" Som screeches. I hear her jamming the restroom door into the sturdy sofa as if attempting to beat it into a pulp. "If you're in here, you better come out now. Some of us have more urgent business to attend to!"

"Speak for yourself," I say, exiting the stall with Vahe trailing behind. "Our business was pretty damn urgent."

"I knew it!" she declares, victorious, as we put the couch back in its rightful place and remove the out-of-order sign. Som waves the rest of the glam fam over. "Betches, in here—I won, I won, I won! Twenty-four karat gold facial—here I come."

Casey leans over Som's shoulder, noticing the confusion on my face. "We wagered a free spa day for whoever located you two lovebirds." She frowns. "Tori, I thought you'd be in a pickup truck kind of mood."

I break out into a grin. I'm glad I wasn't the only one who found joy in making a fun bet. "Sorry, you're about two months too late on that one." I grab Vahe's hand, giving it a squeeze. "But once we find our own place in the city, we'll be hooking up there for the foreseeable future."

The glam fam squeals their support, yanking us out of the restroom and onto the dance floor. As we bounce up and down to the beat, I can't possibly think how anything could top this moment—until I catch Queenie shaking her booty, waving her cane in the air. We lock eyes, and at the sight of her grandson's hands around my waist, she winks at me.

I blow her a kiss. It'll take time to win over all the Derderians, but for now, I feel so lucky that this is the family I wandered into. "I guess Queenie was right," I say out loud.

"She always is," Vahe agrees. He cocks his head. "Did she tell you she fired me?"

"What?" I shout over the blaring music. "I—I thought you'd be franchising Dikran's Deli. Why the hell would she kick you to the curb?"

He flashes a smile at the matriarch, no bad blood between them. "Maybe because she knew I needed to leave the nest once and for all. Or maybe she got sick of me moping around the customers because I was heartbroken over you." He pulls me in close. "Either way, it's for the best. Whether it's Tania making her donation or Queenie giving me the boot, I don't accept help until it's forced upon me. If it weren't for gutsy, headstrong women like you all, I don't know if I'd ever make the leap."

In that moment, I'm struck by Queenie's words before she convinced me to wax her coochie: *I'll give him the push he so desperately needs if you promise to catch him.*

Damn, I'm not sure I completely agree with her Machiavellian methods, but what can I say? All hail the queen.

As I take in the grandeur of Tania and Nolan's wedding reception, a deep sense of contentment overcomes me. I will still miss the closeness I felt with the glam fam when we were younger, before any significant others entered the picture and it was easier to coordinate our busy schedules. But with bonds this strong, I know they'd never leave me behind. Growing older is inevitable, and now I'm not as resistant to making radical change in my life, if it means the people I love are propelling me forward for the better.

"So that's what we'll do," I tell Vahe, taking his hands in mine. "We'll jump together."

∽

Tori Townsend's list of "basic" things she'll now tolerate—and their caveats

Tori will: Drink a pumpkin spiced latte
As long as she can: Use a corny cup name like Seymour Butts

Tori will: Wear Uggs or Crocs out in public
As long as she can: Pair them with sunglasses or a ski mask to avoid being spotted

. . .

Tori will: Listen to chart-topping hits by beloved pop divas

    As long as she can: Find covers by jazz artists or black metal bands

Tori will: Dress modestly for a family-friendly function

    As long as she can: Go commando to sneak away for a much-needed quickie

Tori will: Watch a sportsball game or the five billionth superhero movie reboot

    As long as she can: Jerk off to homoerotic porn parodies afterward

Tori will: Waste time walking around the aisles of a big-box home goods store

    As long as she can: Rearrange the monogrammed décor to spell out profanity

Tori will: Use obnoxious phrases on social media like "the girlies who get it, get it"

    As long as she can: Encourage her followers to send glitter bombs to GOP politicians

Tori will: Take a Boomerang video of cheers-ing at brunch

As long as she can: Never pay for a bottomless mimosa ever again

Tori will: Celebrate Valentine's Day at an overpriced restaurant with her new boyfriend

As long as she can: Pick the dessert and the safeword at the end of the night

epilogue

One year later

With my hand on the doorknob, I turn around to Vahe, fear in my eyes. "I don't want to do this."

He stops in his tracks, bewildered. "What are you talking about? You promised!"

"I know I did, but it wasn't a good idea." The words come out through gritted teeth. God, I wasn't expecting to feel this uncomfortable.

Vahe rubs my back, encouraging me to breathe deeper. "It's not like we jumped into this willy-nilly. Tonight took a healthy amount of communication, planning, and more than one pregame drink to take the edge off. You said you wanted to be open to new experiences, so come on. You can do this."

In case it wasn't clear, we're not taking about baked goods or butt stuff, both of which sound infinitely better than what awaits me. It's Valentine's Day, and I agreed to do something I've never done in my life: celebrate the Hallmark holiday (stop the presses) at an overpriced restaurant (cue gasps), like every other couple in love in this city (the horror!).

My head involuntarily shakes so hard I'm afraid it will detach completely. "Sarma. Sarma!"

Vahe's face crumples into an annoyed frown, pushing past me to open the door. "Overruled. You're not supposed to use the safeword until after dinner. And if you don't get your shit together, there won't be dessert of either kind."

That gets me to fall in line real quick. These days nothing is more convincing than the promise of paklava or a naughty nightcap. You would think after a year of dating Vahe, I would grow tired of both sweets and sex, but I'm as ravenous as the day I met him.

The restaurant we enter isn't what the kids these days call aesthetic. It's not the hottest spot in town. It wasn't difficult to secure a reservation. It's been operating in San Francisco's North Beach neighborhood since 1850, and the decor looks as if it hasn't been updated since then. Our host leads us past the subway-tiled entryway into a narrow dining area lined with tables covered in white tablecloths on each side. Each table sits against a mahogany interior with a mirror that tries to make the room look bigger than it is—a noble attempt when space is so hard to come by in the city.

We're seated towards the back, and when we're handed our menus, it dawns on me that there's a silver lining to coming here. Because this restaurant hasn't been trendy since the nineteenth century, I won't be recognized by one of Alex's diehard stans and incite a manhunt for the social media princess. The only way the cool kids would frequent this joint would be if they were doing so ironically. But you'd never be able to tell from the sheer joy on Vahe's face.

"Do you see that?" he whisper-shouts in awe. "The bar goes down the length of the whole restaurant like those classic soda fountains in diners. This place is an institution!"

His eyes light up at the old-timey dishes listed on the menu, like Oysters Rockefeller, Cosmopolitan salad, and calf's liver steak. None of it sounds particularly appetizing, and if I'm going to spend forty dollars on an entree it better be a work of modern art, but hey—I spent my early adulthood subsisting on bodega snacks and jungle juice, so who am I to judge?

That thought would have never entered my mind before I met Vahe, because boy do I love to judge. But seeing how he jumps into everything with his whole heart warms my formerly cold one.

Queenie may have pushed him in the right direction by giving him the boot, but every decision since has all been Vahe's: securing the right investors, downsizing his stuff, and selecting a live-to-work location in the Mission so we could remain close to Som and Glen. We even repurposed our second bedroom into a mini salon so I could have a dedicated space to service clients when I'm not on the road with the glam fam.

In the first few months of living together, I kept waiting for the other shoe to drop. I assumed Vahe would regret making such a huge sacrifice—that it was only a matter of time before his simmering resentment boiled over into another explosive fight, the one that would break us up for good.

But both our shoes stayed on. An important achievement while we completed his restaurant's renovation, at constant risk of stepping on nails and other dangerous detritus covering the dusty floors.

That's not to say Vahe and I haven't had our fair share of disagreements—let it be known that it is fucking hard to combine households with a sentimental baker for whom every redundant kitchen gadget is precious. But it's Vahe's tenacity to make things work in any situation that changed my perspective about our future. If he was determined to make his culinary dreams come true, then I'd roll up my sleeves too. While he studied DIY tutorials on tile installation, I spent hours fighting San Francisco bureaucracy to secure permits and process paperwork.

Eventually, as the weeks went by and our disaster zone turned into a love nest, I stopped asking myself what could go wrong and started imagining what could go right. Like building Queenie's Café and naming it after the woman who showed us what it means to leave a legacy.

Tania was right, after all: My life needed upending. I was so resistant to moving to Fresno because I thought there were winners and losers in love, and I didn't want to compromise. Now I know that for the right person, you'll want to make room for them.

"I don't know why people say relationships should be fifty-fifty," I muse aloud. "I don't think ours ever added up that neatly."

Vahe pauses, amused as our server approaches our table. "So you're saying you don't want to split the seafood platter?"

I lightly smack his arm with the menu before rattling off our order. "Not that. I mean, sometimes you meet in the middle, like sharing a bathroom vanity, and other times you move hundreds of miles because you're a saint and your stubborn girlfriend refuses to budge an inch. I'm not sure what she did to deserve you."

He takes a moment to squeeze my hand across the table. "Hey, to give you credit where it's due, you only had a mini-freakout about doing something *basic* tonight, and it all worked out fine."

As much as I hate to admit it, Vahe makes a good point. This restaurant looks like it's caught in a time-loop, but the food's so tasty, it distracts from the horrid interior. When the last course arrives and Vahe offers his fork, my brain stalls for a second. He's feeding me a bite of his bourbon bread pudding. Mortified by any public displays of cutesy-ness, I open my mouth to refuse such an infantilizing gesture. Vahe beats me to the punch, sticking the fork in before I can complain.

If desserts are indicative of our personalities, then Vahe's choice makes sense. Both he and the alcohol-infused treat are decadent, containing just enough of an edge to cut through the sweetness. Never one to let a man have the upper hand, even if it's feeding me a morsel of pure magic, I bob up and down salaciously—making sure to flick the tines with my tongue so he can't mistake what I'm simulating.

Vahe's eyes glaze over, and he shifts uncomfortably before flagging down our server. "Hey, man, the bread pudding was bomb, but something urgent came up, and we gotta go. You get it, right?"

I pull the fork from my mouth with a lewd pop, winking at the server as Vahe shoves a wad of cash from his wallet into the guy's hands and tells him to keep the change.

"We better come up with a safe gesture," he says, rushing out of the restaurant, "because when I have my way with you, that pretty little mouth of yours will be too full to speak."

Grinning more than I ever thought I would on Valentine's Day, I concede that basic is in the eye of the beholder. And no matter how conventional we seem to be in public, only the two of us will know how freakishly twisted and hopelessly in love we are.

THE END

thank you

Thank you for reading *Love and Paklava*! It would mean the world if you'd consider writing a review on Amazon and Goodreads, as well as recommending the book on social media. Word of mouth has a huge impact on an author's success, and it helps other readers discover new books to enjoy.

Can't get enough of Tori and Vahe? To gain access to a special bonus epilogue from Vahe's point of view, visit alyssajarrett.com/love-and-paklava

recipe for choreg

I hope you appreciated reading about Armenian cuisine and culture. If you'd like a more immersive experience, here is my family's recipe for choreg, passed down through the generations. Enjoy!

Alyssa's Armenian Choreg (makes 50 servings)

Dry ingredients:

- 7 cups flour
- 1 cup sugar
- ½ teaspoon salt

Wet ingredients:

- 2 ½ sticks (20 tablespoons) butter, melted
- 2 ½ tablespoons Crisco
- 5 eggs, lightly beaten
- 1 small can (⅔ cup) evaporated milk
- 1 ½ packets active dry yeast, dissolved in ¼ cup lukewarm water

- 2 teaspoons anise seed

Garnish:

- 1 to 2 eggs, beaten, for egg wash
- 2 tablespoons sesame seeds (optional)

Instructions:

- Combine all dry ingredients in a large bowl.
- Make a hole in the flour and add all the wet ingredients.
- Work the dough until it does not stick to your hands.
- Let the dough rise until it doubles in size (approx. 2–3 hours).
- Roll and shape the dough into knots, pretzels, or other desired shapes.
- Paint the knots with egg wash.
- Sprinkle sesame seeds on top, if desired.
- Bake at 350 degrees for 20 minutes.
- Let cool and enjoy!

acknowledgments

They say the third time's the charm, and I had a charming time writing my third novel thanks to the people who helped me bring it to life.

As always, to my editor Kristen Tate at the Blue Garret. Your editorial feedback and extensive knowledge of both SF and NYC neighborhoods have made this battle between cities even more authentic and enjoyable. I'm forever grateful for your partnership on this series.

To Heather Lazare, host of the Northern California Writers' Retreat, and the entire NCWR community, especially to agent Jill Marr and my 2024 workshop buddies Adrienne Barr, Heather Hecht, Laura Hall-Grodian, Leigh Lucas, and Sarena Straus. Your feedback helped me reimagine the opening of *Love and Paklava*, but you can still find the twenty pages you critiqued in later chapters. I hope this book does you proud, and I will continue recommending this retreat to any writer who will listen.

To my critique partners Sophia Le and Taleen Voskuni, and my beta readers Ashley, Brooke, and Jess. Thank you for your ongoing support and enthusiasm for the Glam Fam— you are honorary members through and through. And a special shout-out to Thao for advising me on Vietnamese translation and making every sentence ring true.

To my Bay Area and greater NorCal family, especially to Kit, Jill, and my K.A.S.A. group chat. From South San Francisco to Sacramento, I love you all. I would move two hundred miles away all over again if it brings me closer to you.

To everyone who is in my life because of our connection to the Central Valley. Whether you're a Sanger High Apache, a Fresno State Bulldog, or just someone who reps the 559, I'm one of you. If someone can figure out a way to ship me Chuck Wagon chili, I'd be forever in your debt.

To my best hometown friends, Lily and Celia. We became BFFs in high school because we hated P.E. and loved the same books. It's comforting to know that twenty years later, nothing has changed. If anyone turned Fresno into FresYes for me, it's you two.

To my family, who taught me how to have Hye Pride. I may only be a quarter Armenian, but I'm 100 percent honored by my heritage. My only wish is that my grandfather was alive to see how much Queenie takes after him.

To my brother and cover designer Nick Jarrett. I threw a lot at you with this book's design, but you always manage to turn my half-baked ideas into magic. I can't wait for Tania's brother to get his own happily ever after.

And, lastly, to my readers, wherever you are in the world. Where we live says a lot about who we are. Small-town romances may get all the hype, but suburbs and cities—and the people who live in them—deserve love too. I hope you find yours, along with perfect sunny days and a parking spot whenever you need one. Thank you for joining me on this amazing journey.

a sneak peek

Please continue reading for an excerpt of Book 3.5 in the Glam Fam series, *Love Me Merrily*.

chapter
one

It's blasphemous to admit at this time of year, but the holidays are the worst. As I enter the grand ballroom of the Granite Grove Lodge—Yosemite's second-best hotel according to every travel magazine on my shit list—I find it hard to enjoy the festivities. Per company policy, the open hall has been decked out since November first: wreaths hanging in the windows, poinsettia centerpieces on every dining table, and a massive tree by the far wall, its needles barely visible underneath the obscene amount of ornaments, tinsel, and string lights.

My supervisor, the general manager, is out of town for the week, so as his direct report with the longest tenure, I'm filling in to run things while he's gone. That includes instructing all Granite Grove staff not to refer to our decor as explicitly Christmas-themed—even our tree is a "festive fir," gag. We wish our guests "happy holidays," but I've been working in Yosemite for over a decade, and I've yet to see any concerted efforts to celebrate other holidays. Sure, we host a Thanksgiving dinner and a quickly thrown together costume contest for Halloween, but the second the calendar month flips from ten to eleven, it's all about Christmas until the new year.

As I take in the lodge's color palette of red and green, I begrudgingly admit to myself that the decor does look phenomenal against the backdrop of the ballroom, with its stone interior and vaulted mahogany ceilings. The fire roaring in the granite hearth should be more than enough to keep me warm and cozy, yet my blood continues to run cold.

Because I hate every single winter holiday, and I hate Christmas most of all.

"Summer, where do these go?"

A young, bright-eyed woman gestures to the boxes off to the side, pulling out elaborate Venetian masks in wintry white and silver.

I sigh. As the front office manager, I usually remember the names of everyone working at Granite Grove. But now that I'm on a mission to be promoted to sales director by throwing our first-ever Merry Masquerade, I've had to hire additional seasonal staff, and I can't keep them straight. They're all right out of college, innocent and inexperienced, and I have little patience for their entry-level enthusiasm.

Twelve years ago, I was just like them. Before that dreaded day on the Matterhorn when the love of my life was struck by a large rock and died in my arms. Ryan and I were both experienced climbers—he was a pro at the top of his game, so it's not like we didn't know what we were doing. But I learned the devastatingly hard way that freak accidents don't just happen to amateurs.

"Tape those back up and lock them in the storage closet," I tell her, banishing the memory to the recesses of my mind. "There's not much space left, so the rest of the supplies will have to go in the break room."

My tone must have been steelier than I intended because the woman shuffles off with the box as fast as she can, avoiding eye contact. Jeez, I got to get it together. I may not feel any Christmas cheer, but if I keep snapping at Santa's little helpers, I can kiss my promotion goodbye because I'm going to find myself out of a job.

When I returned to work after Ryan's death, everyone treated me like I was bubble-wrapped. Who wouldn't have sympathy for the girl who held the back of her boyfriend's cracked skull as he bled out?

Most of those colleagues have moved away and moved on with their lives, while I remain frozen in time. Even on days when I'm feeling good and life seems completely normal, in a flash, I can be transported back to that mountain, and my whole mood is thrown off. But if I can't put on a happy face around people who don't know or care about my tragic backstory, then it will be my fault when I'm fired.

It's December twentieth. I only have to plaster on a smile for five more days, and then when the Merry Masquerade is over on Christmas Eve, I can take some much-needed paid time off and be a Scrooge in peace.

I'm going to be a beacon of hospitality. Right after I tell this red-headed trespasser to fuck off.

"Excuse me, sir?" I bark out to the only man not wearing the hotel's uniform. "The ballroom is closed until this evening." I check my watch, which reads a quarter after two. "Dinner starts in about three hours."

When I say he's red-headed, I don't mean he's a natural ginger. I mean his hair is dyed as brightly as the Santa hats we're forced to wear at the front desk this month. And his Kool-Aid hairdo isn't the only thing that stands out. He's also sporting ear gauges, a nose ring, and tattoos peeking out of his black hoodie.

We rarely get guys with this kind of street style—camping types are more minimalist—but there's something about his aesthetic that's familiar . . . do I know him?

I brush off the possibility, since it's obvious why his vibe is jogging my memory. Because Ryan used to look like this.

My evangelical family hated him, a rock-climbing rebel with an orange and yellow fauxhawk who shared my love for the "devil's music." Needless to say, I went very-low-contact when they couldn't even pretend to grieve his passing.

And here's this guy, someone who could be mistaken for Machine Gun Kelly, and all I can think is Ryan's ghost has come back to haunt me.

The hotel guest watches my expression shift from annoyance to apprehension and quickly explains himself. "I'm sorry, I didn't mean to intrude. You must be Summer McKenzie. We're scheduled to meet tomorrow morning, but I decided to drive up from Fresno early so I could check out the space."

"The space?" I repeat, racking my brain for why this dude waltzed into the ballroom. If he's interested in booking Granite Grove for a wedding, wouldn't his fiancée be with him?

"Yeah, for the Merry Masquerade. I'm John Beecher, the brand designer."

He sticks out his hand to shake mine, and it dawns on me where I've heard his name. The same name I've been emailing for months now, the one he shares with my primary point of contact. "Tania's brother? From Beecher Media."

John nods reassuringly, as if this isn't the first time this confusion has occurred. "Yes, Tania's the one who takes all the client calls. You *are* Summer, right?"

"The person who's in charge of this event but is apparently too scatterbrained to recall the co-owner of the marketing agency she hired. How did you guess?"

He averts his gaze. "Tania's always going on about how gorg—I mean, how great Summer looks on Zoom, so I figured you must be her."

John's face turns as red as his hair, and I must be blushing just as hard. Does he find me attractive?

Tania Beecher and I met under antagonistic circumstances

two years ago—back when she stayed at Granite Grove during a corporate retreat and I thought she was a spoiled Bay Area coastal elite. Then my best friend—famed free solo climber Nolan Wells—fell in love with her, and eventually I changed my tune, once I saw her through his eyes. Now living ninety minutes south in Oakhurst, she still doesn't take naturally to the outdoors, but she's got a good heart and great taste in pop-punk music. And she finds every little quirk about Nolan endearing, even his disgusting habit of pissing in bottles when he's too lazy to leave the van on a climbing expedition. Now that they've been married for almost a year, I can't imagine any two people being a better fit together.

That's when it hits me. John Beecher isn't just Tania's younger brother. He's Nolan's brother-in-law.

Nolan only had one sibling—his twin, in fact—and that was Ryan. The man whose life I watched fade from his eyes. My first love who was gone way too soon.

about the author

Alyssa Jarrett is a romance author and tech marketer based in the San Francisco Bay Area. When she's not telling steamy, satirical love stories, she can be found drinking an iced tea or cuddling with her cats.

You can subscribe to her newsletter, Grumpy + Sunshine, on Substack, and follow her @authoralyssajarrett on Instagram, Threads, and TikTok.

alyssajarrett.com
alyssajarrett.substack.com

Follow Alyssa online:

instagram.com/authoralyssajarrett
threads.com/@authoralyssajarrett
tiktok.com/@authoralyssajarrett